MW00640447

New World Order

666 – Mark of the Beast

Volume 1

W.R. Benton

Modus Operandi Press
Paradise, CA

1st Edition
ISBN 978-1-944476-15-1

Author Photos © Copyright 2016 by W. R. Benton, LLC
Cover design by: Rockingbookcovers.com
Book cover © Copyright 2016 W. R. Benton LLC
Edited by: Bobbie La Cour, Daniel Williams, and Kay King

This book was produced in the USA

www.modusoperandipress.com

The *New World Order* series

This series, by award winning Amazon bestselling author W. R. Benton, is the story of war torn America. As the rich and elite of the world move to put the new world order in place across the globe, they understand they must move quickly. At times just as rich and exciting in content as real American history — this is a series of heroism, valor, patriotism, greed, blackmail, sex, traitors, and death, as normal day-to-day Americans make a valiant stand against the takeover. This series is more than just exciting reading, it is the affirmation of the American spirit and our total dedication to a once great nation. It's an attempt of common people to recover their country from those who have unlimited funds, support of the United Nations, and a deep determination to rule the world.

New World Order, 666 - Mark of the Beast, Volume 1

In Volume One, it all starts as the rich and elite move quickly to take complete control of the world and all governments. They attempt to place the whole world under the control of one leader, unidentified, with a totalitarian world government. They hope to have one world bank, one currency, one government, and they promise comfortable lives for all citizens of the world. Countries are invaded by UN troops and martial law is declared, a few weapons are gathered, food is suddenly strictly rationed, no cars, no gas, and no utilities for anyone who is not wealthy and a part of the New World Order. Protection is to be provided by the UN troops, and all is going well as one nation after another falls. This is all part of the Illuminati agenda and things are moving smoothly. That is, until the UN troops step on American soil and the battles start. The Americans are a determined bunch who will not just lay down and allow their nation to be taken over. If they are to lose their country, they will go down fighting to the last man and woman.

New World Order, California Invasion, Volume 2

Facing bitter resistance, the New World Order clamps down on the American forces. It's a fight against global domination with the freedom of the human race at stake.

In Volume 2 of the New World Order series, the Order shows a new U.S. President what will happen if he doesn't do their bidding. These shadowy puppet-masters will sacrifice anyone, even elites in the upper circles of power, and they prove that to the new President in vivid detail. Individual lives mean nothing when their objective is so close they can taste it.

New World Order, Cold Lifeless Hands, Volume 3

The New World Order moves forward with its twisted plans for full disarmament of the world's population. Their chosen method is arrest and 're-education' of any questionable citizens—i.e. those who will not accept a new global government or a micro chip implant for their own protection. The conquered people soon realize every whim of the Order must be swiftly met or overly harsh retribution will follow. This new Civil War is costly. Americans are choosing sides, the battle for their hearts and minds is well underway, and most rebels would rather die than submit.

Books by W.R. Benton

W. R. Benton is a master story teller, with over 40 books, eBooks and audio books to his credit, and his mountain man book, "War Paint," set in 1820, is soon to be a feature motion picture. Benton is known for his action and adventure, along with great character development that makes many readers feel as if they are actually a part of the book. He tells of the kind of bad guys you love to hate, with good guys you root for from the very beginning.

Explore more than 40 WR Benton books, at

http://www.amazon.com/author/wrbenton

DEDICATIONS

This book is dedicated to my "war buddies:"
"Rap" Brown, "Stoney" Burke, Stephen Carrier, and
to the memory of Master Sergeant Thomas Lujan, a
special and good man. I salute you, gentlemen, as well
as others who served with me in Thailand during the
end of the Vietnam war.

To my four children, Lisa Benton Willis, James Hollis,
David L. Benton, and Amie Benton.

A Word from the Author

The New World Order 666 - The Mark of the Beast, Volume 1, is
what happens when the rich and elite of the world manipulate the
United Nations, along with other nations, using the New World
Order. They attempt to place the whole world under the control
of one leader, with a totalitarian world government. They hope to
have one world bank, only one currency, one government, and
they promise comfortable lives for all citizens of the world. Countries are invaded by UN troops and martial law is declared, a few
weapons are gathered, food is suddenly strictly rationed, no cars,
no gas, no utilities, for anyone who is not wealthy. Protection is to
be provide by the UN troops and all is going well as one nation after another falls. This is all part of the Illuminati agenda and
things are moving smoothly. That is, until the UN troops step on
American soil.

In America the "New World Order" is resisted. The President of
the United States, bought and placed in position by the NWO, declares martial law and orders all Americans to surrender their guns
and have micro chips implanted, or die. Without the chip implant,
food cannot be bought, medical services are denied, jobs cannot
be kept, and your whole history, personal, professional, and health,
is saved on the chip. No chip, no food. This micro-chip is advertised as the ultimate safety device and provides a way to find lost
or stolen children and the elderly who wander off or drive away, all
because it will have a GPS tracking capability. It will also send
medical information on all individuals to a centralized computer
system, which will dispatch 911 ambulances to the individual in
the event of a medical emergency. However, it also has a sinister
and dark side as well; it records your very thoughts and the computer system can give the implanted person suggestions, which the
human brain will process as original thoughts.

Conservative Americans have decided to die rather than give up
their freedoms and most see the chip as the Mark of the Beast
from the Bible, but who is the anti-Christ? A full blown civil war
balances with the conservatives battling the liberals, who are as-

sisted by funding from the NWO, along with personnel and equipment by the UN. Soon, the Union dissolves. Conservative states join together to form the CSA, the Conservative States of America. The primary reasons for the split and soon to be fought civil war is over the failure of the United States to follow the Constitution and chip implanting. The CSA feels the Constitution cannot be ignored and mandating the chips is a violation of basic human rights and a violation of individual privacy.

Then, the United States violates Constitutional law by stating the Second Amendment is now void and will no longer be honored. The President of the U.S. is not concerned, because his funds are supplied by the NWO, and his troops by the UN. Additionally, some high ranking military members on all sides are on the NWO payroll.

Today, some of us do not believe in the New World Order, but some of our Presidents do. In a speech delivered on September 11, 1990 during a joint session of the Congress, President George Bush explained his objectives for post Cold War global government, in cooperation with Soviets, and he stated:

> "Until now, the world we've known has been a world divided—a world of barbed wire and concrete block, conflict and cold war. Now, we can see a new world coming into view. A world in which there is the very real prospect of a new world order. In the words of Winston Churchill, a 'world order' in which 'the principles of justice and fair play ... protect the weak against the strong ...' A world where the United Nations, freed from cold war stalemate, is poised to fulfill the historic vision of its founders. A world in which freedom and respect for human rights find a home among all nations."

While considered a silly conspiracy theory by many Americans, the term New World Order suggests strongly of the emergence of a powerful totalitarian world government controlled and manipulated by the rich and powerful, with enforcement by the UN. This conspiracy is often considered a warped view held by a few of the far right, who are paranoid, or by the "Bible thumpers" as the basis for the end of times prediction in the Bible. Of the two, I'm more inclined to believe the Christians. Besides, as the old adage says, "Just because you're paranoid, doesn't mean they're not out to get you."

Sound far fetched? Not really. Just go to any major search engine and type in New World Order and it will pop up thousands of pages and sites. The New World Order Conspiracy is alive and well, but is it fact? Read about it and draw your own conclusion.

Additionally, what I've written here could very well happen. They'd start with a few well planned murders and they'd surely be rich enough to afford only the best in agents. Then some catastrophic event in the states, like a dirty bomb close to the White House. If the NWO has bought the President with billions of dollars, he simply declares martial law.

The towns and caves mentioned in this story are real, including Rolla, Newburg, Licking, and Devil's Elbow, Missouri. I have spent many days running around on the banks of the Little and Big Piney Rivers. The cave where my group initially runs to, is in fact Gourd Creek Cave and I've camped there many nights. Even the store owned by Homer Poor is real, but I've given the owner a fake name, because I have no idea who owns the place now.

So, relax, find a comfortable chair, and get your favorite drink. It's time to read W. R. Benton's, "*New World Order - 666: Mark of the Beast, Volume 1.*" Enjoy.

W. R. Benton
1 June 2016
Jackson, Mississippi

"That one may smile, and smile, and be a villain."
– William Shakespeare, Hamlet

9 And the third angel followed them, saying with a loud voice, If any man worship the beast and his image, and receive [his] mark in his forehead, or in his hand,

10 The same shall drink of the wine of the wrath of God, which is poured out without mixture into the cup of his indignation; and he shall be tormented with fire and brimstone in the presence of the holy angels, and in the presence of the Lamb:

11 And the smoke of their torment ascendeth up for ever and ever: and they have no rest day nor night, who worship the beast and his image, and whosoever receiveth the mark of his name.

12 Here is the patience of the saints: here [are] they that keep the commandments of God, and the faith of Jesus.

— **King James Version**
From the book of Revelation chapter 14:9 through chapter 14:12

CHAPTER 1

Agent X1 was a quiet man who rarely spoke to anyone not related to his work, and even his wife had no idea what he did for a living, thinking he worked in the stock market. He worked for an individual with a high management position in the stock market, but his payments originated in Switzerland, not that X1 cared. Agent X1 knew his Boss simply as Mr. Smith. Payment for his work was always done electronically, with funds that were manipulated by Certified Professional Accountants working for the U.S. Federal Government, and usually only after the money had been moved numerous times by a number of wealthy individuals. The accountants keep the money flowing in his account as government fund transfers, with all sent using *legitimate* payment centers. Some of his payments came from the American Government or other governments around the world.

X1 paid no income tax, his real identity was gone, completely deleted from all computers, and there were no paper trails associated with him. He had a number of unregistered weapons, three of which he carried at this moment. He had access to any drugs, even deadly ones, he needed and could change roles in a heartbeat to complete his mission. In his office at 'work' he had over 30 passports of different nationalities and valid driver's licenses to back them up, along with the identities of 30 different men in the world's computer system. This computer system was linked into the international do not fly listing, FBI, CIA, and the United Kingdom's MI5 and MI6 branches. Each of his "characters" was listed as no security threat, with a small image of an eye within a triangle on the lower right of each file, indicating his working for the NWO.

Agent X1 was an enforcer for a secret organization, in bringing about the New World Order, and he did what was ask him, without question. He was often called to break bones, maim, or in some cases, kill. Murders done by him came in three forms; 1) The victim would simply disappear, 2) a neat and clean assassination, 3) a bloody and gory killing that could be blamed on someone else or create panic. It didn't matter much to him what he was hired to do, because X1 was a professional hit man and had been taught by the very best—the United States Government.

After a stint with the Green Berets, he was offered a job with the FBI, which he took, and learned a great deal about the art of ending people's lives. But when he transferred to the CIA, he discovered countless ways to kill and hurt folks, but only in the service of the New World Order (NWO). It was while with the CIA he became what he was today, a deadly enforcer. What most Americans did not realize was the CIA, the Joint Chiefs of Staff, and all political leaders, were neck deep in bringing the New World Order into being. Even the President of the United States was placed in the oval office by the NWO, not the American people. Each member of the senate or congress was placed there by rigged voting and the vote of the individual American, at all levels of politics, was useless and never counted. Normal crime, terrorist activities, and such didn't concern X1, because his mission was only with the NWO. If caught or arrested, he'd be released within an hour, no matter the crime. His skills were seen as essential to the American Government and the key players of the NWO establishment, who were not located in the United States, but in Europe. X1 was a tool, a very useful tool.

He was currently in the elevator of a high priced penthouse in Houston, Texas, with an assignment. His target, James Mims, was the owner of Mims Aircraft Manufacturing Firm and he was to be terminated because he knew too much and suddenly wanted out of the NWO. X1 was an average size man, wore black plastic framed glasses which he didn't need, and a blonde wig. He had no scars, no fancy rings, absolutely nothing that folks would remember about him. He was dressed in a dark gray suit and carried three pistols with him at all times. He had a silencer rrel of his .38 and if all went well, he'd kill the 0300 and most everyone was asleep in the city. door to the penthouse, he used his lock pick apartment in seconds. He was wearing thin, g gloves as he closed the door behind him. *This place is beautiful, with images and paintings from around the world, and some of the art must be worth a fortune*, he thought.

He moved to the security system, input the code he had and now the alarm system was disarmed. He walked by a fully stocked bar in the huge living room, and dirty whiskey glasses littered the coffee and end tables.

He pulled the .38 and moved to the bedroom. Just as he expected, his hit was laying on top of an oval bed nude with two beautiful women, who were nude as well. One woman lay on each side of him.

Sure is a waste of good woman flesh, but I can't leave a witness, he thought.

He raised his pistol, shot the blonde in the middle of her beautiful face and the back of her skull exploded. The redhead stirred, rolled onto her back, and he shot her in the chest, her death instantaneous. He couldn't help but admire her large breasts with hard nipples. His primary target was still sleeping, so moving close to the man, he shot him in the left eye and not a sound was heard as his body quivered as it shut down. He moved to the man's wallet on the night stand and took all of his money, removed his expensive jewelry from a jewelry box, and took his credit cards, which he'd never use. He'd shred them once back in his office. On the way out, he picked up a Rolex watch from the dresser and left, but only after programming the security system again. Now the death would be reported as a robbery and after a while, the media would grow bored and stop reporting, or they'd be ordered to stop by the NWO, who owned the media too.

James Walker sat at his kitchen table reading the newspaper and shook his head. A minute later, he said, "Honey, there is something unusual about the killin' of that rich Mims guy in the paper here."

"Mims? He owns a company that builds planes, right?"

"Yep, same guy, but according to the newspaper he and two housekeepers were killed last night and his place robbed. I don't see that happening, not with the security he must have had in place. Didn't he have guards? His place, according to the paper, was a million dollar penthouse on the top floor of the Mims Building."

"And just last week a CEO for some big government supplier was found drowned off the coast of Mississippi and there are still no leads. As for Mims, I doubt those women were housekeepers, if you look at their photos." she said as she topped off his coffee cup.

"That drowning was strange, too. The man didn't like water, couldn't swim, and didn't own a boat, and yet his body was found floating almost twelve miles off shore." James said, and then shook his head again.

He was in his early 60s, with a potbelly, still had his rugged outdoor looks, most of his auburn hair, and a salt and pepper beard. He'd retired from the military over 20 years ago and while over the hill physically, he'd never admit it. He had high blood pressure and his doctor was always telling him to lose weight. He'd been an investor while in the military and bought shares of some new computer companies and now was a fairly wealthy man, but you'd never know it. He was dressed his usual, with jeans, ball cap, dress shirt and cowboy boots.

"Well, it doesn't impact me or my little world. I know no billionaires and most of my friends live from payday to payday, trying to make ends meet. We're lucky you invested when you did and selected the right companies." Donna said.

Donna was two years younger than James, had always kept her body slim and trim, so as a result, she still turned heads when out in public. Her blonde hair now comes from a bottle but at one time it was natural. White hair waited until she was in her late fifties before it struck hard. She was popular, had a few close friends, but neither of them socialized on a large scale. She worked for the police department as a dispatcher and before that had worked a 911 switchboard. She didn't need to work, but did it to pass her time.

She stood, bent and gave James a deep teasing kiss and said, "There will be more like that when I get off work. I think tonight would be a good time to have a candlelight supper."

"For sure, baby, if you want. Yes, let's do it. Call me if you have to work late. I'll thaw a couple of steaks and have it all ready when you get home."

"I love you!" she yelled as she moved toward the front door, purse and keys in hand.

"I love you, too!" he yelled back and then added, "Be safe on the way to work."

He finished his coffee and moved to his computer. Each morning he visited a social media site where he met his friends and exchanged information, told jokes and exchanged lies. Most were old military men like him, and a few even served in the Air Force as he had. Two or three had served with him in Thailand, Vietnam, or Guam, and he'd known them for years.

Since he was a retired E-8, most of his friends called him "Top" for top sergeant. While they mainly gathered to joke and clown around, lately there had been some serious conversations about the New World Order Conspiracy and if it was real or not.

"Mornin' all!" he typed, then pushed the enter key and waited. He took a sip of his hot coffee.

"Hey, Top!" Wilson replied quickly.

"Where is everyone this morning?" James asked.

"I don't know. Maybe Homeland Security picked them all up."

James typed a "LOL."

Only it was possible. As veterans they often spoke their minds and to hell with who didn't like it. That's why James liked and trusted them, because they were loyal Americans who had served their nation when many others had not. They didn't look like heroes, but they were exactly the kind of men who once made America great.

An hour later, Bill Blake came online and said, "Thomas and Jerry were both picked up for questioning by Homeland Security. Seems Tom made some comments about the President being a weak dick Muslim and they took it personal. You know how Thomas is when he gets pissed. He meant nothing and was blowing off steam."

"This isn't the first time." He reminded them that Tom had been picked up before for posting images of the President dressed as a rag-head, with a camel, and a desert tent in the background. It was what the President was doing to the camel that got him in trouble. They'd warned him, slapped his wrist and he'd returned home pissed. A day later and he was back doing it again, but this time posting the President as an overweight drag queen.

"I think all of this is part of the New World Order." Blake said.

"Oh? How's that?" James asked, and then laughed.

"We are so weak now as a nation all it would take is one hard puff and we'd fall over. Look, men are dressing like women, and women like men, and our society is so corrupt and full of evil, all ya have to do is read the Bible to know we're in the end of times. Sodom and Gomorrah had nothing on us. We have adults acting like kids because they were never raised, they just grew up. No one has respect for authority, and no one even has self-respect, with piercing and self mutilation the norm. The norm!"

"Not my problem." James replied.

"The President is considering letting the United Nations come in to disarm all American citizens. He claims once the weapons are gone, the deaths from guns will have to go down."

"I see two problems there." James typed, "One, the American people will never give up their guns. Two, most of the murders done today are not done by law abiding citizens, but thugs. You have to be some kind of special liberal stupid to believe criminals will obey gun laws. Oh, at times Tom might find Sally in bed with his best friend and kill 'em both, but you know what I mean."

"On the news today he was saying if the guns were not handed over to the UN, he'd declare martial law and they'd take them from us."

"How'd the military react, or do you know?"

"The Generals, except for a few, agreed with him."

"Of course, they're all damned yes men. Hell, they can't think on their own." James took another drink of his coffee.

"Consider this; They now legally listen to and record our phone calls, they scan our mail to keep track of who sent it and who it is addressed to as well. They often hack our computers, but for what, images of Mary and Frank's wedding? Cell phones are easy for them to hack and so is our computer usage online. How many drones fly over our heads or vans are parked on our street watching our homes?"

"I don't think it's that bad." James said, and then went into the kitchen for more coffee. He returned a couple of minutes later.

"Damn it, James, it *is* that bad. The younger generations are dumber than a box of horse turds and that's the college graduates I'm talking about. I'd be surprised if many Masters level graduates can even read at the senior high school level. NSA claims they're looking for terrorists, but according to the news they've not caught a one, not a one, with all this invasion of privacy bullshit." Blake said.

"Not my problem." James typed.

"Nothing seems to be your problem today, old buddy." Wilson typed.

"It *is* your problem, my friend, and mine too." Blake typed and then added quickly, "Our society is purposely being made stupid. The NWO is doing this on purpose, just like bringing in the millions of illegal aliens and the refugees. They want our economy to go tits up and for the United States to fall, and hard, too. One by one they want the economies of the world to collapse so they can take over. With the Liberals in charge, our economy is doomed, because we'll fall and soon, too. Hell, they've been spending money we don't have for fifty years. But the NWO, they like us doing this stuff."

"What is this and who is they?"

"The rich, James, the super elite rich from around the world. I read they want to brainwash all of us, set up a world currency, one religion, no guns, no resistance, and to kill off millions of folks that are dangerous to the state, or may have serious medical problems. The mentally ill will be gassed to death or used for medical experiments. I read they want to plant chips in each of us, so they can control us, monitor our thoughts, and track us with a GPS."

"Hell, it sounds like Hitler and his Third Reich. LOL." James said.

"Some Christians are calling the chips the mark of the beast, so it's a serious issue, if it's true." Wilson typed.

"I just don't see it, LOL." James replied.

"Not funny, man, they are calling it the Fourth Reich. This Reich will not be on a national level, but a world level. It would operate the same way as Hitler ran his Reich, with concentration camps, mass gassing, public executions and so on. Hell, why do you think FEMA is making camps all over the United States? Huh? Do ya reckon they spend all the money just for hurricanes?"

"You're forgetting all the hunters and veterans we have out there with guns. No, I ain't falling for no NWO conspiracy yet. I just don't see it happening. Do you really think the squirrel of a man we currently have as President has the balls to call the UN in to disarm us? He's only got a few months left and then he's history, and bad history at that. I don't think he could scratch his own ass if he started with his hands in his back pockets."

"It's not his call, James, but the NWO. The President, when elected, was worth almost one million dollars, and he had no solid source of income, not a thing, before being elected. Now, almost eight years later, he's worth over twelve million bucks. How'd he make that money legally?"

"He was a college professor, or so I heard." James replied.

"No college professor is making enough to have a million dollars in the bank and I don't give a damn who they are or what college they teach. The man taught Constitutional law and he's broken it more times than any President in history. Probably more than all the other Presidents combined." Blake replied. "Hell, I thought Grant was dishonest and his administration corrupt, but this President makes him look like a boy scout."

Wilson typed, "Remember a couple of elections back when it looked like retired General Wiseman would win the election? He had all the electoral votes; even the Liberals liked the man, but he lost to Goings, who was under investigation for keeping classified information in her home and on her private email server. Goings should have gone to prison, but she was the hand picked one to be our President by the NWO. Suddenly, as the President, all the FBI charges against her were dropped, and nothing was ever said about her or her email again. I really don't think our votes mean shit and the NWO selects our leaders."

"Look at all the deaths too. Some of the world's richest men and women have been found dead. Some were ruled suicides, others murder, but why? I think they weren't playing by the rules of the NWO or they've pissed them off in some way. Hell, Mims was killed just last night, but why?"

James chuckled, took a sip of his coffee and said, "Wilson, my man, you're reading too many action books and I think you're way off with your thinking. Are you trying to tell me the NWO has hit-men?"

"It's possible. These men and women are billionaires and can call the shots. Nothing, and I mean nothing, goes on in the world without their approval."

James laughed and typed, "Bullshit."

"James, you're wrong, good buddy. The NWO even financed the protesters and looters at all the public speaking events General Wiseman had. Those folks didn't just show up on their own. They were paid big money to raise hell and attack the General's policy on sending illegal aliens and refugees back home. If you remember, not one American flag was carried by the protesters, but plenty of Mexican and Mussy flags. They looted towns, causing millions in damages, blocked traffic on highways, and just raised hell in general. Even the blacks turned against him and blocked traffic in and out of a number of large cities in protest."

"Let any sumbitches try to block me on the freeway and you'll have a mass burial. I don't play that shit." James typed, and then chuckled.

"Pull your head out of your ass and you'll see it all around you. Kids are learning less about religion and few attend church, history has been rewritten and is no longer taught as it really happened, it's getting hard to tell the men from the women, and we're a nation of wussies. Hell, most Americans today are obese and lay on their asses all day doing nothing. Racial tensions are higher now than when Martin Luther King was marching in the

1960's. More and more Americans are getting used to the government taking care of them and that's just for starters. Under the current President, race relations have been moved back 60 years or more." Blake said.

Wilson said, "I see black folks protesting the killing of one of their own and demanding the policeman who killed him to be locked up. The man killed had shot at the officer twice, hitting his cruiser door both times. Hell, like anyone else the cop shot back. They wanted to know why the cop shot to kill and not just maim? Why didn't he use a taser or pepper spray? Now, I may be a black man, but even I don't understand that line of thinking. I'll bet you the NWO is behind all this racial unrest too."

"Just some lazy folks who think they can sue for some big money and come out on top." James typed.

"Well, the current generation is a lazy bunch and that's obvious. But, don't ya see, it's the old adage of divide and conquer. The NWO wants all the minorities in this country at each others throats." Wilson said.

"Interesting discussion, but I need to run some errands. Will you be online later?" James asked.

"Maybe. As a retired detective, maybe I can pull some strings and get the Homeland Security folks to release Thomas and Jerry. Hell, they're not criminals." Wilson said.

"LOL, one day they'll do too much and end up in jail for a spell. I'm actually surprised they've not been sued for slander." James said.

"Or ended up in a concentration camp." Blake typed.

Half a world away, in Frankfurt, Germany, a man sat in a dark office at the very top of a huge industrial complex, with only his desk lamp on. It was cold outside, with the skies overcast and the threat of snow in the air. The man picked up his phone, dialed a number and then said, "Begin phase three, immediately."

CHAPTER 2

Wilson looked at the desk Sergeant and asked, "What do you mean they're not locked up? Are they here, in this building?"

"I have no record of them being arrested, no warrants are on file for either, and no reason we'd pick them up. I can guarantee you, they're not in jail here."

"Run a computer check and see if the Feds have anything on them. They're both retired military men, so it's not likely they've broken any laws."

"I'll do it this time, bro, but keep in mind, this ain't Wilson's police force, okay?" the black Sergeant said, and then laughed.

Minutes later he glanced from the screen and said, "They're clear, and the Feds don't want them either. Maybe they went out for a while. There's no reason any agency would want either of those guys. Oh, and they're not listed on the No Fly List either, so they're clean." The Sergeant then laughed.

Just then, Donna walked in from lunch and Wilson said, "How are you doing today?"

"I'm fine, Frank, and how is Julia?"

"Doing well, and the doctor said the baby is due any day now."

"You just watch and make sure that pretty daughter of yours doesn't try to do too much."

"I will, and say hi to James when you see him tonight."

"I'll do that and after the baby is born, well, maybe y'all can come by the house for supper one night."

"I'll tell her, and look forward to it." Wilson said and then added to the desk Sergeant, "Thanks for the help, Sarge, but those guys are my war buddies."

"Not a problem, but if the Lieutenant catches me doing this for you, he'll have my ass." the Sergeant said, and then gave a big smile.

Wilson walked outside, gave thought to his two friends and then started walking to his car. He'd just entered the parking lot when he saw two men being loaded into a van. One was Jerry, he was sure of it, but his face was black and blue with bruises.

Before he could approach the van, it sped away and was lost from view.

Now, the desk Sergeant either lied to me or had no idea Jerry and Thomas were in the building. If no one has a warrant for either, why have they been taken? Who took them? he thought as he started his car and placed it into gear.

He glanced at his watch, 1312 hours, and then relaxed. His wife, Nancy worked as a nurse at a local hospital and his daughter Julia had mom's car for the day. Seems his daughter's car was in the shop, so Wilson had to pick up Nancy at the hospital, but that was hours from now.

I need to talk with the wives of both guys to see how the arrests went down and take it from there, he thought and drove to Tom's house first.

Tom and his wife lived in a nice middle class neighborhood, with fairly new homes, and well maintained yards. Tom's yard always looked good, because it was his pride and joy, along with his 18 foot flag pole, which had both a United States and Texas flag mounted. He pulled into the driveway and parked behind the 1965 Ford Mustang his buddy was rebuilding.

He walked to the door and rang the doorbell.

A few short minutes later the door opened and Wilson could see that Joan had been crying.

"Oh, Frank, come in, please. Some men showed early this morning and took Tom away."

"That's why I'm here. Did the men say they had a warrant or what did they say to him?"

"No, no, they showed me no warrant, but said they had one. Please, sit on the sofa. I'm worried to death over him."

Wilson took a seat, met her wet eyes and said, "Tell me what you know and remember about this morning. No detail is too small."

"They were dressed in cheap three piece suits, like you'd buy at a department store, and all three were big men. They told him they had a federal warrant for his arrest for threatening the President of the United States, but still didn't show the papers. He gets hot online at times, but I know he'd never threaten anyone. He has been speaking out against the NWO and lately he'd been getting some strange calls and even a few threats. Tom doesn't take threats well and stayed armed even in the house.

It was a little after four this morning when the doorbell rang. I thought something had happened to one of our kids, who all live out of state, so I rushed to the door. When I opened it, three men rushed into the house and handcuffed Tom. They showed me no search warrant, warrant for his arrest, or any paperwork. The only words spoken by them was to him and they said they had a federal warrant for his arrest, supposedly for threatening the President of the United States. How can that be, if they didn't show me the papers?"

"Well, by not showing the papers, the arrest was illegal. What did these men call each other, or do you remember?"

"Uh, some kind of military code. I only remember one man called Agent Poppa Whiskey. One of the men asked, 'Agent Poppa Whiskey, where is the suspect to be placed in the van?'"

"Did you see any badges or name tags, anything like that?"

"I was half asleep and they all wore badges on their belts, to the left of the buckles. I remember seeing an eye in a triangle, with a world globe behind it, but I was never shown one. They rushed in, took Tom, and then left. I'm worried about him, Frank."

"I'm looking for them now. I hope to have him home in time for supper with you." He gave an ill felt smile as he stood.

"I do have a license number for the white van and it's NWO666, Texas state plate." she said as she handed him a scrap of paper.

"The 666 comes from Revelation 13 in the Bible. If I remember correctly 666 is a human number that is connected with the mark of the beast."

"I opened my Bible right after they left, and it reads, 'No one could buy or sell unless he had the mark, which is the name of the beast or the number of his name. Here is wisdom. Let him who has understanding calculate the number of the beast, for it is the number of a man: His number is 666.'" "I think that's Revelation 13:17,18, right?"

"I don't know, Frank, and I didn't write any of this down. The NWO scared me as much as the sixes did."

"Let me know if you hear anything about Tom, okay? I don't care the time of day or night, you call me, understood?"

"I will, and I hope I get him back safe. He's a good man, Frank."

"I know, and I knew him before you, remember?" he replied, stood and added, "I have to speak with Jerry's wife, too, and see how she is doing with all of this."

"She's not home, and is away visiting her grand-babies. Do you think I should call her?"

"No, but if you have her number, let me have it and if they're not home by tomorrow morning I'll contact her."

She walked away and returned a few minutes later with the number. Handing it to Frank, she said, "Anything else I should know?"

"Do not speak about Tom or Jerry being taken on the phone or computer, because both are being monitored, I'm sure."

"This can't be happening in the United States this day and age, can it? Tom's no criminal, just an old retired military guy that drinks too much beer at times and gets obnoxious on the computer. He has very strong opinions about being patriotic and is worried about our county. He's very open about both."

Frank met her eyes and said, "I think it may be more common than we realize. Let's just hope they're both returned safely and soon. I'll do some digging around and see what I can find."

"You be careful, because we have no idea who is behind all of this."

James was out in the garage painting a doll house he'd made for his granddaughter, when Frank pulled into his driveway. Seeing his friend of many long years, he placed the paintbrush on the top of the can and was wiping his hands with a rag when Wilson neared.

"Top, we need to talk and your house is not the place. Let's go for a ride in my car for a bit."

"Okay, but what's going on?"

"We'll talk in the car and it's about a basketball game."

Basketball game? Hell, he knows I can't stand round-ball at all, Top thought as he moved to Wilson's car.

Once they were moving, Frank turned on some music and said, "We'll talk in a minute."

"It's your dime."

He then pulled into a large parking lot for a department store and said, "Let's take a walk."

As they walked, Frank told him all he knew and James was stunned. He'd spoken to a lot of men, intelligent men, who believed in the NWO, but never, until now, had he had any solid proof the organization even existed.

"Is she sure of the plate being NWO666?"

"She even wrote it down."

"I can't believe this; did you run a check on the plate?"

"I did and there is no such plate. Never has been a plate like that made in the USA."

"She's positive about the plate?"

"Her husband was being taken and he was placed in a van, so I'm damned sure she got the right plate. She was terrified and while she didn't say anything about being scared for herself, her eyes spoke a great deal."

"I just can't believe this NWO crap." James said, his frustration obvious over the missing men.

"This is not new, and they've been around since the 1700's, but most people thought they were part of the Masons."

"I had no idea."

"Look, a lot of folks know John Wilkes Booth killed Lincoln, but few know why. See, Lincoln had been meeting with the leaders of the blacks and his goal was to have all of them relocated to someplace else, at the expense of the Federal Government. Lincoln was one of the biggest racists in the history of America. They'd been going over places that were similar to Africa in weather, when the NWO had the man killed. The NWO at that time knew the blacks would eventually demand equality and they did, only it was the 1960's before a lot was done about it. The NWO wants countries to fight internally and collapse."

"I don't know if I can believe that." James said, and shook his head.

"Okay, what if I told you I suspect JFK wasn't assassinated by Lee Harvey Oswald alone, but by the NWO, using Oswald as the trigger finger? JFK had threatened to release some pretty good news in a few weeks and from what I gathered, it was about the elite rich and powerful. He was killed to shut him up."

"Okay, let's say you're correct, what in the world would the NWO want with two old retired military men like Jerry and Thomas?" James asked.

"That I can't answer, unless it's to make both of them an example."

"Let's pray that's not the case or we may never find their bodies."

"I don't think they'll kill them, but they might."

"What now?"

Glancing at his watch, Frank said, "It's 1534, so I have to get you back home and then pick up my wife at the hospital. Her shift ends at 1600." He turned and they started walking back to his car.

"You going to be online tonight?"

"Yep, but don't bring any of this stuff up or even discuss it on the phone." Frank warned.

"No, of course not. Do you think our homes are bugged?"

"I honestly don't know, but we're small time for NWO. I think they just want to shut Tom's big mouth so he doesn't stir up the general population."

"Do you think the President is stupid enough to declare martial law and bring the UN into this country?" James asked.

"I don't think the man is stupid by any imagination, but someone else is calling the shots, not him." He shrugged and then unlocked the car doors.

"Well, I think it would be a huge mistake for him and he'd have a Civil War on his hands that would kill millions. Lawdy, can you imagine the veterans and hunters giving up their guns? Hell, the deep South has been waiting for another civil war and I suspect this would be bloody. I don't see the rednecks or cowboys giving up their weapons, it just won't happen."

"I'll not give up mine without a fight. How about you?"

"No way in hell. I earned the right to have my guns during my military service, not that earning a right is needed. Like most Americans, I feel the Constitution is all the right I need. Carrying a gun to me is a God given right."

"Well, let me get you home so I can pick up my wife from work." Frank said and started the car.

The next morning after Donna left for work, James moved to the computer to see if anything had been heard from the two missing men.

"Howdy."

"Howdy, Top." Frank answered quickly enough.

He must live on this site, James thought and typed, "Any word on our friends?"

"Yes and we're going to take another walk where we did yesterday."

"When?"

"Right now, okay?"

"Sure. Later, Frank."

"Stay safe."

James jumped on his motorcycle and drove to the department store parking lot and saw Frank leaning against his car door. He was smoking and, as far as James knew, he'd stopped smoking twenty years ago.

He parked his bike, removed his helmet and placed the brain bucket on a mirror.

"Well?" he asked as he walked toward his friend.

"They're back, but they ain't pretty."

"Don't you know smoking isn't good for you?"

"Lay off, because I'm in the mood to start drinking again too."

Leaning on the car as well, James asked, "What do you mean by they're not pretty?"

"Late last night, near midnight, a van drove by the house and our two boys were rolled out onto the pavement. Jerry has two broken legs and two broken arms. One of the arms, I think it's his left, is a compound fracture. Thomas looks like hell and lost all the nails on both hands, has a nasty cut to his forehead and both legs are broken. According to the VA doctor, it looks like the breaks were made with a steel pipe. He's got a couple of cracked ribs and he's complaining of his back hurting."

"How do you know all of this?"

"Joan called me last night crying and thinking the broken bones would kill them. I had her call an ambulance and have them taken to the VA hospital in Houston. I visited both of them this morning and had a chance to speak with their doctor during his rounds."

"How do they look?"

"Rough, man, rough. Both are skinned up and bruised. Jerry was out of it when I visited, but Thomas came around long enough to talk to me. He clearly said, 'The New World Order wants 'all veterans to stand down and not interfere in the coming years,' but I'm not sure if it was him or the drugs talking."

"I find this hard to believe, man. This sounds more like a couple of men holding out on a drug dealer or pimp and being taught a lesson. Let me have one of your cigarettes."

Tossing the pack to him, along with the lighter, Frank said, "Now it's like old times, you never did have enough money to buy a whole pack of smokes."

James laughed and then said, "Did he say anything else?"

"Yes, he said for us to watch television tonight, when the President speaks."

"You mean he's been beat to hell and wants me to watch the President lie to us again?" James gave a confused look as he spoke.

"He said he was warned that the comments about the NWO are to stop and right now. He said the President will be talking about the NWO and the UN. Tonight he's to make a very serious announcement to the American people. Thomas warned that all veterans will be declared legally insane and admitted to medical facilities for treatment."

"Facilities, my ass. They'll murder us is what they'll do." James said, his anger obvious.

"Well, let's listen to the President tonight and see what the man says. He'd be pretty stupid to piss off over 12 million veterans by calling them insane."

"You know, he's about useless as a man and even less effective as a leader. I suspect the dumb-ass is going to announce that the UN is coming for our guns, and I hope that won't happen. The second he says that and declares martial law, the people will rise up in revolt."

"Tonight, just like always, when you're online, we'll communicate. If martial law is declared and they're coming for our guns, I'll ask you to meet me for a card game this weekend. Once I say that, you reply with an okay and we'll wrap up the talking. As soon as you're off the computer, bring Donna and meet me at my hunting lodge. I know it's safe to talk there and I've already told a number of people I really trust with this information. Keep the information secret, and tell Donna it's a weekend camping trip."

"Oh, this is going to really mess this country up. I just don't believe this. I pray we're all wrong about this."

"It's real, and my primary concern is how the military is going to react."

James thought for a moment and then said, "Our enlistment oaths have this covered, remember; "I, insert your name, swear (or affirm) that I will support and defend the Constitution of the United States against all enemies, foreign and domestic; that I will bear true faith and allegiance to the same; and that I will obey the orders of the President of the United States and the orders of the officers appointed over me, according to regulations and the Uniform Code of Military Justice. So help me God.'"

The key words are: defend the Constitution of the United States against all enemies, foreign and domestic. And, according to regulations and the Uniform Code of Military Justice. First, the right to bear arms is guaranteed by the Constitution, that's not open to debate; an order given to take our guns away is unlawful according to the UCMJ. I think the military will side with the people on this one."

"Well, I need to get home, but let me know this evening what we're going to do."

"Will do, and you stay safe. I trust no one these days. You carrying?"

"Always, and I have been since I retired. You?"

"I wasn't earlier, but I am now. Later."

At 1800 hours on the dot the President of the United States walked behind a podium at the White House and said,

> "My fellow Americans, it is only after much thought that I speak to you tonight to share a decision I have made. As the man you elected to carry out your wishes, I could not delegate this responsibility to anyone else. After seeing the great progress that gun control has experienced in cities like Chicago, Detroit, Saint Louis, and other places in our great nation, I have asked the United Nations to become actively involved with collecting firearms from all owners throughout the United States, effective immediately. This is with the hope that most of you will voluntarily surrender your guns. Additionally, in order to suppress any violence, and there will be violence, I am declaring martial law throughout the land effective tonight at midnight. The UN is already in place, so all

they have to do is don their uniforms tonight. If you are out after midnight this evening you run the risk of being arrested or shot. Let me assure you, this is no joke and I am being dead serious here. Starting tomorrow, we'll be collecting registered weapons that are listed by owners in our computer system. I am aware that by taking your guns I am violating your second amendment rights, but our safety is more important than allowing a bunch of rednecks and cowboys to have guns. I think by disarming our country we can roll into the New World Order smoothly. I thank all of you for your time."

The man then turned and walked away.

James, sitting on the sofa with his arm around Donna, said, "Awww shit."

CHAPTER 3

Agent X1 walked around the old abandoned warehouse and out of habit, he stayed in the darker shadows. He smiled as he thought of his interrogation of the two old men and how defiant they'd been at first. Near the end, they'd begged him to kill them. He'd worked the two retired military men over hard, and knew he'd gotten carried away with his crowbar. However, before he'd started being rough his brain received a thought impulse to leave the men alone, at least for a while, and to question them. He had no idea this thought was the result of a chip planted in his left arm, slightly below his wrist, in his hand. With the chip installed, every thought of Agent X1 was recorded, and new thoughts could be sent to his brain. Christians in some third world nations had refused to be implanted with the chip, calling it the mark of the beast, and they'd died in large numbers. To date, many who were once Christians were carrying a chip. They'd renounced their religion to save their lives.

He'd learned nothing from interrogating the two men, except they were a couple of old men who disliked the current President, as well as the President elect. They were both hardcore Republicans who were tired of the "free" society that had been created by the Liberals in America. There were now more folks on public assistance than off, and the worker bees were paying out the nose to provide the free support to their fellow Americans. They were both extremely upset that American tax dollars were paying for sex change operations, providing free assistance to illegal aliens, relocating refugees and providing them large sums of money, and supplying free birth control pills for women, while veterans died waiting to see a doctor at their local VA hospital.

Once he'd questioned them, he beat both men hard to teach them they must avoid discussing the New World Order or they'd be killed the next time.

His cell phone rang and he opened it, "Yes?"

A familiar voice only said three words, "Begin phase three."

"I understand, begin phase three."

"Correct." the voice replied and then the phone went dead.

X1 knew his job now was to kill large numbers of innocent people, but he felt no emotion.

He returned to his office, opened his safe, and removed a cylinder marked, "Polonium 210." There was a National Basketball Association playoff game this evening and X1 would need to service the air conditioners.

It is said a single gram of Polonium 210 could easily kill 10 million people if ingested, inhaled, or injected. Another advantage of using Polonium is if the radiation doesn't kill you, which would be rare, you are then a perfect candidate to get cancer. Some scientists claim it's 250,000 times deadlier than hydrogen cyanide, but X1 didn't know or care about that. He had been trained that high doses would result in the victim experiencing confusion, convulsion, and coma within just minutes of inhaling the poison. Phase Three put Agent X1 and all the other agents in the United States into an action mode.

The purpose of Phase Three was to reduce the world's population to a more manageable level. To coincide with X1's basketball game, agents across the states were to bring their various groups into action. All the minority groups would start huge riots, with looting and the killing of police officers, all instigated by NWO agents. Agents in the Republican state militia groups would bring them out of the woodwork to assist the local and state police in controlling the violence caused by the looters. Given time, these agents would eventually resort to shooting and killing.

Even the illegal aliens and refugees had, over time, been infiltrated as well and they would step forward to add their protests. Many of the refugees were Muslims and they'd make their presence felt by using suicide bombers in busy areas, detonation of road side bombs, and through assassinations. There were also a number of dirty bombs owned by the Muslims and they'd not hesitate to detonate all of them. They already had selected locations for the weapons, and now they would be used. It was hoped that a massive civil war would develop in the middle of all this chaos.

Glancing at his watch, X1 went to the garage, took a white van and then placed a large magnetic sign on both sides that advertised A-1 Air Conditioning and Heating. He loaded his Polonium 210, dressed in a pair of coveralls and then drove to the event. By now, it was just starting and he knew people had been lined up for hours, because newsmen had covered that very well on the 6 o'clock news. By looking at the blueprints of the building, X1 knew where the air conditioning and heating unit was located. He'd drive to the entry gate and have a guard let him in. He had a fake driver's license, a fake company ID and even had the gas cylinder marked as R-410A. He'd been taught that R-410A, a replacement for Freon, contained no chlorine and was considered ozone-friendly, so the container would not be suspect. Even if eyed closely, he would gain access, but if he ran into trouble, he'd just kill the guard.

When he neared the location of the game, the streets were filled with folks going to the playoffs, so X1 smiled. None of them suspected that within a few minutes, most would be breathing Polonium 210 and be dead shortly. He pulled up to a gate shack.

"What do you need?" the guard asked; his name tag read Jones.

"I've been sent to top off the Freon for the game tonight."

"I need to see your driver's license, vehicle registration, and company ID."

Handing them to the guard, he watched as the man carefully looked the papers over, entered his name and license plate number and then ran the name through their computer system. The search came back clean, so his papers were handed back.

"I know the heating and ac is on the southwest corner, but how will I get into the building?"

"I'll have a guard let you in, and he'll be with you at all times as you work. When you're done with your task, he'll let you out and then lock up again. Take it easy, and I hope you get to watch part of the game on TV later."

"Thanks, Jones." X1 replied with a big smile. He slipped the van into gear and moved to the southwest corner.

He finally spotted a guard standing by an open door, so he parked the van, pulled his tool bag and his cylinder. He nodded to the guard and said, "Ain't this one hell of a note? I have to check the air conditioning system with a game going on. We were notified the temperature inside isn't as cool as it should be." He then thought, *Once he's inside with me I'll kill him and keep his radio for a while.* The guard was smoking, so X1 suspected the man would enter after he'd finished his smoke, but he'd be a smoker who'd never have to worry about lung cancer.

"I don't know nothin' 'bout no air conditioners, so ya do what needs doin'."

"I will," X1 said and then added, "and it won't take long either."

He pulled out his tools, removed a panel, having no idea what he was looking at, and then waited for the guard to enter. Finally, pulling a step ladder, he moved up higher to look an air duct over.

Pulling a pair of tin snips, he cut a hole large enough to place his cylinder, but bent it upward. Now, he wasn't sure if the guard would come inside or not. He then returned to his tool box, pulled a roll of duct tape, and was just about to pick up the gas, when the guard neared.

X1 had his silenced .380 in the bottom of a large white bucket and when the guard was close enough, he pulled the pistol and sent three rounds through the man's chest. With a surprised look on his face as three long fingers of blood shot from his back, the guard fell to the concrete floor, unmoving. Placing the pistol back in his bucket, he pulled out a full face gas mask and thick gloves. Once wearing the mask and gloves, he moved to the cut in the vent. He opened the nozzle on the cylinder as far as it would go and then placed it in the vent. He then folded the metal down and sealed the cut metal with the duct tape.

He gathered up all his tools, took the dead man's radio and waved at Jones as he left the complex, heading north. Once outside of town, he removed the signs from the van, gathered his tools, the coveralls, and other gear in green plastic bags and dumped them over a wooden fence on a narrow country road.

Another Agent would pick them up in an hour, so he turned the guard's radio on. He could hear Jones trying to reach him and as he drove he realized by now the auditorium was probably filled with the poisonous gas.

Minutes later he heard, "Attention all stations. Attention all stations. We have an unknown number of fans experiencing confusion, convulsions, and going into comas right now. We even have, wait one."

A minute passed before the radio became busy again, "Now about half of both pro teams are on the floor. Jones, alert the police and have ambulances sen—"

"Base, this is gate one. Base, this is gate one. This is gate one to all stations, get all the fans out of the building now! I repeat, empty the building and do the job now. Someone check on Base and see if he's still conscious." Jones ordered.

He then switched channels, "Hospital this is gate 1 at the auditorium at the NBA playoffs. I need all available ambulances at my location. I have an unknown number of people with convulsions, and many in comas. I repeat, I need all available medical assistance at my location now!"

Once again he switched channels and said, "Desk, this is gate 1 and I need assistance at the auditorium. I have an unknown number of victims experiencing confusion, convulsions, and comas. I am lowering and locking all gate guards right now. Report to gate 1 for admission."

Still wearing his gloves, when X1 went over a bridge a few minutes later, he tossed the radio out of his window and into the river below. He gave a loud insane laugh and when he got back to his office, he'd watch the television to see how much damage he'd done to the fans and players.

It was then he saw a red and yellow light flashing behind him and wondered how the cops could be on his tail that quickly. He pulled into the empty parking lot of an out of business grocery store and stopped.

He quickly pulled his driver license, his registration, and proof of insurance card. He then placed his hands on the steering wheel.

X1 wasn't overly concerned because if this cop gave him any trouble, he'd simply kill him.

The officer walked to the now open driver's window and asked, "Do you know why I stopped you?"

"No, sir, I wasn't speeding."

"Your rear right tail light is out."

"Oh, I had no idea."

"Let me see your driver's license, registration, and insurance card."

When X1 handed the items to the cop, the man walked back to his patrol car to see if any warrants were open for this driver. X1 was relaxed because he was in the system and protected as well.

The officer walked back a few minutes later and said, "Uh, Mr. Walker, I have no idea who you work for, but I was just told not to detain you and to release you immediately." He handed all the papers back to X1.

"I'm CIA, and working a case right now. Not a problem, officer. See, I have my badge right here."

When the cop leaned forward to view the badge, X1 fired the .380 twice and bullets struck the man in the face. Shards of skull, brain tissue and blood blew out behind the man's head and he dropped instantly to the ground, dead before he'd even struck the pavement.

Starting the van, X1 gave a loud laugh and after he sobered, said, "The killing has started in earnest now, so let the fun begin."

"Wilson residence. This is Frank."

"It's me, honey. There was some sort of poison gas released at an NBA game tonight and most of the hospitals in town are full. Right now we have no idea if it was released on purpose or accidentally. We have many dead, but I have no idea how many. Frank, I had a little girl no more than ten die holding my hand as we prayed for her recovery. I'd just watched her mother and

NEW WORLD ORDER : Volume 1

father die. What kind of monsters kill kids?" She broke down crying.

"What? My God, that's horrible! Baby, are you okay?"

"No, I'm not okay . . . and . . . and I may never be okay again. I want to stay and work a double shift, because every second counts with these folks."

"No, it's okay, you stay there as long as you feel you're helping. Let me know when you're on your way home."

"Bye, sweetheart, I have to get back. If I learn something important, I'll let you know. It's all over the television right now. Love you, and later."

The phone screen went black, so Frank moved to the living room, turned on a news channel and called James.

"Hey, Frank, how are you?" James answered the phone.

"Better than some. Look, have you seen the news?"

"No, why? I was painting a doll house."

"Turn it on now, and I think this is just the beginning. Looks like peace is dead in America. I was in the service twenty years as a Military Policeman, then twenty years with Houston Vice. Never in 40 years have I seen so much violence and death in one day."

"I'm bringing Donna, and we need to talk."

"Well, martial law is in effect, so if you don't make it quick, you'll spend the night. Hell, this reminds me of Kristallnacht and the Nazis. I'm concerned, and we'll talk when you get here. You'd better be packing too, because this is a dangerous night to be out."

"Okay, see you in a bit." James said and they hung up.

Damn, they have maybe thousands dead from the NBA game, riots and looters in six or seven major cities, the rednecks have attacked Muslim mosques in Houston, who are suspected to have sent two suicide bombers to blow up in malls. *Oh, there it is, the Memphis Mall and a mall in New York City have both had explosions with an unknown number of dead. What in the hell is going on?* Frank thought.

"This is Burt Wilcox of WDBB news, and we interrupt this program to report the possible explosion of a nuclear device of some sort near Washington, D. C. Again, we have reports of the detonation of a possible nuclear bomb or dirty bomb in the Washington, D. C. area. Initial reports indicate there are many known dead; the explosion was so bad, it blew down brick buildings for almost four miles from the explosive center. Right now the police are asking everyone to avoid the area. There is also the risk of fallout from the radiation and the winds are blowing to the east. I take you to Tanya Brown, who is on the scene."

"Burt, I am being kept away from the danger zone by police but complete buildings are gone, to include the White House. It is known the President was in the building earlier today, but the First Lady was visiting Houston, Texas showing support for undocumented aliens and refugees. Houston, which has exploded overnight since the President declared martial law, with the state, county and city police saying they will not and cannot support martial law. So, tonight Texas is not under martial law and many other states, mostly Southern, have followed in the footsteps of the Lone Star State. Mississippi Governor, Bill Spence, said today, quote, 'The White House can go to hell as far as the great state of Mississippi is concerned.' unquote. James Boxer, the Governor of Alabama sent the most chilling comment today when he said, quote, "You can have my guns when you peel my cold dead finger from the trigger." unquote. Burt my first glance indicates that the While House is truly gone."

The cameraman panned the whole area and the White House was completely gone with no sign it had ever stood. When the camera returned to the reporter, she said, "This is Tanya Brown of WDBB reporting live from Washington, D.C., back to you, Burt..."

"We have been told by a reliable source that the United States military refused orders today from the President to enforce martial law, stating the second amendment authorizes the civilian population to privately own weapons. They stressed they are bound to support the Constitution by their military oath. They have also stated the UN troops that are stationed on American soil have 24 hours to leave or we will consider their presence an act of aggression and an act of war against the United States, and the troops will then be removed by force. These are truly troubled days for the United States of America."

The camera suddenly switched to a different reporter who said, "This is John Steeples, reporting from Houston, Texas, with a special report. We have unconfirmed information that the First

Lady has been killed, beheaded actually, while visiting refugees. Again, this report has not been confirmed, and we have no word from the White House or the President. But witnesses spoke to us of seeing her headless body being dragged around the streets by two men on a motorcycle. There are rumors of her head being photographed and posted on various social media sites." A camera switched to showing what looked like the First Lady's head laying in a pool of blood on a post on a Social Media site, declaring 'the witch is dead.' It was a color photograph, but it left little doubt in Frank's mind the President, if he survived the blast, was now a widower.

The camera returned to the reporter, "Again, none of this is confirmed, but there seems to be heavy fighting with the local state militia, local cowboys, and others against the Muslims in the city. If you listen closely, in the background you can hear the gunshots. This is John Steeples reporting; back to you, Burt."

"We're going to take a station break, so stay tuned to WDBB, Houston. We'll keep you up to date on local, regional, national and international news as it happens."

Frank heard his doorbell, pulled his Ruger .45 and, moving to the door, he asked, "Who is it?"

"It's me, and I brought some beer." James said.

Frank unlocked the door, let James in and asked, "Where's Donna?"

"She got called into work. Seems the Houston cops are having a full day on the job."

"Have . . . have you seen the news?"

"No, I was working on a dollhouse."

"The shit has hit the stump and I mean all over. It looks like the President is dead, along with his wife, the cowboys and rednecks are attacking the Muslims, and. . . and much more."

Opening a beer, James smiled and said, "Well, aren't you going to give me the bad news?"

"Damn it man, I'm not joking. Some fools set off a damned nuke in Washington, D.C., the Southern states are leading us to another civil war, and the armed forces have more or less told the President to kiss their asses."

"I thought the President is dead." James tossed a beer to Frank.

"He's *thought* to be dead. If he is, that leaves that dumb weak dick of a Vice-President calling the shots."

"Sounds to me like no one is in charge, then. Brill isn't smart enough to run a scout troop, much less a nation." James took a long drink of his beer.

"I'm worried, man. The blacks are rioting all over the nation. We have the whites, blacks, and Mexicans all shooting at each other and all of them are hunting Muslims. Damn me, what a mess. The news said a few minutes ago that over 2,000 were dead at the NBA game alone, but many more are expected to die. It's a friggin' mess."

"So, what do we do?" James asked.

"Here in about thirty minutes, as soon as we finish these beers, we're taking my Jeep and going to get our women. I know they'll not want to leave, but we need to get them and get the hell out of Dodge, man. We'll go to the hunting lodge for a couple of weeks."

"To hell with waiting to finish the beers; take them with us. I don't think there is a cop in town tonight worried about an open container or of us driving and drinking. Both women may lose their jobs, but it beats losing their lives, Frank."

"You hot?"

"9 mm in a shoulder harness and four magazines, you?"

"My Ruger .45, with four mags too. It's a heavy gun to pack, but if I hit you with it, you'll stay down. Come with me into the bedroom and we'll take my other weapons, too. We may not get to come back this way for a while. Grab the ammo cans on your next time in here, because I have 1,000 rounds for each weapon, except the .45, and I have, oh, close to 5,000. Let's load this stuff and get out of here."

"I'll hit your cupboards and bring all your canned goods, too."

CHAPTER 4

The Houston General Baptist Hospital was full, and the sick and wounded kept coming in. Patients lined the hallway on gurneys, and now stretchers were being used, the gurneys full. The parking lot near the emergency room door was established as a triage, where Nancy Wilson decided who'd live and die, based on the severity of their problem. She was sorting and allocating aid on the basis of need and selecting those likely to benefit from medical treatment and those who would not survive. Some were beyond help and were placed on a blanket on the closely cut lawn, to wait for death. In most cases, the ill and wounded were 4 to a room now, and there was no end to the patients seen. The National Guard was working out behind the facility to setup a number of large tents.

She squatted by a man with half his head missing and using her lipstick she place a large red C on his forehead; the soldiers from the National Guard moved the injured man to the grass to await death.

She'd just bent over to evaluate a young boy, when she heard Frank say, "Come with me, baby."

"I . . . I can't, and why are you here?" She stood and met his eyes.

As he explained the news, he could see the fatigue in her face. Once finished he asked, "Well, do you see my line of thought? The United States is going down hill fast, baby, and I want you with me when it falls."

"I can't and won't leave right now! I have injured people here to see and I just can't walk away from them like everything is fine. What about these people?"

Frank, angry now screamed, "I don't care about these people. I don't love these people like I love you. Are you coming, or not?"

"Let me finish this shift, two more hours and then I'll leave with you. I can't last much longer than two hours anyway, because I'm exhausted. Please, baby, I'm the only hope some of these people have."

"Okay, but be ready to leave when I get back in two hours." Frank said, his frustration obvious, but deep down inside, he knew his wife was right. She was a compassionate woman, which was one of the reasons he loved her.

He returned to the parking lot, found James and explained what was going on. He then asked, "Is there anything else from your place we might need? I think we should get my other weapons, along with all my ammo."

"I have some foods saved, mainly for hurricane season and tornadoes." James said, and then removed his cowboy hat and ran his hand through his hair.

"What kind of foods?"

"Mostly dry stuff. You know, beans, pasta, dehydrated meats, veggies and fruits."

"Do we stop for Donna now or after we get the foods and guns?"

"Let's do it after and I'll get my two dogs too, maybe. Now, I'll bring the motorhome, because I can tow the Jeep and the motorcycle mounts on the back."

"I need to call my kids and tell them what's going on, and you need to call yours too."

"I'll do that as soon as we're at my place." James said and then kick started his motorcycle.

"You lead and I'll follow you." Franks said and moved to his car.

At James' house all was quiet on his street. They'd encountered no armed groups and no battles as they'd driven, so far, this night. Since the drive was a little over 20 miles to the hospital, they'd loaded up all the weapons, ammo and food in the camper. It was a smaller previously used camper, but had the advantage of being driven and not pulled. Glancing at his watch,

James saw it was 2300, so he had another hour before he picked up Nancy.

James' cellphone rang and he heard Donna say, "Turn on the TV now and watch the News. Something has happened at the Houston General Baptist Hospital and it's serious. We have officers enroute to the place now. I have to go, but I love you."

He pushed a button on the remote and the TV came on.

" . . . have no idea of those responsible for this attack, but we had a reporter on scene prior to the explosion, filming the National Guard's efforts to erect tents for the wounded, and here is the footage he shot. I do want to warn our viewers this video is extremely graphic and is not recommended for viewing by children."

The station switched to a U-Haul truck moving toward the hospital at a high rate of speed. The reporter said, "An unknown truck is really moving toward the emergency room as so many others have this evening. He seems to be gathering up speed. I know he's moving over 50 miles an hour right now. Get the camera on the truck, not on me, on the truck! Something is not right here!"

The truck was seen running over the dead and injured in the grasses, moving toward the double doors, and it was then when a few military police began shooting at the truck.

The cameraman caught a loud male voice screaming, "Allahu akbar!"

The truck was seen striking two medical orderlies coming out with a gurney and then plowing into the building. A second or so later, a huge explosion was seen with bricks, medical equipment and parts of bodies flying through the air. The secondary explosion was even bigger. The cameraman was knocked off his feet and he was heard asking the reporter, "Are you okay?"

"Help me up, and keep filming."

The camera view was out of focus with the grass seen, then the sky, smoke, and finally a shot of a bleeding reporter's face.

There was a loud explosion on the other side of the hospital and more screams were heard.

"It looks as if a suicide bomber, oh my God, maybe two have struck the hospital! Look at all the wounded running from the place! It looks like a bomber has managed to explode a truck loaded with explosives on the ground floor of the Houston General Baptist Hospital. Right now, we —"

"Run!" the cameraman screamed as his footage showed the six story building starting to collapse. The camera lens suddenly showed pavement and concrete as he ran. The sounds of the building falling, screams of fear and pain were heard, and then silence.

"My God, the whole building is down." the cameraman said as he filmed the carnage. "Send any help you can to the Houston General Baptist Hospital and do it now!" A large cloud of smoke and flames reached for the sky as the cameraman kept filming.

"I don't see Dick, my reporter, and I suspect he may have fallen victim to this atrocious act, which in my eyes is a d*eliberate* act of war. I'm not sure what caused the explosion on the other side of the hospital, but that would be the main entrance to the building. I'm going to sign off now and look for Dick and help any survivors I can find. I think we need some additional crews here to cover this catastrophe." The footage stopped.

Frank stood in shock, his eyes on the television.

"Grab your coat and come with me. We'll take the motorcycle and go look for Nancy."

"I don't believe that just happened. We were just there!"

They made excellent time getting to the hospital. Because of the heavy emergency vehicle traffic blocking all lanes, James was forced to weave in and out of the lanes and at one point even drove down a sidewalk.

"Good Lord, it's a mess!" Frank said as they stopped in the parking lot. They both moved toward the last spot they'd seen Nancy and over the next hour they helped all they could and continued looking for her. It was James who found her.

"Frank! Over here!" He waved his arms.

Frank ran to James and saw Nancy on the pavement, her eyes open, and she was breathing. James squatted beside her and asked, "Where are you hurt?"

"My left thigh was stuck by something."

Frank knelt and ran his hand down her well shaped leg. Finally, he said, "It feels like a piece of metal completely through your leg. Now, Jim and I are going to wrap your leg tightly to prevent blood loss, then pack you to your Jeep. We'll then take you to his house, where we'll look you over better. He and I have plans to leave town and move to the hunting lodge for a few weeks. Baby, if we stay here, it may be many long hours before you're treated."

"Be . . . beside me, you'll see my canvas medical bag, so bring it. Before you . . . move me, look in the bag and hand me a syringe . . . marked morphine. I . . . I have some serious pain."

Frank, pulled out the syringe and asked, "Want me to give it to you?"

"Yes, the . . . pain is . . . rough."

By the time she was at the Jeep, her pain was gone, but now she was sleepy. They placed her in the front seat, slipped a seatbelt on her and then James moved to his motorcycle.

The trip back was rough due to traffic, so more than once James drove his motorcycle on sidewalks, and Frank followed him with the Jeep. At the last street, they'd pulled off the road and moved over a high school football field, coming up behind James' house.

Nancy was packed into the house and placed on the dining room table. Closer examination showed it was a piece of wood through her thigh and not metal. Using booze and rubbing alcohol, Frank cleaned around the wound, and then pulled the wood out. He poured whiskey into the hole in the leg and then sewed both the entrance and exit wounds closed with a curved needle in his first aid kit. He'd soaked both the needle and thread in rubbing alcohol. He covered both injuries with triple-antibiotic ointment and then bandaged her tightly in a torn up pillowcase. Thanks to the morphine, she'd slept through it all.

"We'll put her in the motorhome when we leave. I just spoke to Donna and she's on her way home. According to her, the whole city is a war zone."

"Any idea when she'll be here?"

"Traffic is congested in some parts of town, as you know, so it may be an hour."

"Turn on the TV again and let's see what's going on now. I can't believe this is happening in America."

The remote button was pushed and the TV came on. A male reporter stood outside the Houston General Baptist Hospital as he said, ". . . no one has claimed responsibility for the suicide trucks yet, but authorities are estimating well over two thousand pounds of explosives were used by each truck. The second truck, which crashed through the locked main entrance doors, was a good hundred feet or more inside when the driver set off the explosives. Authorities now say this was not a quickly thrown together plot to kill, but a conspiracy to strike tonight, when the hospital was working well over full capacity. Which leads me to believe, the mastermind behind the attack was also involved with other violence throughout the United States this evening. There have been over two hundred attacks against our nation this evening, mostly hospitals, police stations, and military bases and the list of dead and injured keep growing."

James pushed a button and another news reporter stood by the main gate to Scott Air Force Base, Illinois.

"John, Sergeant Brooks, Senior Airman Thompson, and Airman Joyce were all three gunned down less than ten feet from where I am standing now. Initial reports from the base public affairs office, after viewing the camera tapes from the main gate, is that six unknown men pulled up to the gate, tried to gain access and when Sergeant Brooks told the driver to turn around and leave, the airmen were shot and killed by a passenger, armed with an AK-47, in the back seat. The six men then drove on the base and two attempted entry to headquarters Air Mobility Command, while two others did briefly gain entry to headquarters United States Transportation Command. However, all four were killed during their attempts, but one managed to detonate a vest of explosives he was wearing. Three airmen were injured and none killed when that vest exploded. The guard outside the facility had shot both men, but neither fatally, and was himself shot in the shoulder."

"Uh, Mark, any idea where the remaining two men are at this time?"

"John, there has been no word released by the public affairs office, but unofficially the two are said to be dead, with one killed near the 375th Force Support Squadron and the other killed out by the Fuels storage area. We are —"

"We interrupt this broadcast to bring a special announcement by the President of the United States."

A gaunt and tired looking President move to the podium and said, "My fellow Americans. I speak to you tonight with a heavy heart, and it's with great sadness that I inform you of the death of my wife, April, who was killed while working with Muslim refugees. We don't have many details at the moment and no one has been arrested for this crime. The facts are, she and her security detail were surrounded by an angry mob as she made her way to the car, and then . . . and then." The President waved to the cameras and left the room.

A spokesman moved to the podium and said, "As you can see, he is taking the death of his wife very hard. I will tell you what we know to this point."

"How was the First Lady killed?" a reporter asked.

"That will be released at another date and time, once an autopsy has been completed. I will say this: she was decapitated at some point, but it remains unclear if the act was the cause of her death or done after she'd died."

"Can you say if the act was the result of radical Muslims?"

"I am unable to comment on that at this time. I will say, however, The First Lady was in Houston to assure the Muslim population, those recently resettled there, that they would be provided for and their short and long term needs met. She was there to guarantee these relocated families that a humanitarian effort was being made on their part by the President of the United States. No more questions, please." The spokesman held his hand up and walked from the room.

The camera went black, but then focused on a Hispanic man standing beside a reporter outside in the darkness.

"Burt, I have with me, uh, Mister Thomas Garcia, who claims he was near the crowd when the First Lady was killed. Mister Garcia, please tell our viewers what you saw."

"I was like standing on the sidewalk, because all of these people suddenly started showing up around me. I was feeling uncomfortable because they weren't dressed like me and it was dark. Then these men in suits, with this rich looking woman, suddenly pulled their guns. Shots were fired by both sides. The men with that woman were down and some men in the crowd were beating on them with their fists and iron bars and stuff. Then two men grabbed the lady and pushed her to her knees. I was shocked when a man wearing a mask walked up behind her, grabbed her hair, pulled her head back, and cut her head off with a hunting knife. The man wearing the mask, he did the cutting, and he held her head high in the air and screamed, 'Allahu akbar!' I blended into the bushes and got the hell out of there then."

"How many would you estimate were in the crowd?" the reporter asked.

Donna entered the house, the TV was turned off and James said, "Pack quickly baby, we'll be leaving the city for a couple of weeks." He then moved to her and gave her a hug and a kiss.

"Good; the world as we know it has gone completely crazy." she said.

"Frank, let's get Nancy in the RV and then we'll leave."

"Is something wrong with her?" Donna asked.

"She was hurt when the hospital blew up." Frank said, but quickly added, "We brought her here, fixed her up and we're ready to go. I want to bring my Jeep, as I said earlier, in the event we have to leave the lodge in a hurry at some point."

"Sounds good to me." James replied with a smile.

CHAPTER 5

The man in Frankfurt, Germany smiled as he watched the news and sipped the very finest in cognac. The room was dark, with only a single candle burning on an end table. He was thrilled at all the deaths and turmoil in the United States.

"Sir," the butler said, "your 1800 appointment is here. Shall I show him in?"

"Yes, please."

A man dressed in a black suit, holding his hat, entered the room and moved to the sofa.

Before he was near, the man on the sofa said, "Have a seat in a chair and we will talk in a moment. Cognac?"

"Yes, please."

He leaned over, poured a bit of the drink into a glass, and then handing it to his guest said, "It looks as if phase 3 is moving very well. Most of the civilized world is now in upheaval. I must say it's progressing much better than I'd ever dreamed."

"But will the UN troops leave America on time? I think the American military is very serious about war."

Crossing his legs, he thought for a moment and said, "Let them start the fight and we'll bring the whole force of the UN against America. I'd hoped the dirty bomb that exploded would kill their useless President, but if nothing else, our agents did get that worthless bitch he called a wife. I am angered that we placed that squirrel in the position of President and now he ignores our orders. See that our Houston agents responsible for her death are given a handsome bonus, say a million dollars each."

"I'll see it is done. I'm here, sir, to determine how long you want phase three to continue."

"Oh, for at least five years. We still have millions to kill and I want all resistance by the survivors to be dead. They must be like zombies when we take over their governments, because the next step is planting chips in each survivor."

"Some will resist."

"Of course, it's expected. I think when we start killing those who resist, then that foolishness will stop."

"Any areas that you see that need special attention?" The guest swirled the cognac in his glass and then smelled it.

"I want things doubled in the Southern states of America. Increase the attacks on military bases, get the black and Hispanic folks out on the streets rioting, and if you have any dirty bombs, use them where we'll reap the most good, but with care. I don't think the Southern states will be easy to convince that fighting is useless, because all those damned Rednecks are hard-headed. It may be a good time to use biological warfare and spread some diseases. I want you to hit Texas twice as hard as the other states. Now, if the UN troops are attacked, let them die to the man or woman. We want the world outraged with the United States because of their response to the world's peacekeeping force. If the US does not attack, I still want some or all of the UN troops killed, if possible. This must be made to look like the Americans have turned against the United Nations. Any questions?"

"Uh, no sir. I take it if we're given a chance to kill the American President, we do so?"

"Yes, the Boss is very upset with him. After grooming him most of his adult life, spending millions to see he was made President, he suddenly chooses not to follow our orders. We cannot allow him to live. If he walks away from this unharmed, how many others will try the same thing? The Boss wants him dead."

"Does it matter how?"

"Well, I don't think we'll have another opportunity like we had with JFK in Dallas, do you? The NWO took him out and no one was the wiser, with all blaming Oswald. No, how he's terminated is of no interest to us. But, let me warn you, no one outside of the United States must be involved in his killing. See an American makes the hit or blows his ass up for all we care. The

NWO is willing to pay ten million dollars to see this job done, but we want it done right."

"I will handle it personally, sir."

"Good, but let me warn you, if anything goes wrong, we'll come after the heads of all involved, including yours."

Knowing the conversation was finished, the guest gulped his cognac, stood and said, "It shall be done, sir, and soon."

The man on the sofa moved his left hand as if shooing a fly and the guest left.

Pulling his cellphone as he was moving toward his car, the guest dialed a number and waited for a reply.

"Hello?"

"This is Frankfurt."

"How may I help you, sir?"

"The payment for your job has been approved."

"Excellent, sir."

"The amount is ten million, but that includes all labor, parts, and material to do the job."

"Good, I'll start working tonight."

Both men closed their phones.

"The President will leave in the morning on Air Force One to go to Houston, pick up his wife's body, and then fly to Miami for a private internment ceremony. An autopsy has confirmed her cause of death as decapitation. This statement was released by the White House just moments ago. The President of the United States has declared war on radical Muslims and has ordered the United States Air Force to increase bombing of all known extremist targets where they may be found. He wants it made clear that, quote, 'Most Muslims are a peace loving people and we should not allow the barbaric behavior of a few to ruin our wonderful relations with the whole group,' unquote."

"Bullshit!" James said and then gulped down the rest of this beer.

"Keep the noise down, because I want to hear this." Donna said.

The reporter said, "So far, the death count at the NBA game in Houston has reached 3,000 and it's expected to climb. Medical authorities today said Polonium 210 is responsible for the majority of the deaths, which was confirmed through urine testing, but how to treat the victims is somewhat of a mystery. It's confusing to medical personnel due to there not being any documented history for exposure or treatment. Members of the Military Medical Studies Group will be meeting with the doctors at some point overnight to work out a medical treatment plan. The President stated the attack was going to be treated as an act of terrorism."

"Next up, the FDA issues a serum recall after more than fifty children are hospitalized after getting Mumps, Measles and Rubella (MMR) immunizations. Additionally, there have been 10 deaths related to these inoculations since Monday across the nation."

Hours later, they were resting in the RV while Frank and his wife had the lodge. The lodge was a single story log cabin made from a cabin kit years ago. It was a two bedroom building, with electricity, running water, central air and heat. It also had satellite internet and TV, which worked better than most of the services back in the city.

James got up and got another beer from the fridge. He sat back down and listened to other things going wrong in the country, and then the reporter said, "In medical matters tonight the Center for Infectious Diseases reports three cases of the Black Plague in Denver over the weekend and they are stumped by the reappearance of this highly fatal disease. Black Death, as the Plague used to be called, was thought to have been eradicated years ago, so these new cases are causing heath officials to raise eyebrows and scratch their heads."

"Why are all these things happening all of a sudden? Everything from a dirty bomb going off to bad serum for kids, and it's all occurring at once." James asked, not realizing he was alone.

"We interrupt this program with a special announcement. We now take you live to Sandra Gates, who is on the scene. Sandra?"

"Burt, I am standing in front of the Jackson, Mississippi VA Hospital, which is in flames behind me. Approximately four hours ago a bomb threat was called in to the officials here. The police responded with dogs, but found nothing, and shortly after that a dump truck police believe held thousands of pounds of explosives, plowed through the front door and exploded.

Now, I was told the staff evacuated with patients to the parking lot almost an hour later, and three car bombs in the parking lot exploded. The police tell me that the driver of the truck cried out, 'Allahu Akbar' just before he set off the explosives. At this time, we do not have the number of dead or injured from the hospital or parking lot. The building remains standing and many surviving veterans have been transferred to other local hospitals."

The camera moved around to show the destruction of the VA building as well as the parking lot, and then it returned to the reporter who had an older man wearing a Vietnam Veterans ball cap on his head.

"Burt, I have Mike J. Gibbs with me, and he was a first hand witness to the attack. Mr. Gibbs, when did you first notice an attack was in progress?"

"When that *beep* head came toward the hospital door like a bat out of hell in that truck. I think his intention was to go as deeply into the building as he could before exploding. He yelled something I didn't understand and then blew himself and that dump truck to hell and back. What in the world has happened to this country? We need to turn back to God, get the illegal aliens and refugees out, and start taking care of our own. Until we do that, this *beep* will continue. Hell, it doesn't take much to determine who's responsible for this *beep* act, now does it? Homeland security needs to get up off their *beep* and do the *beep* job they are beep paid to do."

"Uh, thank you for your comments, sir. This is Sandra Gates, WDBB, reporting live from the VA Hospital in Jackson, Mississippi. Back to you, Burt."

"In other news tonight, stores report doing well with consumers grabbing foods off of shelves almost as fast as they are stocked. The big items purchased are bottled water, toilet paper, frozen foods, and snacks. There has also been a huge jump in soft drinks and alcohol, with sales doubling within the last week."

James turned the TV off and then said, "I don't like this, none of it, at all. It's almost as if some outside power is influencing all of this, but that's not possible, right?" Donna had returned to the RV as the footage of the VA was being shown.

"We've expected the Muslims to start trouble, and I think they're responsible for the dirty bomb that wasted Washington, D.C.."

"Do you think they also poisoned the folks at the NBA game?"

"It's more sophisticated than their usual operations so I have to say no, but it's possible. So far, they've shown themselves to be a crude bunch, mainly using suicide bombers."

"I think the Liberals are starting to wonder if allowing the illegal aliens or the refugees to stay was a smart decision. I knew something was wrong when I noticed all the refugees were of military age and healthy. If these men don't have the guts to stay and fight from their own homeland, we sure as hell don't want them here. I think every single one of them should serve a four year hitch in the US military."

"Then, the illegals have the balls to come on TV and shout they've broken no laws and they are not criminals. Bullshit, just by being in our country makes them criminals and as such, illegal to be considered for citizenship. The immigration laws are there, they just need to be enforced, so we can send these people packing. We should send them all back home along with their anchor babies and then bill their governments for the transportation costs and the hospital bill for the kids."

"I agree, but what worries me is the cost of keeping them here. How can a nation, with a deficit of trillions of dollars, suddenly open their arms to millions of new people? Right now they are being provided for, and well, I might add, as some of our veterans sleep in the streets, die for the lack of medical treatment, and our elderly can't afford their medications. At some point in the past, all our elected officials lost their common sense."

"Politicians are bought, baby, and by the highest bidder. Some of those folks are hired as CEOs of large companies, paid millions, and have never seen the office they supposedly work in. I consider the lobbying of our politicians as bribes, and it should be illegal. Those boys and girls need to only make the money the government pays them. Then we'd see fewer upper middle class entering into politics and retiring a few years later as millionaires. There is no way that can happened legally. Corruption is what has started all of this. I also fear the New World Order is behind some of this, too."

"When do you think we can return home?"

"Not until things smooth out some. I suspect the next thing to happen will be riots in the streets, planned killings of cops, social unrest with minority groups, and more bombings. Even right now the President is still demanding our guns, the military has ordered the UN out of the country, and they have sworn to protect our rights under the Constitution. There will be a civil war. The liberals will be the first to die, too."

"Why? They don't believe in guns."

"Most Liberals don't own a gun, but when the war breaks out, it will be between those who want to keep guns and those who do not. Those that want to keep guns already have them, with some households owning a half-dozen or more. Can you imagine starting a war over guns and you're unarmed? Oh, I suspect some Liberals have guns, but there will not be enough of them to impact the outcome. They'll depend on the UN to protect them, only I suspect they'll have their hands full with our military. You'd better hope we win too, because if we don't, I suspect the mark of the beast is next."

"Oh, that frightens me. Do you think it will be a chip implant like we've read?"

"Why not? They could then locate us by GPS, maybe listen to our thoughts, control our minds, and each of us would be counted and under surveillance all the time. As a Christian, I'd refuse the implant and that'd mean death."

"I heard officer Smith at the station say when they implant the chip, everyone's forehead will be tattooed with a blue 666. I won't do that, no way."

There was a knock on the door and when James opened it, gun in hand, Frank stepped in and said, "Just got a call from Jerry.

He and Thomas want to join us out here. They're both useless, but last night they both had their sheds and garages ransacked, and with them broken up like they are, there was nothing they could do."

"Have them bring both families, but in one car. I don't want this place to start looking like a used car lot. I think since they're still out of commission with broken bones, they can have the lodge and you two move in here with us."

Frank pulled this cell phone, dialed a number and said, "Hey good buddy, the poker game for this afternoon is on. Carpool and only bring one car, okay? BYB and pick up some snacks. Okay, bye."

"What'd he say?"

"Well, they'll be here today, and they'll load up on booze and bring some large containers of foods. Jerry has been prepping for years and he has 5 gallon containers filled with beans, jerked meats, pasta and such. I know both men own guns, so they'll bring them as well. I spoke with Jerry the last time I spoke to you in the parking lot. They fear resisting the NWO will bring a fight and I agree with them. After they get here, we'll go back to Jerry's place and load up on all the stuff he's hoarded over the years."

"Once they've healed some, you and I will move deeper in the woods here and taking some chainsaws, we'll make a new cabin. I suspect my lodge is on all topographical maps the USGS makes."

"So?" Frank asked.

"When things turn bad and the civil war starts, we may not want to be found for a while. Food will stop being delivered, gas will become scarce and expensive, and I think folks will start to kill for a meal."

"Do you honestly think it's going to get that bad?"

"Yes, I do. There are too many terrible things happening all at once in this country. I think the New World Order is behind these things. I think over the years our Presidents were elected by the NWO and not the people. As a result, we've had year after year of moral decay from weak leaders. Those leaders had no interest in anything, but lining their own pockets with cash. Everyone was on the Liberal financial bandwagon from transgenders to the NAACP, and all got a cut of the funds. I think the goose that lays the golden egg has died. I think now NWO is coming to collect."

"Do you think the leader of the NWO is the anti-Christ?" Frank asked.

"If they start embedding chips and placing tattoos with 666 on our foreheads, yes I do."

"Well, there won't be anything we can do to prevent this, because it's all in the Bible."

"I'm not sure about that but ask Jerry, he's got that religious stuff down well and even fills in for the preacher when he's unable to conduct services."

"I'll do that. Oh, I got some information on the killing of Mims. Seems it was a professional hit. The security alarm was still on when the cook arrived for work at 7 am; nothing was taken except his cash, jewelry and credit cards. There was a Rolex watch taken, too. All three were killed with one shot; two were head shots, the other a chest shot."

"Sounds like a robbery to me."

"It was no robbery. When a house is robbed, professional robbers pull out drawers, check between the mattress and box springs, and look for wall safes, but there was no trashing of the place like in 99.9% of all cases. In a robbery, more people are wounded than killed. Which leads me to think the killing was a professional hit and all were caught asleep."

"Okay, dead is dead, so why was he killed?"

"I'm still thinking on that aspect and I have no suspect or motive. He was a multi-millionaire, intelligent, powerful, and traveled a great deal. A check made on his phones revealed a lot of calls to and from Frankfurt, Germany. All the calls are being checked, but so far the German phone company is saying the numbers are not good now, and they were not working on the days when the calls were made."

"That sounds like a cover up to me."

"It could be. Then again, maybe NWO has folks working for them that can in some way activate unused numbers temporarily. I know using a VPN on my computer hides me and I can use a server in Spain, France or anyplace in the world. It assigns me an IPN for that region that is not in use. Then as I move around on the internet, no one knows where I'm really from. So, maybe phones can be done like that."

"You mean someone in America is making the call, but in some way the calls are routed through Germany?"

"Or the party could be located in Germany or any other place in the world, actually."

"Wow, I can barely grasp a thought like that."

"The world is changing, my friend, and rapidly too."

"Much of what I see indicates it's changing alright, only it's not improving."

CHAPTER 6

Agent XI rented an apartment on the 6th floor of a run down high-rise in Houston, using a fake name and driver's license. He'd spent some time earlier that morning with a makeup artist, who added twenty years to his appearance, and he now wore black plastic framed glasses. He was wearing old clothes, gym shoes, and a beat up stocking cap. He carried only a few things to his apartment once the lease was signed. Another agent dropped him off later in the day with what looked to be a box of long stemmed roses and some shopping bags with food.

He was a little less than a half mile from the morgue that held the First Lady's body. From his perch in the living room he had a perfect shot all around the service side of the building. The word he'd received was the President would identify his wife's body, claim the remains as her next of kin, and then have her transported to a waiting ambulance. They would then drive to the airport and take Air Force One. He suspected he'd get a shot as the man entered or left the building.

He placed a steak, salad, and drinks in the fridge. He opened a pint bottle of quality bourbon, poured two fingers worth in a glass, and sipped his drink. He sat in an old overstuffed chair and pulling his binoculars, began scanning the morgue. He watched workers come and go, saw the trash taken out, and a new body brought in.

Near 6 pm, when it grew dark, he began using his rifle to check out the area, and the mounted night scope was better in the dark than glassing the area. His sniper rifle was a Russian ASVK / KSVK 12.7 mm large caliber sniper rifle, fitted with a night scope. The shells were 12.7x108 mm, .50 Russian, and the rifle held five rounds in a magazine. His rifle was bolt action, so he wanted his first shot to be a killing shot.

As he waited he raised the window, cooked his meal and ate, and then screwed the silencer on the end of the barrel of his rifle. He washed the dishes and placed them in the dish rack to dry. He poured another two fingers of bourbon and then placed the bottle into his backpack. He would have no more drinks this night, unless his hit was successful. He threw some radical Muslim leaflets around the room and tacked a black ISIS flag on the wall of a bedroom. He then slipped the drinking glass into his pack.

Right at 7 pm a black SUV pulled into the parking lot and a couple of motorcycle cops moved their motorcycles to block all access to the building. A helicopter was seen hovering over the building. The two front doors of the SUV opened, agents scanned the area well as they walked, and then opened the rear doors. The chopper then began flying 360 degrees over the morgue.

When the President stepped from the vehicle, X1 lined up the sights, took a deep breath and held it. This target was seen in a pea green circle, and in a few seconds he'd be a dead man. As he slowly released his breath, he kept the cross-hairs on the man's chest, and began to gently squeeze the trigger. The shot wasn't loud, more of a loud *thump*, but he realized he'd missed his target and hit an agent by mistake. One of the men from the front of the SUV had stepped into his line of fire at the last second. He was down on his back screaming, blood spurting into the air, as one agent was talking on a radio and another had his body over the President, protecting him. X1 fired two more shots hoping one would strike his target. He knew he struck the man on top of his target, because his body jerked each time a big bullet struck him. The big bullets had to penetrate the agent and some injury must have been sustained by the President.

Finally, out of frustration, X1 aimed at the very top of the President's head and squeezed the trigger. In the scope he saw a shard of skull fly into the air, followed by a long finger of blood and brains, and the two bodies went limp.

Having worn his thin leather gloves at all times inside the room and keeping his stocking hat over his short hair, he knew he'd leave nothing for the cops to find, except an ISIS flag and some propaganda from the organization. He disassembled his rifle, placed it in a long flower box and then wrapped a red ribbon with a bow around it. Donning his pack, he stepped from the room. He walked from the apartment and then flagged down a cab.

His next stop was an apartment he maintained on the other side of town. This apartment was where he came to change or clean up after a hit. Weapons were hidden in the walls here, a couple of more identifications were hidden, as well as a variety of clothing in the closets. He removed the auburn wig, showered, shaved and then changed into suit and tie. He then washed and dried the clothing he'd worn earlier and placed them in his closet.

"Hello, baby. I'll be home in a few minutes. Why don't you light some candles and turn on some soft music? Great, I'll be there soon." He then placed his phone back in his pocket.

Agent Joda May of the Secret Service, had jumped into action the second Agent Acker fell with a chunk of his backbone blown out of his back. As he lay screaming, May had contacted the chopper and reported they had a man down from a gunshot wound. The problem was, he'd heard no shot or seen any muzzle flash. One of the cops ran to the agents while another contacted his dispatcher to let him know there was an attempt on the life of the President. He requested an ambulance with a doctor to be rushed to the morgue.

A number of shots were fired and May only found out where they were coming from by seeing big holes suddenly appear in the body of Cox, who was protecting the President as well as he could. Cox began to scream as the pain registered on his mind, but then the President took a bullet to his head and for all practical purposes, it was all in vain. He quickly contacted the chopper by radio and it flew in the general direction of Agent X1's apartment. But few thought a sniper was that far away, so their search was in the general direction of the shots.

May ran to the President, rolled Cox off of him, and pulled him to the driver's side of the SUV. As he moved him, blood, pieces of skull and brain stained the concrete of the parking lot. He then ran to Cox and Acker, pulling them to a spot beside the President. He looked the President over closely and while he was still alive, the bullet that hit him must have been a .50 caliber because half his head was missing. He pulled a first aid kit from the truck, wrapped the President's head tightly, and then looked for other injuries. He had a huge hole in his thigh, another through his shoulder. He bandaged both. Acker was dead, his unseeing eyes open, and his mouth twisted in pain. May moved to Cox and found the man alive, but shot through the shoulder and a hole through his thigh as well. He'd just wrapped him up when two ambulances arrived.

The three were evaluated by a doctor who said the President didn't look good, Cox was expected to live, and Acker would remain deceased. When the President was loaded in the ambulance, May jumped in the back and pulled his pistol, because he was still responsible for the man's security. The ambulance had the two police motorcycles as escorts, with one in front and the other bringing up the rear. The other two ambulances were right behind the President's and when they rounded a corner, they met a road block by an illegal alien group.

May glanced out the front window of the ambulance, which he could see from the back, and yelled, "Go through them! Now!"

The driver began to weave and move slowly. The doctor said, "He's going to die on us, unless we move faster. I don't have what I need to keep him alive here."

"Driver, plow through these people and do it now." The agent yelled to be heard. People were banging on the ambulance, hitting it with clubs, and suddenly the windshield shattered from a thrown brick.

The driver floored the vehicle and those inside heard screams as the ambulance ran over protesters as their speed increased. One man was struck straight on and his body rolled up and over the hood, then over the windshield, to lodge on top of the cab.

On they continued and when May glanced out the back glass in the doors, injured protesters were scattered all over the ground.

Using an iPad, the doctor sent a message to the hospital staff, so all he needed would be in the operating room. The motorcycle in front went down, the cyclist either shot or struck with a brick. The ambulance didn't stop, not with the President injured. The second motorcycle cop helped the downed cop onto his bike, and then both weaved through the crowd to catch up with the ambulance, with lights flashing.

At the hospital the ambulance was unloaded, the cyclist was brought into the emergency room, and all were seen immediately. Acker's body was sent to the morgue and the President was immediately sent in for surgery. Cox entered surgery as did the motorcycle cop and a physician moved to May and spoke with him. Seeing the agent was still on edge, the doc gave him some meds to relax him, and a small bottle of sleeping pills to allow him to sleep in the coming days. He'd annotate in a chart to have May evaluated for PTSD further down the road.

It was then the southwest regional director of the Secret Service, Robert Holley, arrived and moving to May asked, "What in the hell happened out there? Listening to the radio it sounded like a goat roping to me."

"A long distance sniper took out Acker, struck Cox at least twice, and while the President was living when we brought him in here, he'll never be normal. Looked to me like a .50 round from a sniper rifle struck his head, almost center of the cerebral cortex and took most of the left lobe of the brain. Since the man is right handed, and the left side of his brain is used most for those who use that hand, he'll be changed, if he survives. Once he's stable, we'll figure out the angle of the bullets flight path and determine where the shots came from. I do know the shooter was up high and had a clear view of the parking lot."

"Joda, the nearest high buildings are almost a half a mile away. That's a long shot, even for a trained sniper."

"No, not really, Boss. In Iraq, while in a combat unit, our sniper consistently struck targets a mile away, with most marked as confirmed kills."

"How do you know this is true?"

"Because I was our sniper. A mile is nothing for most snipers, but it's my limit for accurate shooting. In my twelve months, I killed 301 men, most well within a mile. At distances over a mile, windage, the drop of the bullet, and other variables becomes complex and you almost have to be a math professor figure it out. If we find out our shooter was within a mile, which I think he was, it was easy shooting for a trained killer."

"Ummm, what concerns me now is we must have a security leak in the agency, because we're the only people who knew the President was coming here this time of night, going to the morgue and not the hospital, and the agents assigned to his security team were all combat veterans."

"We also know the rifle used had a flash suppressor and a silencer installed. I looked and not once did I see or hear a shot fired."

A tired doctor with blood splattered on his lab coat neared, gave a weak smile, and said, "The President of the United States is alive and his prognosis for a full recovery is poor. In his current condition he'll be lucky to feed himself, if he recovers, but he is alive. I honestly suspect he'll recover but be unable to speak well, he'd drool a great deal, and he'll be in no condition to lead himself, much less a nation."

"I think we'd be smart to report him as killed, swear in the Vice-President, place the President into a private institution. Do him just like we did JFK." It was then Holley's phone rang. He moved away from the group, talked on the phone, and closed it and placed it in his coat pocket.

"Everything okay?" May asked.

"It depends on how you look at things. That was the Boss and he wants the President put down, if there is no hope for a full recovery."

Boss? I thought you were the boss, May thought and then wondered who the real Boss was.

"No, he'll never be the same man if he survives. However, as a doctor, I refuse to take his life." The doctor said and then shook his head.

"Give me a syringe filled with morphine and by God, I'll do the job." Holley said.

Ten minutes later the President was dead and an empty morphine syringe was on the tray beside the dead man's gurney.

"Sir, the press are outside waiting for a comment on what happened and the condition of the President." an attractive nurse said to the doctor.

Holley said, "We'll not release his death yet. You, doctor, will say he's alive but has taken a serious injury to his head. I, in turn, will give a few details of the assassination attempt. We'll announce his death later this evening. Right now the American people need hope and we'll see they get it."

They walked from the hospital and the doctor told of the man's wounds, that he was in a stable but critical condition, and his prognosis was poor. He then refused to answer any questions and re-entered the hospital.

Holley stepped to the podium, explained what had happened, spent many minutes building up Cox and his attempts to save the President. He also made it sound as if Acker had positioned himself in front of the President to take any bullets intended for the leader. He was obviously looking for hero status for his fallen agents.

From the press a question was yelled out, "Who is responsible for this?"

"These are difficult times, so we have no idea yet, however over the next few days, we'll follow up on the leads we have. The fact the President just recently installed martial law and threatened to take all guns from gun owners opens up a whole bucket of worms. Right now, anyone and everyone is a potential suspect. No more questions please, we have work to do."

Holley entered the building and left the press asking each other questions.

Once inside, he moved to May, pulled out his phone and dialed a number. The party must have answered in German, because he said, "Die Torte ist im Ofen, komm nicht zu spät zum Abendessen." He then closed his phone.

May had seen him dial 011, the United States exit code, then 49, the country code for Germany, and then the area code. He was unable to see any of the other numbers. *So, the Boss is in Germany*, May thought, and the code used when Holley spoke didn't surprise him at all. They often spoke in code. May spoke fluent German and he knew the Boss had said, "The pie is in the oven, so don't be late for supper." He assumed he used that code to tell the Boss the President was dead.

"May, I want you to stay in the Houston area, since you live here, but take a few days off and get some rest. All that you've seen and heard here tonight is classified Top Secret and not to be spoken about to anyone now or ever in the future."

May drove home and since it was in the middle of the night, he decided not to wake his wife, but to shower and go straight to bed after he had something light to eat. He entered the house quietly, showered in the guest room bathroom, warmed up supper, ate and then took a sleeping pill the doctor had given him. He then moved to the bed and spooned up against his wife. He was asleep in a few minutes.

At nine, while preparing to go running, his phone rang. Glancing at the number he saw it was from his adopted brother, Frank Wilson. As a youngster, May had been raised by the Wilson family, but he'd retained his own last name. There were many reasons for that, but the biggest was he wanted to show the world that a May could be a productive member of society.

"Yo, big brother, what's up?" he asked.

"We need to talk and it's not about family. When you have some time, meet me at the lodge that James has."

"Are you okay?"

"I'm fine. I'll tell you more when you get here."

"Should I come alone?"

"No, it doesn't matter, not really. If Theresa can come, bring her and we'll throw some steaks on the grill and down a few brews."

"What time?"

"Say 1600, how's that?"

"Good, we'll both be there. Love you man, bye."

Strange Frank didn't give me a subject about the talk he wants to have. He's a smart man and may want to talk about anything. Well, I'll run, then relax a bit, and go see him. I'll find out what he wants to talk about when I get there.

When May and Theresa arrived, Joda was surprised so many people were there. The last thing he wanted or expected was to be around a bunch of people. The women were sitting outside as the men sat in the living room sipping on cold brews.

"Joda, what do you make of all this violence and disruption going on across the country?" James asked as he handed the agent a beer.

"We've had it all before, except for the dirty bomb, and we are certain that was an act of Muslim extremist, like ISIS. We think it was done to take the President out of the picture."

Frank said, "We've never as a nation had a First Lady killed and that, along with the dirty bomb makes this year different."

Donna stuck her head in the door and said, "Turn on the TV, it looks like the President was just killed!"

"I suspected this because the American people will never give up their guns." Frank said.

The screen was suddenly showing the parking lot behind the morgue and Directory Holley was speaking. "Agent Acker was killed instantly when he moved in front of the President to protect him, and then Agent Cox took two rounds while lying on the President, protecting him with his own body. The weapon that fired the rounds has not been found, nor the brass from the shells, but it was a bullet almost the size of a .50, which is huge. We were able to find one bullet, which our lab identified as a 12.7x108 mm, which is a Russian make. However, that does not mean the killer was Russian."

"Can you speak on the status of Agent Cox?"

"Agent Cox expired just a few minutes after the President. At a press briefing later today, a doctor will explain his death."

"Uh, what of the missing Agent, uh, Agent Joda May?"

"We have video footage, from the cameras mounted at the rear of the morgue, of him doing absolutely nothing during the shooting and at this time he is wanted for questioning. The footage even shows him shooting the President in the head. We know Agent May was an active partner in the killing of the

President of the United States, but we know little of this conspiracy. Once an autopsy is done, his service pistol may have very well fired the final killing shot. Right now, there is a three million dollar reward for May, dead or alive. Keep in mind, we have actual footage of May firing his pistol and that will be released later today at the press meeting."

Joda sat there in total shock. Holley was lying his ass off and had obviously killed Cox too, to keep the story unknown. With all witnesses dead, the director could say what he wanted.

The room was quiet as the reporter said, "The images you're seeing now is of the room or apartment where the primary sniper fired the shots that killed Agents Acker and Cox, as well as fatally injured the President of the United States. It is believed the shots were fired from the window you see now, and the apartment has ISIS brochures and a large flag on the wall. The FBI and CIA are treating the President's death as an assassination and Agent Joda May is the primary suspect. If you know this man or where he might be, call the number on your screen and speak with a Special Agent. Remember there is a three million dollar reward for Joda May, alive or dead. This is Robert Wilkinson, reporting live for WDBB, Houston."

"Now, ain't *that* some shit?" Frank said, and then looked at his brother.

"My pistol wasn't even fired! I don't understand any of this. Why are they framing me to be the killer? Hell, Holley killed the President with an overdose of morphine."

"You may know way too much, little brother."

CHAPTER 7

Agent X1 was with his wife and kids at a park when his phone rang. Answering it, he heard a man he knew well say, "The money for a job well done is in your account. My sources say the man wasn't dead when he arrived at the hospital, but died later of complications. It's a shame when one of our workers dies, but his wife has been taken care of as well."

"Yes, sir." X1 said, but thought, *His wife was decapitated.*

"You have a new task, and it's in the middle drawer of your safe. It will be a simple job and will not take you long. This job must result in the termination of this individual. He can no longer be trusted, so the company no longer needs him. Payment for this job is one million dollars, so you know it's an important task. Let me know when termination is completed."

"I will let you know."

"Good. Auf Wiederhören."

"Yes, goodbye." X1 closed his phone and began to wonder when the company would grow tired of him as well. The New World Order was the most powerful force on earth, bar none, with unlimited money.

Then the chip in his arm sent a thought to his mind, *you are a tool for the company and you'll be kept as long as you work. Then, you'll be retired with respect. Now, go to work and finish the mission you have in the desk drawer.*

He took his family home, pulled his wife close and whispered, "When I finish this project I have at work, just the two of us will go to Thailand. I've saved some money and we can afford a good trip, and we can leave the kids with my mom or yours."

"Oh, I've never been to Asia and I'll love it! It's your old stomping ground though. I know you spent some time there when you were in the army."

"I didn't have any girlfriends, if that's what you mean. I lived in the woods with the rest of my team. We trained with the Thai police and special forces. Feel like a long trip? Don't forget, I speak the language so we'll really have a good time.'

"Yes, let's plan it."

As he drove to his office, he didn't like the way his Boss had said, 'My sources say the man wasn't dead when he arrived at the hospital, but died later of complications.' It was almost as if he was warning X1. *Do not continue this line of thought, it is wrong and false*, the chip sent to his brain. He blew the thought off and concentrated on his driving.

At the office, he removed a plain brown manila envelope, about 10 inches by 12, and opened it. He sipped a good bourbon as he pulled the package from the container. On top was the image of a black man. His face was rugged and long, his eyes clear, nose not as wide as most African Americans and lips that hinted of white blood somewhere in his line. The man was handsome, clean, and neat and reminded X1 of black soldiers he'd seen that were sharp dressers in uniform. Men like them always made a good impression. Then, raising a paper with a bio, the agent thought, *Wanted for killing the President of the United States; now isn't that rich?*

"Married, no kids, currently not at home and on the run. A GPS check of his phone places him on private land owned by James Walker, an Air Force retired E-8, see map." he spoke aloud, unknowingly. He pulled up a map, studied it for a moment, and then tossed it aside. "At the time you move against May, the United States will enter into combat with the United Nations, without the approval of the new President. Of course, the small detachment of UN troops will be slaughtered, which will start World War Three. The Muslims will rise up, anti-United Nations countries will join the United States, including China. The goal of the NWO is to lower the world population.

You must take May out, because he is the only man alive that knows the New World Order killed the President. While your bullet fatally injured the man, he was helped along by one of our agents. The name of that agent is not important to you. Your mission is to kill May within 24 hours."

Walking to his safe, he opened the door, pulled out a passport, driver's license, and biography of a completely new man. He also removed $10,000 for expenses. He placed the information on May in the safe and then locked it. Someone would return in less than 8 hours and removed the data from the safe.

As he walked to his car, his mind suddenly thought, *It'd be easy for someone to blow me up or shoot me. But, why would anyone want to kill me?*

He suddenly became uncomfortable as the man who killed the President. It made sense to him that the NWO might not want to keep him alive. Dead, he could tell no one who he'd killed but as long as he lived, he was a danger to the organization. *Do not think this. The organization needs you and your skills*, he thought.

I must think of this later, not right now. I will kill May and then give consideration to all of this, he thought, but another thought came to him quickly, *You work for the organization and they need you.* He started his car and was soon moving for the lodge.

James was firing up the grill, holding a cold beer in his left hand, when off in the far hill, something flashed in the early morning sun. It was a little early to be drinking beer but they'd brought all they needed except coffee. James needed something to give his morning a lift, because he had a hangover, so he sipped on a beer.

Looked like metal flashing, so it may mean someone is coming for Frank, he thought and then said, "I just saw sunlight flash off of metal to the west of me, so we have company."

Joda said, "Frank, pull your pistol and come with me."

"Take these boys, too." Blake said and handed both men a 12 gauge pump shotgun. "They're both filled with buckshot."

"What about me?" Richard "Dick" Williams asked. He was an old 11 bravo, or infantry man from way back in the 70's.

"Can you handle a 30.06 with a good scope?" James asked.

"Sure I can."

"There's one right above the door in the lodge. Fetch it and see if you can help them from the patio if you can."

Dick was soon sitting on the patio, glassing the area, rifle close by. Joda and Frank were long gone. Suddenly, the sound of a rifle shot was heard, followed almost instantly by two shotguns. Then it grew quiet.

Dick using the field glasses said, "They have a man down, but I can't see if he's hurt bad or not."

"One of our men is down?" James asked.

"Nope, looks to be a man I've never seen before."

"Blake, take the four wheeler ATV to 'em and see if they need help."

"Sure thing, because I love drivin' a four wheeler."

Thirty minutes later, X1 was on the patio, leaking from a gunshot wound to his left leg. His Russian sniper rifle was gone, all his pistols were gone, and his hands were handcuffed behind his back.

"Who are you?" Frank asked.

"You have my wallet, it's on my driver's license."

"What were you doing up there, and don't tell me hunting."

"I was hunting, but hunting for a spot to try my new rifle. I did nothing wrong and —"

"My land is posted no trespassing, and you saw the signs." James said.

"The rifle you have is a professional sniper weapon and not designed for hunting."

"Go to hell. Call the police, so I can go home."

"Donna, ask your friends at dispatch to run a background check on an Anton W. Cash." James handed his cell phone to his wife and the man's driver's license. Tell them we caught him trespassing a few minutes ago."

Franks wife, Nancy, moved to Agent X1 and using a pocket knife, cut his pant leg so she could see his wound.

"You're a very lucky man. I see only four holes with buckshot, and you could have been killed." She then used tweezers to pull the lead from his calf.

As she doctored the man, Donna was on hold with the dispatcher. She'd given X1's name and information, so now she was waiting for the computer check.

Nancy cleaned the area with Hydrogen Peroxide and then smeared triple-antibiotic ointment on the four holes.

Donna began speaking and in a minute closed the phone.

"He has no warrants, he's a college history professor and he's an important member of the NWO, according to Sergeant Hanes. His computer documents all have the triangle with the eye in the middle of the image. He is to be released immediately by the authority of the President."

James said, "The President is dead so he has no authority over me, and I'll not release him."

Feeling brave now, Agent X1 said, "I demand to be released right now. I am a simple university history professor."

"Name one Indian that attacked General Custer."

"Look, you know I'm harmless and even the President waives my arrest. I am no threat to any of you."

"Shut up," James said and continued, "because you're not what you seem to be. I can't see a college professor, usually a damned Liberal, running around on my land with a sniper rifle unless you were out to kill one of us."

Frank said to X1, "Stand."

When the man stood, Frank looked his forearms over and said, "He's been implanted with a chip. We'll get nothing out of him as long as the chip is in him. It has GPS tracking too, controls his thoughts, records his thoughts, and controls him."

Nancy said, "I can remove it with a scalpel. I can give him a local to kill the pain."

"Frank, bring his ass over here and bend him over the table. We'll do the job there." James said and then opened another beer. "Give him a local if you want, but I don't care one way or the other."

Frank and Joda held Agent X1 over the table, Nancy administered the local and then taking her thumb located the chip. She then took the scalpel and sliced down to a small plastic capsule looking container. Using a pair of tweezers she removed it and James threw it in the BBQ grill flames. Nancy cleaned the small wound and wrapped it.

"It's an admirable thing you have accomplished, but all you've done is place this whole place on the New World Order's death list. They will suspect I'm dead now, so even if I do show, I will soon be dead. Damn it to hell, you've just killed everyone of us. You fools!"

"Do you feel differently now?" Joda asked.

"I . . . I can think better, clearer, and we're all in serious trouble."

"Why are we in trouble?" James asked, and took a swig of his beer.

"If the NWO determines I'm alive, they'll move mountains or wipe out nations to kill me. I know too much."

"Oh?" Frank asked.

"I was, until just now, a professional killer for them. I went to work for the CIA after I got out of the Army, got a GPS chip implanted as part of my indoctrination into special ops, and have not had any emotions or thoughts of my own in years. At some point, I was transferred from the CIA to the New World Order, but don't remember how or when that happened. It's as if my long term memory is gone, completely. I know I have a wife, kids, but know nothing beyond that. I know my address but can't even give you the name of my wife or a child's name."

"How do we know he's tellin' us the truth?" James asked.

"I'll try truth serum on him in a few minutes." Frank said, and then smiled.

Taking a swig of his beer and then wiping his mouth off with the back of his hand, James asked, "Does sodium pentothal really work?"

"Yes and no. He'll talk, but we'll have to separate the truth from the bullshit. In his case, I think most of what he speaks today will be truth." Frank said, as Nancy nodded in agreement.

"It won't hold up in a court of law." May said.

"I don't think we want to even try to take the New World Order to court, when they are some of the richest and most powerful people in the world." Dick said.

"You can be sure, they own most judges." Blake said and took a sip of his brew.

Four hours later, after X1 had rambled on for hours, everyone was loaded in the motor-home, jeep, and Frank was on the motorcycle. The lodge had been locked up, windows boarded up and all the supplies, including food, were taken. Even the top of the RV had boxes and boxes of various items secured, because they would all be needed. They headed north by east, moving from Houston, Texas to Southern Missouri. James owned some land in the Ozarks and on his land was a fairly large cave. The cave was the final destination.

Gas stations were still open, but prices were insane, at $10.99 a gallon, but all filled up. All but James had emptied their accounts at ATM's. Agent X1 had less than eight thousand dollars on him, but knew if he took money out of an ATM, the NWO would know he was alive. James drove into town and transferred all his cash into gold bars, except for $5000 in cash, all of which he brought to the camper with him. X1 wanted to stop and get his wife, but then remembered she'd been part of his cover and had a chip implanted too. The children had been implanted by NWO just months after their births. Finally, feeling he could not trust his wife, he continued on with the rest.

Then he remembered the times with his wife before the chip was installed and his deep love for her. Neither had the chip then and life had been so good. Suddenly, he was flooded with emotions, because he loved his wife and kids, but none could be trusted. Tears began to fall harder as he, the big hit man, cried over the loss of his family.

James, tired of the man's crying, drove to X1's house. When Carol answered the door, Frank, X1, and Dick quickly moved inside and gagged and handcuffed her. The two kids were still small, so they were all taken back to the lodge. At the lodge, each was given a local to kill pain, and the chips were removed. Each child was then medicated by Nancy to help them sleep.

Carol was confused, but knowing X1 was her husband, she moved to him and he placed his arm around her shoulder. He turned to her, lifted her face by using his finger on her chin and he asked, "Do you remember who you are?"

"I am your wife and I love you; we have two sons."

"What is your name?"

"Carol? I think."

Hugging her, he said, "And, your last name?"

"Hall, and you're Ben." She then kissed him on the nose.

"Okay," James said, "we're on our way to the Ozark Mountains."

As they drove, they watched TV and the news was disturbing.

"This is Burt Wilcox and our top story for today is the FBI, working closely with FEMA, arrested more than four thousand Christians over this last weekend. According to the FBI, those arrested have violated the law of separation of religion and private businesses, by refusing to provide services or sale goods to those they feel violate their religious beliefs. Those arrested were immediately moved to FEMA camps and this was done to insure their safety. The FBI further stated that the Christians would be released if they accepted the controversial chip implant, which many Christians are calling the mark of the beast. This implant, just slightly larger than a medical capsule is being refused by most Christians, stating it's a sign of the devil or 666. Be sure to see our special tonight when I will show the chip is not the mark of the beast nor associated with the Biblical numbers 666. I will also discuss my personal implant and the almost completely painless procedure. The use of the chip will make identification for services or goods easier and faster as it confirms each person's identity and status instantly."

The camera switched to a female reporter sitting beside Burt, who said, "Good evening, I'm Jessica Williams. In other news today, the Chairman of the Joint Chiefs of Staff stated that a battle with the United Nations troops has begun. The UN troops were originally brought in to collect guns from American gun owners who would not voluntarily surrender them. The US military, which is sworn to protect the Constitution, as old and useless as it is, refused to allow the UN to move. The military stated private citizens of this nation have a right to bear arms and that right will be protected by them. The UN has threatened the United States with a world war, if their troops were attacked. That attack against the UN was launched at approximately 1400 Houston time."

The camera switched back to Burt, who said, "Today NSA announced a great month for the security of our nation. In the last 30 days, over 10,000 people using social media have been investigated and only 376 have been brought in, interrogated, and then released. The remainder have been locked up in FEMA camps, local jails, or prisons. The judicial system will soon be swamped as each state slowly starts to agree to follow the imposed martial law. Now the weather."

"Interrogated my ass! Those bastards beat me and almost killed me!" Thomas said.

Ben Hall remembered hurting the two men, but he'd had a hood over his face, so he knew he'd not been seen. It was not something he was proud of now.

CHAPTER 8

The wind was blowing little snow devils around and around, and the temperature was below freezing, as the Head of the American Secret Service met with the Boss in Darmstadt, Germany. It was early evening, with snow still falling, but dark already.

"So, X1 is no longer available. What has happened to the man, or do we know?" the Boss asked after many long minutes of silence. His breath looked like smoke as he spoke.

"His chip showed him being captured, the Infrared sensing device in the chip picked up the heat of two individuals, substantiated by his recorded thoughts. He was escorted about two miles away, maybe, and we encountered difficulty sending thoughts to him, until finally, his chip went dead. I think it was burned, because the registered temperature sent to us was that of a fire."

"And, what would cause his chip to die?"

"Only a few things; his battery died, which is very unlikely, or his arm was destroyed, or he was blown to pieces, or it was removed and tossed into a fire."

The Boss stopped walking, turned to face Holley and asked, "Of the three, which do you suspect?"

"X1 was no normal agent, sir. He may have gotten wind that he'd been selected to be hit as well. As the only man who'd thought he'd killed the President he may have quickly realized he was a dead man."

"Not exactly true, Holley, because one of your own Agents, Joda May, also knew you killed two men that night in the hospital. So, we now have two people loose in the United States, and both know you are a killer. I taunted X1 when I talked with him and told him someone else had killed the President. I was sure he'd seen you, but was told later he had not, so I'm unsure. My question is, what are you doing about this and when will they both be dead?"

"We are picking up the signals from Agent X1's wife and two boys at a hunting lodge just outside of Houston. We know the devices have been removed from all three, because the chips temperature was less that the normal 98.6 degrees Fahrenheit and then they stopped working. We have reason to believe they are all there, along with a retired Air Force Security Policeman by the name of James Walker, and his wife Donna."

"What was the rank of this Walker while in uniform?"

"An E-8, which is just a Senior Master Sergeant. Why?"

"Less than 3 percent of the US military attains the E-8 and E-9 positions. So, this James Walker is not a stupid man by any means. I want the lodge hit, and hit hard. I want no feet on the ground, so see an aircraft takes the place out."

"Aircraft? I might be able to have a bomb dropped on the place and then claim the bomb came loose and accidentally fell on the structure."

"You heard my wishes, now make them come true. Also, what is the status of Agent Joda May?"

"There is a reward for him, and his image is being flashed all over the country on television. There have been no leads so far."

"Double the reward, because money talks. Make it enough his own momma would turn him in for the cash."

Holley nodded and said, "Both will happen as soon as our talk is finished."

"This talk is finished." the Boss said, turned, and then walked off into the darkness.

Holley's room was at the Frankfurt Airport and was a suite paid for by United States tax dollars as he traveled. He wondered about the "Boss" and who was the real money and power in the NWO. So far, his intelligence information led him to this single older rich gentleman in Germany. He knew the Boss owned a number of pharmaceutical companies, part of a railroad, and a number of manufacturing plants. He was obviously worth billions of dollars, but his senses warned him the Boss wasn't the top dog. He'd find out one day.

He poured a couple of fingers of Kentucky bourbon into a whiskey glass and moved to the shower. He showered, shaved and threw on some lounge pants and a tee. He'd called room service for a supper and had it delivered.

There was a low knock at his door. Looking out the peephole, he spotted two gorgeous women.

They must have the wrong room, he thought as he held his whiskey in his left hand and opened the door. He met their eyes and asked, "Yes?"

"Are you Mister Holley?"

"Yes, but I don't know you, either of you."

"The Boss sent us over to make sure your evening was relaxing and entertaining."

"Uh, well, I don't know. I am a married man."

"At least let us have one drink and if you're not absolutely charmed by us, we'll leave, okay?"

"Okay just one drink. Come in."

Both were wearing furs and they placed them on the sofa. They moved to the bar; Holley poured them both a whiskey, and looked them over closely.

One was blonde, maybe 110 pounds, short, well shaped, long neck, short hair, big blue eyes, with pouting lips and large breasts. He found her glossy lips attractive. She was the quiet one.

The other had auburn hair, weighed maybe 120 pounds, about 5 feet and seven inches tall, nice rump, shapely breasts, which were just slightly smaller than the blonde's. Her lips were also glossy, and she had the habit of running her tongue over her bottom lip.

They were truly beautiful, but the last thing he needed was to take something home to momma he didn't come here with.

The two women were sitting very close together and the Blonde said, "I'm Gretchen and this is Molly. We're live entertainers and would love to help you pass a few hours."

"I have no protection." Holley said.

"We brought some." Gretchen said and then placed a box of condoms on the bar.

Molly leaned over and kissed Gretchen deeply; as she started undressing her, Holley moaned.

Dawn, 0600 hours, near James Walker's lodge, a prior United States Air Force Combat Controller sat on a hill about a mile from the structure. He was wearing face paint, a camouflage uniform, Boonie hat, camo gloves, and an M4A1. He blended in well with his surroundings and he had a military radio in his hand.

"Razorback 1, this is Eyes 1, over." he said, after glancing at his watch.

"Roger, Eyes, uh, how does it look?"

"Same-same as on the map. I count three vehicles outside, no in or out traffic. Uh, what is your ETA?"

"Three minutes, Eyes 1. I'm coming in from the west, and will dive to deliver the egg."

"Roger that, copy. What is your load?"

"I have napalm or MK-82 bombs."

"Use the napalm."

"Copy, one shake and bake coming up."

The aircraft came screaming toward the lodge and at the last second pulled up as the pilot released two metal containers that looked like fuel tanks to most folks. The containers were spinning end over end until they struck about a 100 feet before the structure. An explosion was heard and a wave of flames, still moving from the jet's momentum, rolled over the lodge and then fell. Within seconds a long line of flames was burning in the valley below. The building that was James Walker's pride and joy was an inferno.

"Razorback, nice bar-be-cue, and have a good flight back."

"Roger that, Eyes 1, and remember, you call and we haul. Razorback out."

The man on the ground dialed a number into his cell phone and then said, "Roast beef."

"Copy, Roast Beef."

He placed his phone in his pocket and waited for the flames to die down. If no fire trucks showed, he'd go down later and look for bodies. Right now he pulled out a flask, took a long drink, and then smiled. He'd just earned an easy $500,000.

On a hill opposite of the lodge, Agent X32, was watching the Combat Controller through the scope of his sniper rifle. He was in a prone position, with the bi-pod on the front of his rifle to assist him in keeping the weapon still as he sighted in his target.

On the other hill, the man was thinking of the things he could buy for his family with the money just earned and decided to call his wife and have her ready to go out for supper later. He was dialing the number when the phone slipped from his hand. He bent over to pick it up when the tree he'd been leaning against took a rifle round, sending bark in all directions. He heard no shot. Knowing he'd just been shot at, he began running, knowing a moving target in a forest full of trees is almost impossible to hit. He moved into the protective cover of dense pines and oaks, and at times he'd hear a round strike a tree.

His forearms were scratched and bleeding, but he knew that was nothing compared to a bullet so he took the pain without thought. At times he fell or stumbled, falling to the ground, and when he came to a small stream, he ran through it without thought. By the time he could see his car, he was bleeding from multiple scrapes and gouges from his run.

He ran until he reached his car.

Opening his trunk he threw his gear in, along with his rifle, checked the safety on his .45 auto and unlocked the door. He moved behind the steering wheel, put his seat-belt on and turned the ignition. There came a split-second in his mind when he knew he was a dead man. His world abruptly exploded into lambent flames and austere pain, and then he knew nothing.

The sniper heard the shattering explosion and waited until he saw the oily black red flames of the bomb and gas from the cars fuel tank rolling into each other. He chuckled, because he'd wired the car before he'd even gotten into position. He'd been with the organization for over ten years, and he always killed his target, *always*, but not always with a rifle. He stood and then moved toward his horses.

In Frankfurt, in a darkened room with a map of the world projected on one complete wall, the Boss was sitting at a table. Twelve other men and women sat at the table, with most sipping expensive cognac, and listening to a presentation by a young man dressed in a high-priced suit. The man talking ran the intelligence section for the New World Order.

"The Russians, Chinese, and Americans are being very resistant to the implementation of the NWO policies. Our largest problem is with the Americans, since they now have a weak Vice President who will run the show for almost a year. However, we are making some progress bringing him into the fold and his price is one billion dollars, which as we all know is small change. We must get him to enforce the martial law throughout the land and start taking guns away.

There are enough registered guns in American for each person to have 2.5 weapons. That, ladies and gentlemen, is a force larger than any organized army in the world. Then, consider the millions of hunters, veterans, and others that keep small arms for home protection. I suspect there are even more older weapons, still in excellent shape, that have been in families for years and they are not even registered. The registration of firearms is relatively new in the United States, and their resistance to turning over their guns is high. Many Americans, especially those over 40, have a cowboy mentality and it's a dangerous attitude for us to face. It is my opinion they will not give up their weapons without a fight."

The Boss interrupted and said, "We expect a fight, especially in America, but it means little to us. Collecting guns and fighting those determined to keep them will be a job for the UN. The UN is on our payroll, so let's have them act in a few days. The time has never been better for implementing the New World Order, so let's make this happen. If a redneck or cowboy gives us trouble, kill him or her. I want the American NSA system to start working harder too, because the director has been bought and paid for, to start rounding up those who speak out against our plans, the UN, gun confiscation or raising hell over what is happening. I want all phone calls, social media, and letters monitored."

The young man said, "That has started, sir, yesterday, as a matter of fact. Those arrested are having chips implanted before they are released. If they refuse to take the chip, they will disappear and end up in a mass grave. However, on a more serious note, intelligence indicates ISIS is about to detonate another dirty bomb on American soil."

"By God, that we cannot allow. They'll turn the whole country into a place we'll not be able to live in for hundreds of years. I want us to detonate our own dirty bombs, within 12 hours, and do so in four of the largest cities under ISIS control. Have them informed, afterwards, if they use one more nuclear bomb of any sort on the United States, NWO will have all ISIS leaders drawn and quartered. This crap must stop. Have the UN declare that they've uncovered evidence that ISIS detonated the dirty bomb in the US and I want death and total destruction to hit ISIS. Use Russian bombers, American B-52s, and carpet bomb the whole area! They've been more of a pain in the ass than a help to us, other than reducing the world's Arab population."

"Yes, sir, it shall be done. One last note of interest. Since combat started between the US and United Nations, the American people seemed to have put their differences aside and joined together, if nothing else spiritually, to resist our efforts. The state militias are well armed, patrolling their states, and even the good ole boys and cowboys have joined in this action. The US has limited its strikes against us to ground troops only and the commander of the UN forces informed me if the aircraft are brought into the fight, he may last at most two days."

"Good, because once the US massacres the UN troops, we'll have legal grounds to attack with all our might, again. Here the United States requested UN assistance to confiscate arms and then they attack us. It makes them look bad. Tell the current President his requested billion dollars will be granted, if he wipes out the UN. If he disagrees or wants more money, eliminate him, but make it look like an accident."

"Yes, sir. The weather folks wanted to remind everyone the area around Washington, D. C. is radioactive and will be long after we are all long dead. The winds in that part of the United States can be unpredictable, but our best estimate is one million died from the initial blast, with an additional estimated two million dead from radiation poisoning. Many Senators and Congressmen and women, were killed too, so there are some changes taking place in the states too."

The Boss asked, "Are they still refusing to comply with martial law?"

"Yes, sir, and it's supported by their military. The military refuses to support the confiscation of weapons, because gun ownership is a second amendment right in their Constitution. Seems when all military members of their services join, officer and enlisted, the oath states they'd defend their Constitution against all enemies foreign and domestic. The United Nations is foreign and the President is domestic, sir."

"Contact the Joint Chiefs of Staff and tell them if they don't do something about all of this gun bullshit, we'll replace all of them with men and women who will act as instructed. I can't believe they can't act and order their troops to do as instructed."

"The individual American soldier, sailor, airman, or Marine is not required to follow unlawful orders and they're even taught how to decline such orders legally. As I stated with the start of day one of our pushing the establishment of our New World Order, the United States of America will be the most difficult country to bring into line. They, as I said earlier, have a different mentality and as a nation are a strong people."

"Get the liberals on the bandwagon and pay them what you must so we can use the influence of their people now, as the United Nations attacks them. Play on how they don't want the US turned into a wasteland with zillions of dead babies laying around or some other bullshit story. We cannot use the FEMA facilities as gulags, start mass killings, or rape Americas resources, until those fools give up their guns. I don't understand how they think, because normal folks would be afraid to be invaded. I get the impression from you that the Americans might even enjoy it."

"They will never give up their guns, Boss, never. I will try and do my best to make it happen, but they are a stubborn bunch. I suspect we'll have to take the arms from each house, one by one."

"We are way off track here in this conversation. You see to what you have been told to do and report to me privately as each step is started and accomplished. This meeting is over." The Boss stood and walked from the room.

CHAPTER 9

James and the small convoy drove straight through to the Ozark Mountains without stopping, except for gas and one roadblock. Ben was very anxious, and worried that his being with the group would get them all killed. James kept telling him the NWO had no idea where he was, because without the chip, they *couldn't* know. Only Ben knew the organization had a long reach and knew things no one else knew. They'd had to hide Frank once, when a roadblock checked them looking for the man. Since he was wanted for killing the President, they used the GPS and CB radio in the van to avoid most roadblocks.

At the roadblock, they'd hidden Frank in the upper shelves and placed canned goods and boxes in front of his body. Of course, the cops hadn't moved the dry goods or canned goods and he was not discovered. While the police searched, since all those fleeing Houston were armed, they were prepared to start fighting at any moment. In their collective minds the United States had gone to hell, and those working in law enforcement were just enforcers of those with money. Corruption had progressed to the point in politics that the average American was disgusted.

James and the rest knew it was just a matter of time before a full blown civil war would erupt. The people were tired of being abused by politicians that treated their voters like so many blind sheep. The voting system was rigged, those in government were dishonest, and Americans were fed up. James figured it'd be Liberals against Conservatives and the positive side was most liberals didn't own a gun, whereas Republicans usually owned a couple or more.

The land James owned was south of Rolla, Missouri on Route 63 South, at a small town named Vida. They turned right at Vida and drove down a macadam road. A few miles later they turned on the gravel road and continued until they ran into a fenced in area with a gate. James unlocked the gate, let everyone in and then locked the gate again. Off their right, as they drove toward the cave, the remains of an old cabin stood, and no trespassing signs were posted frequently. They passed the house, went down a hill and stopped right in front of a small stream. Vehicle engines were turned off and James yelled, "The cave is to the right, oh, maybe 200 feet."

All walked to the cave and it was much larger than imagined by most of them. The RV would have been able to drive in the thing, except trees blocked the approach.

"There are a number of reasons I came here. First, in the event of a dirty bomb, the only protection against radiation sickness is shielding, and there is almost 500 feet of dirt and rock from the cave to the top soil. Second, it is impossible to freeze to death in a cave, because the temp stays pretty close to 68 degrees all year round. Third, while the locals know of this place and it's listed on all USGS maps, few would think of looking for a group from Houston here. Missouri has thousands of caves, so that helps. Later today, we'll drive into town and get new phones, and destroy the old ones. With our old phones, we can be traced right to here, if we make or take a call. So, no talking or accepting calls on your old phones."

"Once the camper is unloaded and everything moved to the inside of the cave, I'll park the camper in the old barn beside the ancient cabin on the hill. I know with the doors of the barn closed, no one will know it's there. The Jeep and motorcycle we can hide here. The cycle can actually be parked inside this place. The Jeep we'll cover with some camouflage netting I use to duck hunt. My concern with all the hiding is to keep the place empty in the event the NWO has access to satellite images."

"They have access to anything the UN has, and satellites are used when needed. I'm sure they'll have men and women working around the clock looking satellite images over. They'll come to understand some folks will go into hiding. They will mark all known spots, so they can check them." Ben said.

James grinned and said, "Now, I have solar panels on the top of my camper for power, gas generators, as well as a battery powered radio and television. To conserve power, we'll listen to the radio at noon, then the TV at 6 pm each day. At some point this next week, we'll remove the solar panels from the RV and rig them up outside, for use in here. I'm not sure if we'll be able to pick up many radio stations underground like this, so we'll have to check. We also need to cover the front of this cave to help avoid detection. I have a chainsaw with me, so we can cut and place logs across the front, leaving just enough of an opening to come and go. Eventually we'll make a swinging door."

"What about a bathroom or place to wash?" Carol asked.

"For the first day or two, move out about 100 feet to do your business, and wash in the stream at the bottom of this road. Eventually, we'll build outhouses and a shower room of some sort. While in town today, I'll look for a 55 gallon drum we can use to fill with water and then modify into a shower. Things will be a little primitive for a while, but we can all do it."

Four hours later James, Dick, and Blake, along with Donna and Nancy pulled into the parking lot of a huge department store in Rolla. They loaded up on non-scented bleach to treat water, batteries of all sizes, a lot of different sources of protein, including 100 pounds of dried beans and cases of peanut butter. Cases of shells were purchased for pistols, shotguns, and rifles. Hacksaws were purchased, arrows for compound bows, and camouflage makeup as well. A dozen individual first aid kits went in the cart along with two cases wide sanitary napkin pads used by women. The pads worked well to slow the flow of blood from a gunshot wound.

Camouflage colored tarps were thrown in the cart, along with portable shovels, toilet paper, large containers of salt and pepper were added, and two cases of non-scented bars of soap. Lighters, matches, and even flint and steel kits went in the basket.

Of course, James picked up 8 cases of beer and 10 quarts of whiskey. No, the hard alcohol was not for a party, but to be used as a painkiller, once the medications Nancy had were gone. The beer would be consumed on special days or after an especially difficult day. It was the only luxury item purchased.

Nancy had been in the medical supplies section of the store and picked up cases of medications to treat a variety of minor illnesses from diarrhea to tooth pain. She loaded her cart with rubbing alcohol, cases of multi-vitamins, vitamin C, and repair kits for glasses. As a nurse practitioner, she wrote out prescriptions for James, Blake, Dick, and Donna. She had them get 90 day supplies of antibiotics, painkillers, sleeping pills, Xanax, and other drugs she thought she might need. Over the next week, she'd write more scripts, so she could stockpile the drugs for any emergency.

In the outdoors section of the store, two plastic fifty-five gallon drums were taken along with various types of tubing, clamps and rope. Full size shovels were also purchased, along with nails and a complete tool box full of tools, including a hammer.

Once back at the cave and the supplies stored, James sawed the barrels off most of the shotguns, issued ammo, face paint, and other gear. He then said, "From tonight on, we'll have guards and everyone will pull guard duty, women included. I figure one hour shifts, since we have so many people, and that should be easy on all concerned. Now, if I catch you sleeping on guard, the first time you will be warned, but the second time you'll be banished from the cave and the group. Any questions?"

Silence.

"Carol, I'd suggest you start teaching your children now. It will keep them and you busy and doing something productive. Over the years, they'll learn a little from each of us, which will improve their knowledge." James said, glanced at Nancy, smiled, and continued, "Didn't you want to say a few words?"

"If you start to get ill or suffer an injury, come and see me then, and don't wait until later when it has turned more serious. Most illnesses and injuries are easy to treat if we get to them early enough. Now, while this looks like a prolonged camping trip, try to stay clean by bathing at least every other day, change your clothing often, and keep your hands and feet healthy. Hands will collect splinters, small cuts, and torn nails; take care of them by using your individual first aid kits. Feet need to be cared for too, and that means clean socks each day, and if they get wet, change your socks as soon as you can. Keep your feet dry or they'll start to crack and bleed on you. If any doubt about an injury or illness see me."

Dick asked, "What about security?"

James grinned and said, "As a retired security policeman, I'll run security and we'll have a guard on the high ground, right above this cave 24/7. From the top, all approaches to the cave can be seen and it's in a wooded area, too. The guard will carry a telephone and will be able, maybe, to report anyone coming to visit."

"Maybe?" Frank asked.

"Yep, maybe, because I'm not sure how well the phones will receive signals in here. If they do poorly, we'll have to rig up a warning of some sort."

"We'll come up with something." Frank said, but then asked, "How were things in town? Did people seem concerned about all the changes going on now?"

"Not a great deal, and I don't think most folks will realize things are going to hell, well, until it's too late to do much. I think tomorrow you, me, Ben and Carol need to run in and get some prescriptions filled and buy more ammo."

"Sure, but if I get any medications, then the NWO will know exactly what town I'm in and the same with Carol. Also, you can be sure the FBI and CIA are checking all they can on Frank, as is the NWO. Any activity on his medical records, ATM, or other computer files, will send a red flag."

"Damn, I'd not given that much thought, so that's out, unless you just want to go look around."

Sitting on a log they'd packed in for a sofa, Ben said, "No, I'll not chance it, and suggest Carol and Frank stay here, too. We need to lay low for a long time, and the less seen of us the better."

"Okay then, I'll take Fred, April, Tom, Joan, and Dick with me. The idea is to stock up on medical supplies that we may need during the long haul. Before we leave in the morning, Nancy will write all of your prescriptions for the meds she will need the most if this lasts a long time."

Dick, quiet most of the morning said, "The news this morning said black folks have taken over Detroit, Chicago and most of St. Louis. Large numbers of whites, Hispanics, and Asians were reportedly murdered. Then, the Texans went on a rampage, and those cowboys burned every mosque in the state. There are reports of thousands of Muslims killed and hanging from trees and telephone poles. What in the hell is going on? I think it's looking more and more like a civil war is coming, and I don't like this at all."

"But, who against who?" James asked.

"As I've heard said before I think Liberals against Conservatives. The Liberals are the fools that riot over sending the illegal aliens home, raise hell every time a cop kills a black man, no matter if the dead man was dangerous or not, wanted millions of Syrian Refugees in the country, and have spent and spent until there is little left to spend." Dick said, and then gave a weak smile.

"What of our military?" Carol asked.

"Most are conservatives, but when the government can no longer pay them every two weeks, how long do you think they'll keep coming to work? That will happen with the police, fire fighters, and EMTs too. Once the money stops flowing, folks will start to walk off their jobs. I think all community resources will dry up, grocery stores will soon empty, hospitals will no longer be able to care for patients who will be sent home, or abandoned in their beds. Someone will have to rescue them or they'll starve to death."

"You can be damned sure the New World Order will be watching this country closely. They're patient people and won't move until after our civil war is over. Once the smoke clears, they'll come into this country with all the power the United Nations can provide, with all the speed and force they can muster." Ben said, and then poured some coffee into his cup from the pot on the small fire.

"Well," James said, "we'll worry about that when it happens."

It was close to 6 pm, so they turned on the television, which was running off solar power and discovered they only received one station clearly and two others with a lot of snow on the screen. They finally tuned into the clear station.

"Federal authorities announced today that starting next week all legal citizens of the United States will begin to get microchips installed. Your personal information, medical history, banking information, credit rating, and driver's license will all be stored on this chip. It will also transmit your body temperature, vitals, and other information to a monitored computer, which may save lives by sending emergency medical assistance to you before you have a stroke, heart attack, or other life threatening emergency. It also has a tracking GPS, which will assist the police in locating missing persons. However, this order does not come without some resistance. Harold Glover reports for WGXG in Jefferson City. Harold?"

"John, I am standing in front of the First Baptist Church and as you can see behind me, the chip offends some people. Christians as a whole are refusing to have the implant and referencing the scripture pertaining to the Mark of the Beast in the Bible. They claim the number of the beast is 666. Federal authorities are attempting to persuade them that it is nothing, except a better way to store information about any individual and only those places that have need can access the individual's information. Starting the first of next year, those without the chip will not be able to access ATMs, medical care, cash checks or accomplish banking transactions of any kind. There will be many places the chip is required, like voting, shopping or selling merchandise in any way. Also, those on public assistance or receiving disability, military retirement, or other checks from the United States Treasury will not be able to have them deposited until the chip is implanted. Food stamps will also be denied to those who do not have the chip. The chip is free and being implanted at all hospitals, police stations, and clinics. This is Harold Glover, reporting for WGXG."

Ben shook his head and said, "They are fools if they get the chip. It's not being done for the good of people, but to enslave them. As for saving lives, the NWO wants to reduce the world's current population to a much more controllable number, so that's all bullshit."

"I reckon," James said, "folks that live in the country, cowboys and cowgirls, Christians and others who know the Bible will refuse the chip; then what?"

"They'll be taken to a FEMA camp, kept until there are enough of them and then used for slave labor, or they'll be taken into the countryside, shot and killed. There is no room for those who do not conform." Frank said, and then shook his head as he said, "That chip will lead to civil war. The Republicans will refuse it, but the Liberals will see it as another free lunch."

"So, what do we do?" Donna asked as she looked at James, and he could see her fear.

James reached over, patted her hand a few times and then said, "We'll get by here, in the cave, until we see how this split happens."

Dick said, "This is insane, because we have racial splits happening, religious splits, political splits, so how can we tell which is which? How do we separate the good guys from the bad?"

"We wait, is what we do. Soon, very soon, the change will take place and the TV will cover it all."

"Look," Frank said, "all of us are veterans, except for the women. Why don't we try to make contact with an active duty unit or with the state militia?"

"Is there an active duty unit around here?" Dick asked.

"There is an Army base about 30 miles west of here, and maybe tomorrow two of us can go there and at least see what's going on. Once on the base, we'll buy more ammo, food and medical supplies." James suggested, and then winked at Donna.

"I like that idea." Ben said.

The phone rang and James answered, "Yeah?"

A minute passed and then he said, "How far? Okay, stay where you are no matter what happens, okay?"

"Good, bye." Looking around he said, "There are two men wearing camouflage making their way toward the entrance of the cave. Blake said they know what they're doing, which usually means ex-military, and he only spotted them when the sun flashed off something. Both are carrying sniper rifles and they're about half a mile away — to our south."

Ben neared and said, "They're after me to be sure. Let me get on top of the cave and I'll take them both out with my rifle."

"How do they know you're here?"

"They probably raided your place in Texas, found it empty and then they just ran a computer check to see what other properties you may own. This one came up."

"Okay, move, but let neither of them escape." James said.

Ben grabbed his rifle and was gone.

"I want the rest of the men outside, hiding in the bushes. All women and the kids need to go back further in the cave to where it turns. Stay there until we tell you to come out. Men, take a rifle and pistol, but remember to hide well. I think from now on, we need to wear pistols at all times."

As the men left the cave, Donna wondered how many would be alive in an hour.

CHAPTER 10

The two snipers on the hillside opposite the cave mouth, were FBI and learned to shoot while in the Army. They'd both received special training and as one shot, the other would spot for him. As a team, these two had hundreds of kills behind them, and since they'd joined the FBI, they had added another couple of hundred. They tried hard to use one shot for one kill, but truth be known, some hits took more than one bullet. In the field they rarely spoke, but used their hands to communicate, and they'd been on so many missions before, they could almost read each other minds.

Their mission brief stated that Ben had turned rogue and left the CIA. Neither questioned the briefing, because they'd had the chip implanted, so all was fine with them. They were told where the suspected target may be and that was it. Then, using a government C-130 running between bases on the east and west coast, they'd left the airplane at 20,000 feet free-falling and then opened their parachutes at 800 feet. Commonly referred to as HALO, High Altitude (jump) Low (parachute) Opening, they'd landed less than two miles from the cave in a large hay field. Near the Little Piney River, they'd thrown their parachutes and other jump gear under a ledge and then collapsed it to cover all traces of their jump.

Neither had spotted Blake or Ben on the very top of the cave. By the time the snipers glassed the roof of the cave, Ben was in a prone position scoping the two snipers. Once Blake heard Ben wanted to take out the snipers, he'd hidden as well as he could near the man and would spot for him. He disliked all snipers and while he didn't think of them as cowards, because he'd seen some brave ones, they didn't fight fairly in his eyes. He'd served with some brave snipers, very brave men, who'd spend days sneaking up on a ripe target. To them it was part of the job, but he disliked their job and could do without snipers on either side.

Ben was having a real hard time finding the man with the rifle on the far ridge. He'd found the spotter easily enough, but the sniper eluded him. Of course, the spotter wasn't Ben's primary target, because the man with the trigger finger would kill. While the Federal sniper did not see his targets, either Agent X1 or Joda May, the missing Secret Service Agent, he did see over a half dozen old fat men, only they didn't interest him.

Finally, the spotter wrote on a sheet of green paper, "ten feet off the left side of the trail leading to the cave, is a black man. Looks to be May. He is approximately ½ the distance from the stream to the cave. Behind a huge walnut tree."

The sniper nodded and then looked for Joda. Finally, he spotted the man and confirmed he was in fact Joda May. Black male, 28 years old, short hair, thin, small scar on his forehead. He laid the cross-hairs on his targets head, right in the middle of his face, and then took a deep breath. As the sniper slowly exhaled, he began to squeeze the trigger. The shot was more of a light thump than a crack or boom, and when he'd checked his target, he could not be seen.

Whispering, the spotter said, "Bullet must have struck a branch or twig, because your shot was deflected, wide."

"Okay, let's just kill all of them."

"You sure?"

"Why not, they're with wanted men, so they're harboring fugitives, right?" The sniper thought that killing all of them was the smart thing to do. Of course, his thought came from the NWO master computer.

Ben had known a shot was fired, because he saw just a touch of smoke and the hint of muzzle flash. He glassed the area again and finally spotted the sniper.

As the Federal sniper was lining up Thomas in his sights, Ben smiled and thought, *This sniper will never have to worry about getting a microchip implanted, because he's about to be implanted with lead.*

Both the Federal sniper and Ben fired at the same time. Thomas screamed, grabbed his chest and fell to the forest floor near the trail. The shot had taken him dead center of his chest, with a lead slug pushing a chunk of backbone with it as it punched a hole through the man. Blood was seeping and oozing from the small entrance hole, but a carmine stream was flowing freely from its exit wound. In a matter of a few short seconds, he was lying in a growing puddle of scarlet blood. His feet kicked and his fingers scratched at the soil.

A split second after Tom screamed, Ben's bullet struck the sniper's scope and continued down the long tube, to exit already flattened. The misshapen lead struck the Federal sniper in the right eye, continued through his brain, and then exited at the rear of his head. Blood, brain tissue, gore and shards of skull splattered on the bushes behind him. His bloody Boonie hat was knocked from his head violently as his head was snapped back from the force of the bullet.

As the sniper lay jerking and twitching, the spotter grabbed the sniper rifle and moved further up the slope. He finally moved behind a big oak tree. Crawling very slowly, the man moved away from the tree to a dense clump of brush off his right side, where he hoped to hide until darkness; then he'd kill his target.

Ben and Blake knew where the man went, but had no idea he was moving. The new sniper was moving so slowly, even those watching for him did not detect any movement.

The spotter had almost lost his professionalism when the sniper was killed. Never had the two taken so much as a slight injury, until today. They were obviously the target of another well trained sniper and he suspected it was Ben. He'd been briefed that Agent X1 was a very deadly man.

"I've lost him." Blake said, his voice full of frustration.

"I think he's still behind the oak tree, but he'll move soon. Sooner or later, he'll make a mistake. When he does, we'll take his ass out."

Picking up the phone, Blake asked, "Anyone hit with that shot?"

Ben knew a well trained sniper didn't shoot until he had a clear shot. There were very few victims of snipers that were just wounded.

"Understand." he said and then closed the cell phone.

"Well?"

"Thomas is fatally injured. He took what looks like a 30.06 shot to the middle of his chest and is living right now on borrowed time. According to James, his lungs and spine were hit, and they can't get the bleeding to stop."

"If that ever happens to me, just shoot my ass. I see no need to suffer excruciating pain for long minutes or even hours, with no hope of recovery."

Picking up the cell phone, Ben dialed a number and then said, "It will be dark soon and we need to take the other man out, or he'll change to a night vision scope. Once he does that, we're dead meat."

"What do you suggest we do?"

"Send two men toward the sniper, but from opposite directions, and when he moves, I'll smoke his ass. He'll see the movement of one or both of them for sure and he'll either hole up or take a shot. If I were him, I'd take a shot. Tell your men to shoot to kill."

"It'll be me and Frank." said James. "We both have 30.06's with scopes and sidearms. We're moving now."

Minutes later, both men were seen slowly moving toward the sniper, from different sides. Both men fully understood what they were up against and it was very probable the sniper would take one or both of them out. However, they also knew once it grew full dark, the sniper could kill more of them than in daylight. Folks using the woods as a toilet, gathering more wood, or anyone near the fire in the cave would be fair game. It was likely the sniper had Night Vision Goggles which allowed him to see in the dark, but he'd see everything in an eerie green color. James knew, once dark, they'd never find him.

The going was rough and the slope of the hill was steep. It didn't help James that he'd been drinking beer and sitting on his ass for a couple of years. He was out of shape and his mind was on edge, knowing the next second may be his last. While not really a religious man, he found himself silently praying they'd take the sniper out with no cost to them.

Frank had just stepped on a rock and as he moved, the rock rolled and down he went. At the instant he fell, he heard the bullet zing past his head, less than an inch from his ear.

"I have movement." Ben said, "In some bushes."

"Moved to some bushes? I never saw him move from the tree."

"He moved to the clump of bushes to his right, or our left. He's right in the middle."

"Frank is down, but I have no idea if he's hit or not. Can you risk a shot?"

"Better than that, I'm going to take the man out, but watch him in case I miss."

"I have him visual now, so shoot when you want."

Ben lined up his sights, grinned, and as he squeezed the trigger, he said, "Bye and say hello to Saint Peter for me." His rifle gave a muffled thump as it fired.

The sniper on the hill was lining his rifle up on James, when he suddenly felt a searing pain go through his chest, and he was knocked violently to the ground.

I've been hit, he thought, as he tried to remove a bandage from his first aid kit, only to discover his hands and arms wouldn't obey his brain. He was able to open the first aid pouch on his web belt, remove the bandage, but he couldn't tear the paper it was packed in. He did pull the morphine self-injecting syringe, from the first aid kit, and struck it on the side of his thigh. He felt the needle enter the meaty portion of his thigh and just seconds later, all pain disappeared.

His bloody rifle lay by his side, but he lacked the strength to pick it up, which confused him. He felt no pain, but his back was resting in water, he thought. The wetness he felt was his blood, not water, and the puddle was growing larger with each beat of his heart.

He was thinking of his days as a child, floating homemade sail boats down ditches following a hard rain. Suddenly, he was a child again. He pushed his boat to the middle of the trench and watched the current grab the wooden toy. Then slowly, his world turned from full light, to light gray and then, minutes later, it turned black. The last man of the sniper team sent to kill Joda and Ben was dead.

James made his way cautiously toward the sniper and then got a phone call.

"Yep?" he asked as he stopped for a breather.

"The threat has been terminated."

"You sure?"

"Positive; now strip those two men of anything you can find. Bring their watches, guns, packs, and all but the clothing they're wearing or the bodies."

"Copy, and will do." James said, and the line went dead.

Once back at the cave, Frank and Joda went through the gear and supplies. They discovered two sets of NVGs with extra batteries, and three more doses of self-injecting morphine. Thomas no longer needed it; he'd died minutes before the last sniper. Six MRE self-heating rations, two 9 mm hand guns and two Russian sniper rifles, with one day and night scope, the other had been destroyed, and four magazines of ammo for each rifle. Small binoculars, and some other small items each man liked to carry, such as pocket knife, chewing tobacco, and so on, were found too. Neither man had any identification and each carried close to a thousand dollars.

James waited a bit and then said, "We need to move again, but we're lucky, because we're in the Mark Twain National Forest. Tomorrow, Frank and I will scout the area and look for another cave or spot to make a home."

"Why move, honey? This place is nice."

"It's obvious the Feds, knowing of my land here, figured this is where we'd be. So, we need to go where they won't expect us. Now they have lost two snipers, they'll soon send more men and we don't want to be here."

"It's time for the evening news." Frank said, and then turned the television on.

"Our top two stories tonight, the US treasury to remove 'In God We Trust" from all American currency. The removal is the result of a joint lawsuit filed by the organizations, Atheists Have Rights Too and the American Civil Rights for Muslims. The

Supreme Court voted the words do in fact violate the separation of religion and government. Christian organizations, especially our nations Southern Baptists are angered by the ruling."

The camera traveled to the other reporter sitting at the desk and moved in for a close up shot as she said, "Federal Health authorities are confused by the increase in the number of Plague victims since the first victim died ten days ago. In the ten days since his death, 2,000 others have died. The Black Plague, long thought eradicated, has suddenly become a major health concern. Not to mention 276 new cases of Ebola, and almost a thousand Zika victims. Homeland security is involved to determine if this is not an act of terrorism."

"Breaking news! Just minutes ago, it was announced the United States military defeated the United Nations teams sent here to take guns from gun owners. The President of the United States is to speak to our nation in a few seconds. Lee Johnson is currently on the scene in Los Angeles, where the temporary White House is located, and covering this item. Lee, what can you tell us about the President and his speech?"

"Confidential sources close to the President tell us he is requesting many more UN troops and is determined to confiscate all guns from Americans. This action is, of course, illegal with the Second Amendment of the Constitution guaranteeing the right of every American to keep and bear arms. He has also —"

The camera zoomed in on the new President of the United States as he walked to the podium. He removed his speech from his coat, cleared his throat, and said, "My fellow Americans, we are facing times of increased gun violence across the nation, and this cannot be allowed to continue. Therefore, I have once again asked the UN to provide me with enough troops to disarm all Americans. I have asked the United States Military Services to release any and all members of our military who will not follow my orders. My orders to our services will be to place those who refuse to follow my orders in FEMA camps for their own protection, to guard these camps and to assist the UN in collecting weapons. Those who resist will go to our camps and their families will join them. Individual states who fail to obey my martial law decree will see their Governor and other elected officials sent to

FEMA camps as well. Individuals who fail to follow my orders, fail to enact martial law, and those who refuse to surrender their guns will be identified as criminal felons. My goal is to follow the New World Order and take America to places and new levels it has never achieved before. This cannot be done in a criminal environment where every mentally disturbed veteran can buy a gun, and they are all dealing with serious PTSD issues, or where wannabee cowboys can arm themselves in just a few minutes. Along with taking guns, I have passed a new law that makes the selling of any gun, by anyone, a very serious offense that carries the death penalty. As of this minute, guns will no longer be made in the United States. I will not answer any questions at this time. Thank you." The President of the United States walked from the room.

"John, it's clear the President can collect guns, as part of martial law, but once the state of emergency is over, the guns will have to be returned to their owners. It's difficult to see the need for martial law, but there have been some violent riots in some of our larger cities. This is Lee Johnson, on special assignment with the President. Back to our studio."

"Thank you Lee, and I now take you live to our Governor, who will comment on the President's speech."

"Missourians, the great state of Missouri has activated the National Guard, our Reserve units, and our state militia. I feel the President is out of bounds by declaring martial law and is clearly, as well as intentionally, violating the second amendment to the United States Constitution, the same document he swore to defend. Therefore, I am soliciting impeachment proceeding against him at this moment. In the event he will not accept an impeachment ruling, the State of Missouri, along with many Southern States, will once again secede from the Union. As of this morning, we had 30 more states willing to leave the Union as well. Those states that did not join us are primarily Liberal states and are not really welcome to be a part of us. We find the New World Order to be dangerous, powerful, and not something the state of Missouri or the United States would find in her best interests to be involved with. I will not answer any questions at this time. Save your questions for tomorrow's press briefing; thank you."

The camera man followed the governor and his bodyguards out of the building. Cameras were clicking and video cameras were moving to the best positions for lighting in the early evening darkness. The group climbed into a black SUV.

The driver turned the ignition and the starter was heard turning, then came a huge explosion as hundreds of pounds of conventional C-4, placed under fertilizer and flour, exploded. Additionally, items in the trunk included nuts, bolts, and over a hundred pounds of nails placed loosely on top of the explosives. The occupants of the SUV died instantly. The top of the vehicle, as well as the trunk, where the FBI agent had place the explosives, blew high into the sky, twisting and turning as they moved upward. Over forty bystanders were seriously injured and eighteen killed. The United States was starting to look like Arab countries, where car bombings were a daily occurrence.

"John, we have our camera man down and I . . . I think . . . I think he's dead. Back to you."

John gave a fake smile and said, "We'll keep you updated on that assassination as soon as more information becomes available. I repeat, the governor of Missouri, the honorable John Hains, was assassinated just moments ago by a car bomb. Join us later tonight for our 10 pm newscast and we'll provide you with the latest up to date information on his horrible killing."

The camera switched to a woman reporter in the studio who said, "The stock market closed today after taking its biggest loss since the great crash of the 1930's. Worldwide, other markets dropped too, and financial experts feel the loss is due to people not trusting their governments and fluctuating currency exchanges. There has been a huge rush to sell stocks, with very few buying them. The Asian Stock market fell to its lowest level in recorded history. Economists claim if the markets continue to drop and stay that way, we will soon enter a great Depression."

The camera switched to the male anchor who said, "The FBI and CIA have both stated that Joda May and Ben Hall are believed to be traveling together. Both May and Hall are suspected conspirators in the assassination of the President of the United States one month ago. Take a look at both of these images and if you see either man, you are requested to call the FBI or CIA at the numbers showing on your screen. Currently, there are large rewards offered for either man. These men are considered armed and dangerous, so do not approach them. We'll take a short commercial break and will be right back to bring you the latest weather."

James turned the radio off and then said, "Shit, what a mess."

CHAPTER 11

In Frankfurt, the boss was in another dark room, being briefed by his senior man in intelligence. So far, he wasn't impressed at all.

Finally, the briefer asked, "Any questions, sir?"

"Yes, I do have a few. Are you telling me that two FBI snipers were killed by some over aged men with beer bellies?"

"No, sir, because a ballistics check of the bullets used to kill both snipers were determined to have been fired by Ben Hall's government issued sniper rifle. He has turned rogue, sir."

"I don't care what he has turned into, I want the man dead! Do you understand me? Or the next time you brief me, we will have a death —yours. Bring the force of the NWO down on his head."

"Uh, yes, sir."

"I also want to know when we'll start killing Christians. I gave the order last week and you just told me it cannot be done. It *can* and *will* be done, understand me. I want it started as soon as this meeting is finished."

"How can we kill them in the United States without revealing our true goal, sir?"

"Our one true goal is to establish a global government, with one currency, one religion, and one ruler. Some have or will call our ruler the anti-Christ, but any person with a brain does not believe in God or the fact he was killed and rose again. Once dead, we stay that way. I want the killings to start in America, or they will soon start in Germany. Understood?"

"Yes, sir."

"Good; now get out of my sight and next time I want to hear some results, or you'll be giving your last briefing to anyone. Make things happen, my friend." the boss said as he stood, put his coat on and then donned his hat.

Once the room was empty, the man pulled his cell, dialed a number and said, "Begin operation Bratwurst."

"Begin operation Bratwurst? Are you sure?"

"Ordered by the boss."

"Mein Gott. Auf Wiedersehen."

Thousands of miles from Frankfurt, near the small town of Enid, Oklahoma, the phone rang.

"Hello?"

"How many Christians do you have in your FEMA camp, Colonel?"

"Approximately five thousand, General."

"We want you to offer the chip to them once more. If they refuse, kill them."

"Kill all that refuse, sir?"

"You heard me correctly, sir, kill them. We want them all dead by dawn."

"And, what do I do with the bodies?"

"Bring in a bulldozer or backhoe and make a long trench. Bury them in the trench."

"I see, sir. Yes, while I want to go on record as being against this, because it violates the Constitution, the job will be done."

"I understand Colonel, and I promise this is the last time you will ever have to do this for us."

"Thank you, sir. I didn't become a soldier to kill civilians."

"I'll see you are taken care of immediately, Colonel. Contact me when the killing is finished." The voice said, but thought, *Right after the executions, you'll be a dead man.*

"Yes, sir. Goodbye."

Over the next few hours, the Christians were told to take the chip or die this day. Out of five thousand, four changed their minds. While the interviews were being done, a trench, six feet deep and a hundred yards long was dug near the camp. The bulldozer then parked behind the barracks, the driver knowing the hole would need filling at the end of the day.

A machine gun was placed in front of the trench, ammo cans were stacked, and three new gun

barrels were placed on a poncho. All the enlisted men knew, as they guarded the prisoners, was their guests were criminals. The guards had no idea the only crimes they'd committed was not getting the chip implanted because they were Christians and felt it was the sign of the devil.

Calling his men together, the Colonel said, "I have been ordered to kill the prisoners. Each was found guilty earlier of acts against America and sentenced to death. We will lead them out in groups of 100 and use the machine gun on them. Others will be led to showers, the doors locked, and the exhaust fumes from our trucks will be sent by plastic pipes. Our work will be hard and long, because all five thousand need to be dead by morning."

One young Sergeant said, "Sir, you mean to stand there and tell me almost 5,000 people have been given fair trials for crimes against this nation, and I've heard nothing about it on the news? I'm not, with all due respect sir, calling you a liar, but I don't find your order legal. I have sworn to obey the Constitution, as you have, and I feel their rights have been violated. Have these folks been denied due process?"

"Uh, I have no idea of the legal classification of any of these people. The documents I have read say they're all convicted of heinous crimes against the government."

"Colonel, I think you damned sure need to know before you start murdering our fellow Americans. I cannot believe for one second that these women or children are involved with grievous crimes. I, sir, refuse to kill my own people, because some day, I'll have to stand in front of the Lord, my God, and explain my actions. I feel, Colonel, your orders are illegal."

"I refuse too, sir." a young Lieutenant said and moved to stand beside the Sergeant.

Then, one by one, others moved until four men remained.

Giving a loud sigh, the Colonel said, "I guess you have a valid point, Sergeant, so instead of killing these folks, we'll turn them loose. Only, I suggest all of you gather up your families and go into hiding. I told the General I didn't like the idea of killing these people just because they're Christians. To be honest, I can't do this to my own people. Just like you though, if I'm caught, I'll be shot."

"Where do we release them?" the Sergeant asked.

"Take them east, Chicago or even New York, and turn them loose and leave tonight. I think they can hide better in a large city. Those that do not want to go, can leave here by foot. You men can either go with the Sergeant or change into civilian clothing and leave. Remember, if they catch you it's likely you'll be shot for deserting, but the orders we received to kill are not lawful. Or that's my opinion."

"You heard him, men, let's get all the trucks loaded and get ready to move."

The Colonel started to walk away when he said, "Give each released family a case of MREs to feed them for a while. Good luck to each of you."

The Colonel went back to his office, pulled out a bottle of Scotch and poured three fingers worth in his glass. As prisoners walked by his building he heard them talking and laughing, which confirmed in his heart he'd done the right thing.

He sipped his whiskey as he waited until early the next morning when his phone rang.

"Hello, this is the Commander speaking."

"Has your mission been completed, Colonel?"

"Oh, yes, hours ago."

"So, all 5,000 are dead?"

"No, I didn't kill a soul. See, as I gave thought to your orders, I realized they were not lawful, so they are not binding to me. Besides, I had a message from my Supreme Commander and he told me to not listen to your orders."

"Who in the hell is this Supreme Commander?"

"God, my lost friend, God. One day you'll have to explain your actions to him."

"There is no God and you, sir, are a dead man."

"You're wrong in both cases for right now. Have a good day, and I'll pray for you and your salvation."

The phone went dead. The Colonel loaded a case of grenades, carbines, ammo and all sorts of other military gear in his SUV. His wife had died years back of cancer, so he had no reason to return home. They had no living children, their two beautiful baby girls had died as infants, which still bothered him at times. He had some cousins down in Missouri and he'd head down that way to hide out.

He then spent a good hour pouring gasoline all over the FEMA structures and as they burned, he started the bulldozer. Once the dozer was moving, he knocked down the fence, and ran over it, then pushing it into the flames, rendering it useless.

He'd then climbed into his car and drove south.

Out on the main freeway, he spotted a military convoy heading north, most likely to his old assignment. They'd not find much now, but blackened soil where a FEMA camp once stood. He prayed he wasn't stopped, because he'd go to jail or be killed for what weapons he had alone. Jail wasn't an option; his country needed him, and he didn't want to kill an innocent policeman or woman.

They'll not find much when they get there, he thought and then chuckled. *I just hope my cousins remember me, because I've not seen them in years. Times are fixing to turn really rough, I think.*

He drove straight through, stopping only for gas in a small Oklahoma town near the Missouri border. His camouflage uniform caused a bit of a stir, but he found it great that some people still appreciated his dedication to keeping America strong and protected. He left there smiling and waving at the old man who followed him to his car. The old man was a Vietnam veteran and as far as the Colonel was concerned, old vets like him were what made our country great.

In between exits, at one point there was a roadblock, and he heard his heart pumping loudly in his chest. There was no way to turn around, so he was caught in traffic. The police were checking driver's licenses, looking in cars, and checking for drunks. He'd sobered up since he left the camp, so he waited his turn, hoping he didn't have to use the cocked pistol beside him, covered with a blanket.

"Can I see your driver's license, sir?" a state trooper asked.

"Sure, give me a second." He pulled out his military id and his driver's license.

"Are you on active duty, sir?"

"Yes, and I'm in a bit of a hurry to get to Fort Leonard Wood, Missouri. I've been recalled from a TDY."

"No, problem, Colonel, I'm a Captain in the National Guard. You're free to go, sir."

"That's it?"

"Frank, this man is a full Colonel, so let him through!"

"Sure." Frank replied.

"That's it, and have a safe trip, sir."

The Colonel almost had a heart attack when he first stopped and even now, as he drove away, his hands were shaking. It took him almost an hour for his body to get back to normal. *Damn me, I've not been that scared in years. I just knew I was going to jail*, he thought.

He kept his speed legal, not wanting any attention drawn to him and soon pulled into the small town of Rolla. It had changed some, grown out, but not up. There were no super high-rise buildings, no hurry up attitude, and life was slower here. He stopped at the same department store James and the rest had been using. He bought whiskey, beer, canned meats and peanut butter, and the last two for the same reasons James did— protein. While he'd brought some MREs, they wouldn't last long when shared with others.

His short drive to the old homestead showed no one there, but an RV was in the barn. The Colonel knew of the cave and suspected they were there. They'd often played there as kids. He knew James as a smart man, and one with a great deal of patriotic pride. There was no way his cousin or the rest of the Walker family would sit back and let this nation fall, not without a fight.

He drove down a trail that was as rough as an old logging road, full of ruts and mud holes.

He parked his car by a Jeep, another car and a motorcycle.

Stepping from the car, he heard a voice say, "Stop, that's far enough. Who are you?"

Realizing he was still in his camouflage fatigue uniform, he said, "I'm Colonel Robert 'Bob' Walker. I am a first cousin to James Walker, and he owns this land."

James walked from the woods, gave a big grin, and then said, "Relax guys, I know this ugly ass Colonel, and he's kin."

The Colonel said, "I'm sure they can see the family resemblance in our handsome faces."

"What are you doing here, Bob?"

The two cousins shook hands and then hugged.

Bob told his story and then said, "I think I'm a wanted man now and if they catch me, I'm facing death. But, there was no way in hell I could kill all those people who refused what they think of as the Mark of the Beast."

"Did you get one, an implant?"

"No way in hell. I'm not a deeply religious man, but I have to agree with the die-hard Christians, it's the mark of the Devil in my opinion, not the Beast."

"The Bible says Beast, not Devil."

"I know what the Bible says, but I think of it as the Devil. They have two different chips now. Workers and poor folks get a barcode inserted under the skin of their foreheads, while the elite get it put in the left hand. Those with only one hand or other missing limbs are killed. Those past 65 are going to be killed when they develop any medical problems that require hospitalization, and anyone diagnosed with a serious illness, say cancer, if they're not one of the elite, they will be killed too."

"How long can you stay?"

"As long as I can. I suspect a civil war is coming, and it will make the last one look small. Now, in my car you'll find all kinds of military weapons, explosives, and gear. I also purchased canned meats and peanut butter for protein." He opened the trunk and heard James whistle.

Soon, the men had the gear in the cave and once the M-4's were handed out, along with a couple of bandoleers of ammo, not an adult in the place lacked a rifle and pistol. They had grenades, mines, and an old M-60 machine-gun, along with six boxes filled with ammo for the weapon.

Blake said, "I love shooting a LAW, and you have four of them."

"Listen we all need to move, and this morning. The two snipers we killed are surely missed by someone now. While I took the chips and sent them floating down a stream, they know exactly where we are. Now, when we leave here, we're driving out. I know where we're going and I won't be bringing the RV, because it's too big. It may take us more than one trip, so let's get everything loaded; use Bob's car too."

Once loaded, they moved back to the main gravel road and drove east for about two miles. James turned to the right and stopped in front of a long metal gate. He jumped from his motorcycle, and cut the lock off with bolt cutters. He placed a new lock on the gate and then led the men to where they would camp. Once all the gear was unloaded, they returned to the cave.

It was when they'd finished loading that James' cell phone rang.

"Yep?"

"I see a group of about five moving toward us, but can't tell who they are yet."

"Once you know, call me back."

Five minutes later, his phone rang again.

CHAPTER 12

A Learjet 75 rose from the runaway of the Frankfurt, Germany Flughafen and then once sufficient altitude was gained, the aircraft banked hard to the left. On the aircraft was the Boss and three other people, who did not exchange names. The interior lights were dim, the passengers sipping on rare liqueurs, as the men smoked expensive cigars. All were wearing big-ticket clothing; the men in tailored business suits and the lone woman was wearing a business blazer with a skin tight black skirt.

The men were all over fifty and all carried a spare tire, but the woman was still stunning and in her mid thirties. She wore her red hair short, little make up covered her face, but her pouting red lips were glossy. Her nails were painted and matched her ruby red lipstick. She was a small woman, five feet two inches tall, a hundred and fifteen pounds, and every inch of her was ruthless and cunning. She was an intelligent woman, who made her first billion dollars by the age of thirty. While her eyes were green, they carried a coldness in them that spoke of power and wealth, as well as evil.

"So," asked one of the men, "how many guns have been rounded up in America?"

"None, and I mean not a single weapon." The Boss said and then continued, "the United Nations troopers sent to assist were either killed or captured by the United States Armed Forces."

"And," the woman asked, "What have you done about the slaughter of our troops?"

"First, the UN has, just minutes ago, openly declared war on America, the President has been bought for one billion dollars, and the top Generals were paid one million dollars each to allow the United Nations to get a foothold in the country. As you know, most of the politicians are already on our payroll, those that have any power, anyway. The American Government has been bought like a toy in a store window."

"And the chips? How many have been implanted?" she asked as she leaned forward, knowing her cleavage excited most men. She knew the buttons on her blouse were straining due to the size of her breasts.

"Uh, well, the chip implants are progressing well, with the Americans pushing it as a good thing, because it will allow lost or kidnapped folks to be found, monitor health of their aging and —"

"That's enough. My question was how many?"

"Last count I had briefed was over five million and the list grows daily."

"Good, once we have the chips in most of them the resistance to our take over will slow and then die. Above all things the implants must continue."

"I was also briefed that Christians and some others are leaving the towns and cities and moving to the country, where they cannot be found. Most of them have sworn to fight to avoid the chip. They call it the Mark of the Beast, from the Bible."

"Exterminate them when you find them, Herr Thierse."

"Please, ma'am, no names. I must insist you always call me by my position, Boss."

"You are the boss of our operations, not the overall program, sir. However, I agree, my use of your name is a violation of our security. I will see it does not happen again. But, as I said earlier, kill them where you find them."

"We are doing that, but it's not easy because American citizens have strange ideas about massacring thousands of people who have not had their day in court. They have a high sense of fair play and all are equal in their nation. All of their rights are guaranteed by their damned Constitution and they live by it, and demand their rights as well."

"I want no more excuses, none of us do." a portly man pushing 300 pounds said. "Squash all resistance and start the executions of all who refuse the chip."

"I will see it is done and quickly put in place." the Boss said.

"Good, because you are a very useful man to us." she said, then met his eyes as she slowly ran her tongue over her lower lip.

He felt himself quiver.

"How is your budget holding?"

"I'm doing well, and suspect I have much more money than I'll need."

"Keep account of who is paid what and make sure you continue to send the financial statements as you have been."

The Boss nodded and then said, "I have a short video for all of you to watch. It is what is taking place in America as we speak."

He stood, moved to the wall mounted TV and turned it on.

Long lines were seen at hospitals, grocery stores, and even shopping centers. Empty shelves in stores, the result of fuel going up to twenty dollars a gallon, because no trucker could afford to pay and stay in business. The price of gas and diesel fuel was determined by this very group watching the video.

It then showed executions of some Christians for refusing the chip. Most were shot, but some were hanged, others were burned to death and a few were decapitated. It was a small FEMA camp in New York City that caught their attention, because the victims were all crucified on crosses.

The woman laughed and said, "Now, I call that justice."

"I have ordered no more crucified, because when these people were found later, a riot developed that destroyed blocks and blocks of businesses. There were over 500 dead from the riot alone."

The woman laughed again and said, "Start them again. Why do we care if they kill each other? It simply keeps us from having to kill them later."

"I'll allow them to continue doing it, then." the Boss said as he met the eyes of the other men.

"No, you'll do more than that, you'll suggest it to other FEMA camps, too. They must learn we will be obeyed and nothing will stand in our way, nothing." the portly man said, picked up a phone and said, "Return us to Frankfurt, please."

Once the plane landed and taxied to the stop, the woman moved to the Boss and asked, "Do you have time for a drink?"

"Here or in the airport bar?"

"How about my place? It would allow me to slip into something more comfortable."

"What of my wife?"

"If she's open minded, invite her too. I think we would all three have a good time."

"Uh, no, she must never know of this."

"Good; now come with me, my driver is waiting, and I'll warm you up on the way to my house."

The President of the United States was facing a dilemma. He had over a billion dollars in a Swiss bank, but was starting to worry if he'd live long enough to spend a dime of it. The military had threatened him with a coup, the FBI and CIA were up in arms, and Congress wanted to impeach him. He was in a world of trouble and was so worried about being killed by so many different people, he'd started drinking heavily. Each time his driver started the car, he cringed with fear.

This evening he sat in his Presidential office thinking and realized any attempt at disarming American citizens would result in a civil war. No matter the reason, guns could not be taken from the country, so the next best thing was to try to make guns illegal in some states. He knew the Liberal states were willing, but the problem was, most liberal states didn't have money. *Just look at California*, he thought, *biggest liberal state in the union, but broke as hell. Just a few years back they were a wealthy state, then the liberals took control and now their deficit is insane. I'd not be here now if the original White House was still standing.* He was a liberal too, but he got into politics for the money, not to help anyone.

His personal wealth was over twelve million dollars, not counting the billion in Switzerland. He knew he was stressed and his personal physician had placed him on medications to help him, but he didn't take them, because then he couldn't drink. Drinking made his problems disappear for a few hours.

"Are you coming to bed?" his wife asked as she entered the room, wearing a robe.

"In a bit. I'm worried about taking guns away from these crazy people. Three days ago, when I spoke to a group of veterans and hunters, they turned so violent I was escorted to safety. But, the guns must go."

"We both know if you try to take guns away from hunters, veterans, farmers, cattlemen, and other conservatives, you'll have one hell of a big war on your hands. Americans will put up with a lot of political bullshit, but not the taking of their guns. If I were you, I'd relocate those who don't want to be around guns to different states. I'm warning you, when the first UN soldier steps on US soil to take guns, the civil war will start. So, invite them here to assist with the relocation. This last time the armed forces took care of the problem for you, but now many more have chips implanted so they'll do as they're told. Then, once the two peoples are separated, send the UN into the areas with the guns and use our forces to back them up."

"I . . . I don't know if that'll work, because we're already at war with the UN, only they've done nothing aggressive yet." He poured another drink.

"It's worth a try, so give the task to someone else to deal with and lets you and I take a vacation for a few days."

"Vacation, have you lost your mind? Hell, half the country wants to kill me."

The lights flickered a few times, a bright light flashed across the sky, followed by a loud crack of thunder, and then rain began to beat on the window panes. The President stood and walked to the window. His hands were behind his back as he watched a single rain drop run from the top of the glass to the bottom. There came another bright flash across the black sky, followed by the sharp crack of thunder. The lights flickered again.

There came a loud boom, but it didn't sound like thunder. It was then a Secret Service agent ran in and said, "Both of you come with me, and now." He had his pistol out and the hammer back.

"Why?" the First Lady asked.

"We're under attack by an unknown force. Now, move, please."

"To where?"

"To your car. Once in the limousine you'll be safe. It's built like a tank." Suddenly a man dressed in black walked into the room, rifle in hand, and the agent fired. The man screamed as he fell and began to thrash on the floor.

"Move!" the agent yelled.

There came a loud explosion, followed by gunshots, and the building shook violently.

They encountered two more men in black and each was killed by the agent. They continued to move toward the limo. Gunshots were heard now and much more frequently.

Just as they neared the car, there came a shot and the agent fell screaming and kicking. The President squatted, saw the man would live and dragged him into the limo. He placed the agent in the back seat with the First Lady, and he would drive.

"See to his wounds. It looked to me like he took a bullet high in the left shoulder and the bullet went through the flesh. Be sure and bandage both the entrance and exit wounds on him."

He closed his eyes, turned the ignition, and expected to be blown to hell, but the limo started. The garage door was closed, so he drove through the door, pushing it off the roller tracks and leaving it a chunk of bent and twisted aluminum in the driveway. He then moved toward the entrance gate.

Bullets stuck the limo and *bang-zing* was heard when they struck and then *zinged* off into space. At one time an RPG or LAW stuck the front right quarter panel, but it didn't phase the limo. Zipping through the open gate, they saw the guard laying in a large puddle of blood, his head mangled.

"Is there a first aid kit in here?" she asked.

"It's in front of you, in the pouch with the red cross."

"Where are you going?" she asked next.

"To Air Force One. We'll get in the air and wait until the White House is cleared and safe. Pour me a double bourbon."

She poured him a drink and passed it to him through the sliding window between the front and rear of the vehicle. He knocked it back and asked for another.

"I think one double is enough, don't you?"

"No, I need another drink because the road up ahead is filled with protesters, so pour the damn drink and I can get it down before I drive over these sonsofbitches. I don't think the cops want to be anywhere around this riot in front of us."

Looking out the windshield, the First Lady said, "My God, if they stop us they'll kill us for sure."

"Keep . . . driving . . . sir. Ma'am, in . . . first aid kit . . . is a round tube. It's labeled mor . . . morphine. Give . . . it to . . . me. Sir, in the . . . center . . . console between . . . the seats is a . . . red button."

"I've located it. Now what?" the President said.

"Push the button . . . when near . . . the . . . protesters. It's a machine-gun . . . that will . . . clear the wa . . . way."

"Here's the morphine."

Holding the auto-injector against his thigh, he pushed a red button on top, which sent a needle into his thigh and injected the drug. Minutes later, his pain was gone, but he was getting sleepy-headed.

"Hang on, baby," the President warned, "We're nearing the protesters. My God, there must be fifty thousand of them."

The unknown agent said, "Push red button now, sir."

The President pushed the red button, and a small screen dropped from the dash. On the screen were camera images of the protesters and a cross-hair. Three buttons were shown, fire, stop, and quit. He pushed the fire button.

A machine-gun popped up from the roof of the limo and began firing, sending empty .50 brass in all directions as it completed a circle of the vehicle. With the windows up, all the occupants of the limo heard was a light coughing of the gun as hot lead passed through bodies, struck the pavement, and then ricocheted into other people.

"Sir, near your GPS screen, uh, I still hurt a little, is a toggle switch marked gas. It's tear gas, mixed with pepper spray, so as we move through this crowd, keep the gas flowing. Switch the toggle up."

The President flipped the toggle and continued driving. When folks got too close, he had the machine-gun send a few rounds into them the computerized system sighted the weapon for him. Most people moved away from him now, because of the tear gas and gun.

He soon broke through the crowd and moved out onto the highway. He discovered that while the limo was like a tank, it had little speed. Even with the pedal to the metal, 60 MPH was the best he could do. He suspected it was due to the limo's weight. He pushed the button on the drop down screen that read 'Quit' and the screen folded back into the dash. Pushing the toggle switch down, he turned off the tear gas.

Picking up the mic from the dash, he said, "This is the President speaking. I want Air Force One ready to leave immediately. The temporary White House is under attack and we will be at the aircraft in approximately five minutes."

"Uh, copy, Mister President, but where is your driver?"

"I have no idea, and don't really care right now. Have the aircraft engines running when I get there."

"Will do, sir."

"Out." the President said and then tossed the mic to the floor. He then added, "Pour me another double, baby, and give one to our agent. He saved our lives."

A minute later, she handed a drink to her husband, and then handed one to the agent. The wounded man gulped it down.

"My dress is covered in blood."

"Once on the aircraft, we'll both shower and change. We have clothes on board."

As he neared the military airport he spotted helicopters in the air and moving in all directions. He went past the gate, as the guard snapped to attention and saluted him. He drove past another gate to the flight line and right to Air Force One.

Five Secret Service men neared, one packed the injured man over his left shoulder, and the President and First Lady were escorted to the aircraft. As the President started up the stairs, a bullet struck him low and in the left leg, so down he went. No one heard the shot because the engines were running on the aircraft. Two agents grabbed him and pulled him in the aircraft, as two bullets hit the side of the bird, near the door. Helicopters began to dive at the suspected sniper's location.

The First Lady was at the door before she collapsed, a bullet to her left arm. She was pulled into the aircraft. The door was closed, the staircase was pulled away by truck, and the pilot applied power.

The doctor on board Air Force One looked the President over and then moved to the First Lady.

"Neither injury is life threatening and both will recover; now, if everyone will take a seat, once we are at a level altitude, I'll work on both of them."

"Tower, this is Air Force One, requesting permission for an immediate emergency take off."

"Uh, Air Force One, this is the tower and your request is approved. Use runway 31 left. Contact me once you are airborne."

"Copy, my take off on runway 31 left is approved." Pings and thuds were heard hitting the aircraft. "Tower be advised, I am taking small arms fire."

"Roger that, Air Force One, and we are alerting the Security Police. Have a good flight."

Instead of stopping and building up power for the takeoff, the pilot pulled on the runway and applied full throttle. The aircraft began to move.

The sounds of small arms striking the plane grew less as the aircraft gathered speed. The pilot watched his ground speed and at the minimal speed for takeoff, he pulled the nose up. As the aircraft shuddered to gain altitude, the wheels rotated and began to move into the wheel wells. A few seconds later, a thump was heard as the wheels moved into the up and locked position in the wells.

"Uh," the pilot said and he quickly switched a toggle, "RPG, I think and it just missed us." He then said, "Tower I'm taking what looks to be either LAW or RPG fire. All have missed due to my air speed and on-board missile defenses."

"Copy Air Force One, we will notify the FBI, CIA, Secret Service and local authorities."

There came a loud explosion, just outside the aircraft, and the co-pilot's head slumped forward, his body held in place by his harness. The pilot, glancing at his co-pilot said, "One of you remove Randy and let me get another pilot up here."

"First Lady and Mister President, Ladies and Gentlemen, I welcome you on our flight and request a qualified pilot, along with a doctor, join me in the cockpit. The last noise we heard was a missile or rocket. My co-pilot has been injured. We are currently passing through five thousand feet and out of accurate range for most ground weapons. We will level off at 30,000 feet."

What the pilot didn't tell the passengers was, he was losing fuel, his console panel was lit up like a Christmas tree, and his co-pilot looked dead. He started a gradual turn, because while his take off was over land, as he climbed he was over the pacific ocean. He wanted to stay over land, so in the event he had to put the aircraft down, he should be able to find an airport.

There was the usual knock at the cabin door and the doctor and a pilot entered. The pilot moved to the empty seat, sat, and then asked, "What do we have here?"

As the pilot explained, the doctor was looking the injured man over closely.

"How's he lookin', doc?" the flight engineer asked.

"Blunt trauma to the right side of his skull, with a concussion, and I need to get him back to the surgical room to be sure. His prognosis is excellent, but he'll have one hell of a headache for a few weeks."

"Doc, can you and the flight engineer get him back there?"

"Sure. Sergeant, if you'll take his legs, I have his shoulders. Sir, as the aircraft commander, please announce the co-pilot will live and is being taken to the infirmary."

"We're losing hydraulic fluid as well as fuel." the new co-pilot said.

"Attention passengers, this is your pilot speaking. Our co-pilot will be fine, and the explosion just outside his window caused a concussion. He is now being taken to the infirmary at the rear of the aircraft, where he'll be treated. Pilot, out."

"Tower, this is Air Force One and I need a tanker on me, and soon. I am losing fuel and hydraulic fluid rapidly."

"Roger, understand. Are you diverting to another base?"

"What facilities in front of me are large enough for a Boeing 747-200B jet to land and take off? I'll also need maintenance, tower."

"Uh, wait one."

"Roger."

"Shit," the copilot said, "the right outboard fire light is on."

CHAPTER 13

James' phone rang again, so he answered, "What do you have?" He was concerned. While all the locals knew of the cavern, few people, except kids and teenagers, ever visited the place. Kids usually came to dig for a fragment of Indian pottery or in hopes of finding an arrowhead. Teenagers came to the cave to kiss and fondle, or even have sex.

"Kids, around 16 years old or so. There are three couples."

"Get down here before they arrive and we'll leave."

"Copy, and on my way."

As they passed the kids a few minutes later, all waved, and James knew they'd find nothing in the cave because it was clean. He had to smile, because he'd often gone to the cave while in high school to 'make out' with Donna. They'd gone further a few times, but it was during a period of his life that was stress free and much happier than now.

At the new location, as they made a home deep in the woods the news was on as they worked.

"The President's new White House, in California, came under attack today by a group of Muslims who destroyed the building, killed fourteen defenders and left twenty agents wounded, twelve of them seriously. The group, estimated at around 10,000 strong, essentially just ran over all the guards. So far, authorities state at least 1,500 of the protesters were killed, an unknown number of injured escaped, and forty are known injured. All protesters discovered to be injured were taken to a nearby hospital, where they were treated and then charged with a wide variety of charges, to include rioting, murder, and conspiracy to assassinate the

President. I take you live to Sarah Gale reporting from the White House."

"Frank, I have with me Ahmed, who refuses to give me his last name. He claims he knows the reason for the attack and, while not personally involved, he claims he saw it happen. Ahmed, tell our viewers the reason behind this attack, please."

"We come to America and find we are insulted for being Muslims. We can no longer remain quiet. Your government once paid and helped us live here, but now, we have no money given to us and we do not eat the same food as you Americans. Your food is unclean and nasty to my people. Our women cannot dress like Muslim women and everywhere we turn we find pork or dogs. Our culture has no use for dogs or pigs. Why do Americans not change for us? We need Sharia law, our foods and our customs in this place we now live. Your God is false and so is your Jesus. We will continue to resort to violence in this country until it is all Muslim. America will be Muslim!"

"You knew before you came here, Ahmed, that Americans love dogs and cats, follow the laws of God, and eat pork. You knew you'd have to live under our laws, not your laws, and eat our foods. If you come to America to live, you should leave your customs behind and become Americans. We already have customs, laws and holi—"

"You be a woman and cannot talk to me with insult!"

The camera man screamed, "He has a knife!"

The blade flashed once in the light from the camera and Sarah Gale's throat began to spurt bright cerise blood. She fell to the ground, jerking and twisting, her eyes filled with fear. With each beat of her heart, blood spurted into the air. Her hands clawed at the dirt and her feet kicked wildly.

Ahmed raised his arms and screamed, "Allahu Akbar!"

"My God, he's murdered her!" the camera man said as he continued to film live.

The killer knelt and began cutting her head off as she shuddered and jerked, her central nervous system shutting down.

Once her head was removed, he gave a big toothy smile, as he raised her bloody face toward the camera and said, "This is what we will do to all infidels. America will soon be our country. Become Muslim or die!"

There sounded two shots, one of which caught Ahmed, in the middle of his back and camera caught the bullet punching a hole through the man. Bone, blood and gore followed the bullet out of the hole blown in his chest, splattering blood all over the cameraman, the flattened bullet just missed him. Ahmed fell to the ground right beside Sarah's body and screamed. He'd been hit a second time in the upper left shoulder, the bullet shattering the flat bone in his back and breaking his collar bone.

A cowboy holding a Ruger .45 auto walked to the downed man, sent a big glob of tobacco juice to the wounded man's face and said, "I saw what you did to this woman, rag-head, and your kind will soon learn, you can't treat Americans like your fellow A-rabs. We're not sheep, there are many more of us than you, so we'll win in the end. You were pretty brave killing an unarmed woman, but try me, you filthy bastard!"

The cowboy was joined by another cowboy who held the wounded man in place, as the first cowboy cut his head off. Ahmed screamed and protested, but the cowboy took his time and removed the head slowly. Finally, holding the severed head by the hair, the cowboy tossed it to the ground. Another cowboy stuck a cigarette between the dead man's lips and put his cowboy hat on his head. He then took photos of the dead man with his cell phone.

"You, cameraman, I have something to say to your viewers." More cowboys were gathering around the cowboy and all were covered in blood.

"You're live." the camera man said, and then pointed at the cowboys.

"America, listen to me, because this is a warning and I'm not bullshitting you in the least." He spoke and then pushed his brown Stetson back on his head before he continued. "My fellow cowboys, who are all combat veterans, have had enough of people coming into our country and expecting us to change to accommodate them. Those days are over. We are on the prowl and when we catch someone breaking the law, justice will be instantaneous. I am just awful sorry we weren't able to save this reporter's life. This is my only warning and it applies to anyone, black, white, yeller, brown, or green. If you're hurting people, burning and looting stores, or breaking the law, your ass is ours. But, so far we've only had problems with these people. If you are a Muslim, be aware we will not tolerate any violence from you. We do not hate you or your religion, but stop the hostility, because it will only breed more bloodshed—*your* bloodshed. For too many years we've chased the devil around the stump, and a time has come to catch 'em." The cowboy leaned over and sent a long brown string of tobacco juice to the ground.

The cowboy walked off camera and said, "Lee, bring the horses. Once mounted, let's move to the center of town, where I heard on my phone a few minutes ago there are some goat humping protesters."

The cameraman panned the two dead on the ground as he said, "Frank, it appears that "Vigilante justice" is now alive and thriving in America. Sarah Gale's body isn't even cold yet, and a group of cowboys have already killed and decapitated her killer. There was not a long wait as the man filed appeal after appeal to higher courts, no waiting as they decided the most humane way to kill him, or twenty years passing before he was executed. The man who did the killing had witnessed her coldblooded murder and justice was administered within minutes of her dying. I for one, am glad the sorry sonofabitch that killed her is dead. Frank, this is Steve Mason, back to the studios."

"Station XWXX apologizes for the graphic content of that segment and it is with great sadness we watched the brutal murder of one of our own. Violence is not unusual tonight and reporter James Thompson reports from a local veteran's group. James?"

"Frank I'm here with a group of veterans who do not want to release the name of their organization, because their efforts are not supported at any level, except for this particular lodge. Most of them are dressed in battle dress uniforms. They are getting geared up for a mission, as the commander said, 'against those who are destroying America.' The commander, 56 year old George, a retired US Army Colonel also said, "We are helping the police now and along with the help of thousands of other veterans, we're taking to the streets to keep our citizens safe."

"Turn that crap off." Blake said, shaking his head.

"Just be glad you're not in a big city right now." James said as he turned the TV off.

Nancy said, "I was so shocked when I saw the reporter killed like that."

"It all started a few years back when our then President brought hundreds of thousands of them into the country as poor refugees. Until recently, they lived here for free, but with our failing economy, our assistance was cut to them. I don't know any of them personally, so I can't comment on them." James said.

Frank spoke, "I know them but not personally, because they killed a lot of my buddies in the sand box. I don't like them as a people; perhaps I am a racist or something, but I have a hard time liking folks who I know want to kill me. They want to kill everyone who's not Muslim, call us infidels, but here they are a minority. I suspect within a few days the cowboys and rednecks will kill most of them."

"I heard they grow up being told to kill all non-believers." Donna said.

"They are a rough and crude bunch, as far as people go." Ben said, "When I was over there as an adviser, the military men I was working with were raping boys, young girls and women. Knowing if I stayed in, I'd end up over there again, I got out. They even stoned a few women to death when I was there, so I'm not overly fond of them either."

"Was that the radical Muslims?" Nancy asked.

"There is no such thing as radical Muslims. Those not doing the bombing and direct killing are supporting them with money, food, labor, or by cheering them on. What that joker said on the TV a few minutes ago about them taking over America, he believes."

Donna said, "The President claimed no radicals were admitted into the USA."

"And, you believed him?"

Winking, Donna said, "Not in the least. I don't have a problem with anyone coming to America to live and become a citizen the legal way. If they come here, let them learn our language, our customs, and our way of life. They need to become

Americans and leave their past behind them. If they don't like our food, holidays, pets, or religions, they can damn well leave."

"When the Muzzies first arrived, and even the illegal aliens, the liberals did a lot of serious ass kissing and made all of the foreigners comfortable, while we had veterans dying in VA hospitals. The liberals were soliciting Democrat votes, by the way. Illegals, mostly from Mexico, were treated better than our combat veterans. I could not believe it, and after all those men and women had done for this country. Can you imagine fighting for America, being discharged due to the loss of a limb or other serious injury, only to be placed on a medical waiting list and then never called? I think our priorities were messed up. Now, with a civil war about to start, I think you'll see the illegals leaving us like cockroaches when the kitchen light is turned on. They like this country, but not enough to fight for it, watch and see, if the cowboys let any of them live. Personally, I don't give a rat's ass about any of them, the refugees or criminal aliens." Dick said.

"You can talk about the cowboys all you want," Ben said, "but they'll be fair and honest about the actions they'll take. I was raised a cowboy and most are good men. Most believe in God, even if they are not practicing Christians."

Joda said, "Actually we're lucky James has us all out here in the woods. While it's just the big cities that are going to hell now, it will spread from the west coast east and in just a few days. Old angers, racism, and crime will see the deaths of many folks. I think we're lucky, damned lucky to be here."

James said, "Speaking of here, tomorrow we'll start making log cabins for all of us. Now, each family will not have a cabin, because we don't have that much time until cold weather hits. There are 13 of us and I think four cabins will work, for this winter. Starting today, we'll have a guard, 24/7 and unless you're sick or injured, you will pull your shift. We not only have to watch for intruders but also helicopters, drones, or other aircraft."

"Do you think black folks and Muslims will rise up against the rest of America?" Jerry asked as he gazed into the eyes of Joan, his wife.

Frank laughed and said, "Some Muslims and some blacks would love to do just that, but together they're maybe, what, 15%

of the population? I don't think that would be very smart on their part, do you?"

"I can understand the anger of black folks, too. A few years back our President had racial tensions the highest I've ever seen it since the 1968 riots. I feel he intentionally wanted folks at each others throats, but why?" James asked.

"He was, as the present one is, part of the New World Order, or bought by them. I think most politicians are on their payroll. Look how many people enter politics with less than a million bucks in the bank. Follow their long careers and see how much money they have when they leave politics. All are worth *millions*, and notice I didn't say, worth a *million*." Jerry said, and then shook his head.

"It's impossible to make that legally on government pay." Blake said.

Ben gave a sad smile and said, "Look, I know how the NWO works and I'm positive most, if not all, politicians are on their payroll and in most cases the man or woman doesn't even know who is paying them. They are paid to vote this or that way and their vote helps the NWO in some way. Most of the citizens of the United States have never heard of the New World Order. Those that have think it is some insane conspiracy by the far right and will never happen."

"Most citizens don't care about much except their weekly football or baseball game, keeping up with the Jones', and having enough beer to last the weekend. I'm talking about those who are the professional baby machines and only care about their assistance payments from the government and food stamps. They sell the food stamps and it buys the beer, while the live-in old man buys and sells drugs. Those with real medical problems are paid a pittance of what they need to survive and live from payday to payday. I have an aunt living on $409 dollars a month, which is impossible, almost, but she had help from family."

"Some of those women on welfare make good money, because they're paid by the child, with each head being so many bucks." Frank said, and then poured himself a cup of coffee.

Donna said, "While working with the Houston police, oh, maybe five years back, they busted a food-stamp counterfeit operation. They were printing the food coupons and then selling $1,000 worth of stamps for $500. They made a mint too, and I think the cops found over $250,000 in cash in the house."

"How'd they discover it?" Ben asked, grinning because he found it funny what people would do for easy cash.

"Most of the stamps had the backs reversed of what they really were."

"Reversed?" Ben asked.

"Upside down. A sharp cashier caught it and had the man arrested. Once in jail, he squealed on the rest and didn't get charged. Later he was found floating around in one of the four bayous in Houston."

A few minutes of silence filled the camp and then Joan asked, "How long is my country going to be messed up? I miss the old days, where we could sleep at night with the window open, we could take a stroll in town late at night and window shop, without carrying a gun. Folks were mostly honest and the kids were innocent."

James said, "I think those days are over, and forever. Now a war will start, there will be many dead on both sides, and before the blood even dries, we'll be rebuilding this nation. Americans are tougher than they realize and only us who'd served in the military understand this. See, the military should be mandatory for everyone right out of high school, or the Peace Corps. Most men who do not serve lack self confidence, self motivation, and they're lazy. The service takes a man or woman as far as they want to go. But the best part is, the service turns boys and girls into men and women, who become productive members of our society."

"I hear ya, brother." Blake said.

Two months later, the cabins completed and things squared away, James, Donna, and Blake went to the super department store to get a few things. They wanted candles, hurricane lamps and fuel, and a few other items. They loaded up the carts, moved to the cashier and began checking out.

When the total was shown the woman said, "Run your hand over the scanner and your banks will show on the screen. Then, okay the amount, push the bank you want to pay with, and enter your pin."

"You must be using the implant chip, but we don't have them." Donna said.

"Keep your voices down, but I can't check you out if you don't have a chip."

"What's the total owed?" James asked.

"Fifty three dollars and 17 cents." she replied.

He handed her a hundred and said, "Keep the change."

"Uh, we don't take cash, either. I'm afraid I need to contact security."

"Contact who in the hell you want, lady, but I've paid you and this stuff is mine. Let's go." James said as he pushed the cart toward the door.

Once outside, a security guard ran toward them, pistol in hand, "Stop, and I *mean now.*"

They stopped and when the guard neared, James asked, "What's the problem, we paid for this stuff."

"You can't buy anything in this country now without a chip. You three will come with me."

The guard was a big man, but in weight only. He was about five feet four inches tall, maybe 300 pounds, and his face was flushed from running a hundred feet.

"What if we don't want to come with you?" Blake asked.

"Then I'll make you."

"You look like a good ole boy, Bubba, so don't piss us off or you'll get hurt. However, with that said, we are not giving this stuff back, we're not coming with you, and if you continue to push the issue, we'll kill you."

"Don't make me shoot." the guard said, and his pistol was shaking as the two men slowly moved apart.

"Holster the gun, son, or start shooting. I have to warn you though, I was killing men in a small country called Vietnam before you were hatched. When I shoot you, I'll place three bullets in the middle of your chest."

"Not me," Blake said, "I want to hit his belly. I'll bet he pops like a balloon."

"Shut up," the guard said and keyed his mic, "Guard 6, I have three people detained —"

Blake and James both pulled pistols.

"Don't shoot me, man. I have a wife and three little kids." he pleaded.

"Load the Jeep, baby." James said to Donna.

"Drop the gun, the belt, and your pants, or we'll shoot." Blake said.

The gun fell and then the belt, which went in the Jeep with the other items from the store. When his pants came off, Blake tossed them in the vehicle. Pulling two plastic ties from his pocket, Blake secured the guards hands behind his back.

All went well until a golf cart with three other guards neared and pulled guns. Blake and James were in the Jeep and as they backed up, the guards began shooting. Blake screamed in pain as blood splattered on James, so he took the guards out, 1, 2, 3, and they fell screaming. The guards had reacted as if they'd never been in a hostile environment before, while James had survived many in Vietnam and Iraq. As Donna floored the vehicle and ran a red light at the top of a hill, James looked Blake over.

"He's still alive, but he'll not live. About half of his head is missing and I see parts of it on the inside of the jeep. I don't think he'll regain consciousness."

"Let's get him back to camp and doctor him up." Donna said, and then started crying.

CHAPTER 14

"Air Force One, this is the tower and we have a KC-135 due to meet you in ten minutes. He'll refuel you and check you visually for damage."

"Copy, tower."

The pilot glanced at the fire light, shook his head, and then pushed 'Agent Discharge', which instantly filled the engine with foam, hopefully putting out the fire. The fire light flickered on and off a few times and then, as the pilot shut the engine down, the light went out and stayed that way.

"Uh, tower, Air Force One."

"Go, Air Force One."

"Be advised I have the President and First Lady on board and I'm declaring an in-flight emergency. I have shut down my number three engine due to fire and most of my console lights are on. Tell the tanker if he's not here in ten minutes, we'll not need him."

"Roger, copy. Right now we have you on radar, and your best bet is to try and reach Saint Louis. Do you think you have twenty minutes of safe flight time remaining?"

"Affirmative, as far as my mechanical problems. If not for my passengers, I'd not be very concerned, but have the tanker on time. Fuel is my biggest worry."

"Roger on the tanker. Saint Louis has the long runway you need to land and take off again, once the repairs have been made."

"Roger, I hear you. This is Air Force One, out."

The tanker was soon spotted, and Air Force One slipped in lower and behind the KC-135. In most cases, a pilot would want to have as little fuel as possible before landing in an emergency to avoid fire, but in this case, he didn't have enough to reach the airport. He needed fuel now, or soon he'd have to put the aircraft on the ground.

"Uh, Air Force One, this is your local gas station, and before we moved into position, we looked y'all over. You have part of your leading edge missing from your right wing, and smoke coming from your number three engine. There is a black spot, about six feet in diameter on top of the same engine. I see where small arms fire struck you, but it didn't seem to pierce the skin."

The Air Force One pilot said, "Roger that, uh, can I get some gas now? We can talk later, Sam, at the O'club."

"I hear ya, Bill. Uh, boom operator, the President is all yours now."

"Roger, sir." the young boom operator said.

From behind the KC-135 a boom extended and a hose seemed to float in the air to the President's aircraft. His Engineer and all watched the fuel gauges as fuel began to flow. As the fuel in their aircraft began to register on the gauges, there came a sigh of relief from the co-pilot.

"I always did like Saint Louis." the co-pilot said with a chuckle. He was holding up the latest popular nudie magazine and letting the boom operator get a nice view.

Many nervous minutes later, the nozzle disengaged, sending a little fuel into the slip stream.

Joking with the boom operator on the KC-135, the pilot said, "Great job you have, just lay on your stomach and pass gas all the time. Can you check my oil and clean the windshield, too?"

"Uh, Air Force One, read my mind, sir."

Laughing, the pilot said, "As usual, a professional job by a crew that works well together. You guys kept me from walking home. Thanks, and when I see you at the club, drinks on me."

The KC-135 rocked his wings, turned gently to the left and was gone in a few blinks of the eye.

"The hydraulic system is still showing the we're losing fluid and while we have a backup manual system, stopping this beast on the runway will not be easy." the pilot said.

"I understand, and both of us will stand on the brakes if that's what it takes. Navigator, what's our ETA Saint Louis?"

"Uh, our ETA to Lambert-St. Louis International Airport is fifteen minutes, on our current heading. You are lined up for a straight in approach."

"Mister President and First Lady, this is your captain speaking. We're experiencing problems with the aircraft and have been diverted to Lambert-St. Louis International Airport and will be landing in about ten minutes. I've had to shut down the number three engine and declare an in-flight emergency but we are currently in no serious danger. The emergency was declared because our President and his lovely wife are on our aircraft. Crew, prepare the cabin for landing."

"Air Force One, you are cleared for a straight in approach on runway 12 left."

"Copy, tower."

"Lower landing gear." the pilot said as they went through the prior-to-landing check list.

"Uh, the nose gear is down but not locked. The light is still in the red."

"Are you sure?"

"The light is in the green for all but the nose gear."

"Uh, tower, my lights indicate my nose gear is down but not locked into position."

"How do you want to handle this, Air Force One?"

"Since I'm leaking fuel and hydraulics I don't have the option of trying to get it unlocked by other means. Please notify the emergency crews I expect my nose wheel to collapse when I land."

"Copy, and all emergency vehicles are in place."

"I'll try to keep the nose level and once my speed is down, I'll let the nose come down slowly."

"Roger, and good luck."

"Cabin Crew, this is the Captain. Our nose wheel will not lock in the down position, so prepare all passengers for an emergency landing. We've been cleared for an emergency landing and we're going straight in. You can expect a lot of noise, bumps, smoke, and perhaps some fire, but the emergency crews are standing by. The first people off the aircraft will be the President and First Lady."

The cabin filled with silence as each person dealt with the emergency in their own way. Few were Christians, but a prayer was heard and when folks looked around, it was the First Lady.

Ten minutes later, the Captain said, "Crew, to your stations and prepare for an emergency landing. We're going in now."

Just before touchdown wind shear struck the aircraft and the wings wobbled as the pilot maintained control, but some of the passengers screamed in fear. The First Lady's prayer became louder and then the aircraft was felt to land with a loud thud; there came a screech of tires, and the aircraft continued down the long runway. The flaps were up, people were bent over with their hands on their heads, and the co-pilot silently prayed.

The pilot played with his throttle, keeping his speed up just enough to keep the nose in the air a little. He slowly reduced his speed and let the nose wheel touch down. He was surprised when the aircraft did not drop on its nose, but now he had to stop this big heavy beast. His hydraulics were all but gone and only with him and the co-pilot on the brakes did they come to a slow stop, with about 100 feet of runway left. Smoke filled the air and the scent of burning metal from the brakes filled the cabin and cockpit.

"Crew, evacuate the President and First Lady, then the rest of the staff and passengers."

Doors flew open, but since most of the passengers were military, there was no mad scramble to get off and it flowed smoothly. The last man off the aircraft was the pilot and when he stood in the door, the passengers, including the President and First Lady, safely on the ground, clapped loudly for him. He waved, smiled, and then slid down the emergency chute.

The pilot stood, moved to the Fire Chief, and said, "Notify the Vice-President that the President and First Lady are alive and well. Also, ask for another aircraft to be delivered here. This one will be grounded a while as they fix the problems."

"Yes, sir."

"Part of our problem, I think, was whatever blew up removed part of the leading wing edge. I suspect part of it was ingested by our number three engine." the pilot said to his co-pilot.

"Yep, the engine needs changing for sure, and the landing gear needs checked closely too. Let's see if we can find a room here at a reasonable price."

Early the next morning, as a new sun rose, a new Air Force One was on the flight line, guarded by military police. The President was driven onto the flight line by a black SUV, and straight to the aircraft. The crew was busy pre-flighting the aircraft and the cabin crew was insuring all was clean, neat, and ready for the President.

As the Sergeant saluted him the President returned the salute and said, "Morning, son. Come with me, we have rain coming in a few minutes."

Passengers and crew entered the aircraft and took their seats. As the engines started and crew was storing luggage and briefcases, from the cockpit the Captain said, "Good morning, Mister President and First Lady, we'll be taxiing in a few minutes and we're cleared for takeoff. On the behalf of the Air Force One crew, I want to welcome any new passengers we have, and assure you we will do all within our power to make your flight a good one. Crew, to your stations, please."

The trip to Atlanta was quiet and uneventful, but the President started his drinking earlier than most days. By the time the aircraft touched down on the runway, he was intoxicated. He was fully in control, and no one who didn't know him would not have suspected he'd had a drop. He was getting better and better at functioning under the influence of alcohol.

They moved to the President's limo, which had been brought in by C-5, and left the airport. They drove to the President's suite at a local hotel, with an escort of four motorcycle riders in front of them and two black SUVs with secret service agents behind them.

About half way to the hotel there came a loud explosion, and demonstrators moved to block the road. The noise had caused no damage and nothing had been seen, so the agents were a bit shocked. They'd later determine it was a hand grenade.

The protesters held signs that read, "No to the Mark of the Beast! God for me and no to 666!"

"Who is behind all of this?" the President asked. "I'm getting tired of this bullshit."

"Intelligence said it's the New World Order funding these mobs." an agent said.

The protesters were rocking the car, striking the windows, and one man was hitting with an ax.

Damn, they're funding me, too. How can this be? Are they wanting violence? he thought as he poured a double whiskey.

"Sir, what do you want to do?"

"Warn them to disburse or we'll use force." the President said.

"Yes, sir."

A speaker mounted on the car began to blast out a warning, but it made no difference to the mob.

"Use the gas." came the order a few minutes later.

Seconds later, people quit beating on the car and began to move away. The limo sped away, striking a dozen protesters as they broke through the mob, sending their mangled bodies back into the crowd.

Just as they neared the Hotel, there was a loud explosion and the car rocked as the four motorcycle cops were removed from their bikes. Three of the four were dead, with the survivor sure to lose a leg and maybe an arm. One of the black SUVs stopped, loaded the man in the vehicle and moved to the closest hospital.

At the hotel, police snipers were on the roof, guards patrolled the building with dogs, an armored personnel carrier was near the front door and a tank sat in the parking lot. The walk in was uneventful and so was the trip to their room. They were on the upper floor, with a guard posted at the door, both inside and out. Two other guards were in the suite. The two interior guards had been working with the White House for years, and learned early in their careers to forget what they heard or saw.

The President turned on the TV, poured a whiskey for the First Lady and a double for him. He turned to a news channel and the world looked to be falling apart at the seams. As he watched the news, he began to wonder if taking the money from the NWO was a smart thing to do. He'd taken it because all he had to do was take guns from Americans and demand the chip to be used. So far, only a handful of guns had been collected, and they were from willing donors.

Of all aspects of the Constitution, the first and second amendments mean the most to Americans, he thought. *I don't know why I got involved with the NWO, but the money was hard to pass up. Of all the times in Americas history, this has to be the roughest, and if what I think will happen happens, I'll soon be facing a civil war, too.*

The First Lady asked, "Honey, can't you do something to stop the rioting?"

"I'm not sure what. If you remember, the agent in the limo said it was the NWO that was behind the protests."

"It just seems to me our intelligence folks could come up with some way to deal with the NWO and prevent riots."

What would you say if you knew I was partially to blame? he thought, but said, "The problem is no one knows who the leader of the organization is, and they have unlimited funds."

"I'd start looking at those in the world who are wealthy and, one by one, weed them out."

"Sweetheart, it's not that simple. We suspect it's a group of wealthy folks operating under a well established business. Of course, there must be a leader."

"Look at the women first. This is so well organized, I think a woman is behind it."

"My staff criminal psychologists disagree with you, but they feel the layout and organization of the NWO was a woman's planning. However, the big Boss is so ruthless, they've ruled out a female."

"That's plain stupidity in my opinion, because women are much more ruthless than men, but men will never admit that fact. Did you know the deadliest sniper in WWII was a Russian woman? The black widow spider is deadly to her mate and the female preying mantis eats the head off her partner after they mate. If you want to be killed, just step between a momma bear and her cubs. There are many more examples, but weak? No way all females are weak. I think if you find a successful business woman, you'll find a woman very capable of running the NWO with cold and cunning orders issued. Simply look for a woman who will not hesitate to kill to gain what she wants."

He walked to the bar, filled his glass, and saw she was still sipping her drink. It was raining lightly and he watched the drops run down the pane of glass. Dropping his napkin, he bent over to pick it up, when the window exploded sending sharp shards of glass flying in all directions. The bullet continued on, struck the floor and went to the room below, which for security reasons was empty. An agent was on the President instantly, protecting him by covering his body with his own.

The other agent keyed his radio and said, "Code yellow, code yellow. Shots fired at big dog, maybe two floors up, south side of the hotel. Appears to be another hotel."

"Copy, we're moving now."

The President's cell phone rang.

The agent moved from him and, sitting up, the President asked, "Hello?"

"You have not kept your end of our bargain, sir. I can see you survived the assassination attempt, but there will be more. The money once in your Swiss account is now gone." a female voice, that at another time he would have found sensual, said.

"What do you want!" he screamed.

"What do I want? Just your life, sir. Your death will please me immensely. You were holding up our progress, so you will be eliminated now, because you know too much. Maybe your replacement will be easier to work with. Oh, tell the First Lady, the pink bra and matching thong she is wearing is very nice. Especially the lace. Goodbye, Mister President." The call went dead.

Looking at the agent, he said, "Take this phone and find out where that last call came from. See who's paying the phone bill, too."

"Yes, sir."

Standing, he gulped down what was left of his drink and moved to the bar to get another. Filling his glass, he asked, "What color is your bra and thong?"

"What? Someone tries to kill you and you want to know the color of my underwear? I'm wearing a pink bra and matching thong, why?"

"That was a female voice from the NWO, and they've marked me for killing. To show me what they knew about us, she told me you were wearing exactly what you just said."

"When did you put those on, ma'am?" the other agent asked, looking worried.

"Right after I showered."

"Control, this is agent one."

"Go, one."

"Our security has been compromised. The President just received a threatening call, and the voice knew the color of underwear the First Lady is wearing. This room was surely checked for bugs and cameras, right?"

"Is her underwear covered by a robe or something? If not, when she passed a window, it may have been seen. Yes, the room was swept and was clean."

Turning to the First Lady, the agent asked, "At any time that you can remember, ma'am, did you walk by a window without a robe?"

"Uh, once I had my underwear on, I did move to the bedroom to get my robe from the bed, why?"

"I'll explain in a minute, ma'am. She only walked around with no robe in the bedroom." the agent replied, and he moved to the bedroom. He then added, "The drapes are open and the blinds have been raised. I think the shooter got a look at her before the shot."

"I agree, close every blind and drape. Control out."

Lowering his radio, the agent said, "Ma'am, I —"

"It's okay, I heard the conversation." She moved from the sofa, walked to the bar and topped off the whiskey in her glass, right to the brim.

The President, knowing he'd never be able to sleep in this room now said, "Alert Air Force One that I want a fresh crew on the aircraft, and engines running one hour from now. Tell them our destination is the Cheyenne Mountain missile complex. I want the facility notified that I want no special treatment, just a room for the two of us to rest our heads, and our visit may be an extended one."

"Yes, sir."

A series of shots were heard off in the distance and then an explosion.

"Lord," the First Lady said, "let me survive the ride to the airport."

The President shook his head and thought, *What a mess. I don't like the NWO on my ass; they hire only the best, and they're ruthless sonsofbitches.*

CHAPTER 15

James looked at Nancy and asked, "How does he look?"

"I don't think he'll survive, if that's what you're really asking me. The bullet struck his forehead and destroyed most of the right side of his brain when it passed through his head. I think within 24 hours he'll be dead."

Ben asked, "Did anyone follow you?"

"Not that I know of, but we were kind of busy. He jerked and twisted violently after being struck, for about ten minutes or so, which is rough in a Jeep. I almost never got a bandage on his injury." James said.

"I suggest we avoid the town completely now." Ben said as he met the eyes of James.

"That means we'll have to steal what we need, then." Carol said.

"So be it." James said, "While I hate a thief, I think I'll have to change my attitude about life a little to survive."

"We'll have to do what it takes for us to live, baby." Donna said, and then shrugged.

"Our biggest problem will be protein, which is things like meat, peanut butter, and beans." Nancy said.

"We have a lot of each, but do we have enough to last all winter?" James asked.

"I don't think so. If we could find a small town that doesn't have the chip technology yet, we could buy all we need easily enough."

James said, "There's a small town, and I know a shortcut that will allow us to use the back roads. It's maybe 8 to 10 miles from here. The last time I was there, they had one cop and a couple of stores, so it's not much."

"This town have a name?"

"Newburg, and it's a small place."

"Who'll go with you?" Bob asked.

"You, if you want, but it could turn to shooting, if we're unlucky. I have no idea what to think of the place now. I don't know if the stores are even still there."

"We won't know if we don't go and see, right? Hell, let's go right now."

"There used to be a butcher shop there, but I think the price of beef may be out of our range. I'm more inclined to get beans and other protein sources."

They moved toward the Jeep, which Ben and Frank had cleaned when the group had returned from Rolla. The chunks of brain and bone were now gone, but the seats were still damp from the water used to wash away the blood. Both men covered their seat with a poncho, and off they went.

The roads James used were mostly gravel and lightly traveled. They drove by the Little Piney river, over the low water bridge and continued moving north by east. The river was low, but gave the whole place a feeling of harmony. Both knew the feeling was deceptive. A few miles later, they turned right on a macadam road, and they could see the small town in the hills on the other side of the river. They drove over a larger steel bridge, crossed some train tracks and were in town. They turned left in town, went down a block, and saw a grocery store. They pulled into a parking lot, with only one other car there.

They entered to see an older man at the counter and he said, "Afternoon. What can I do the two of you out of?"

James immediately liked the old man and said, "We've got a problem. We're both Christians and refuse to have a chip implanted. Do you still take cash?"

"I ain't getting the damned chip neither. I take cash, so just select what ya want, and all is okay with me. The Feds ain't been here hard yet, but when they do, I'll be sent to one of the concentration camps, I reckon. I will not get the mark of the beast, because my God will protect me."

Knowing peanut butter could be stored without refrigeration, James bought four cases of the stuff and three hundred pounds of dry beans. He then bought fifty pounds of lean beef and ten pork roasts. He'd take it back to camp and make jerky out of it. The pork could be used, but the fat would have to be trimmed off first.

He bought 100 pounds of potatoes, the same in onions, five pounds of salt, and 5 gallon containers of unscented bleach, to purify water. He bought all the ammo he had for their weapons, and then got all the bags of hard candy the man carried, because it was hard to beat for energy or heat when cold and tired.

The old timer was smiling as he rang up the total on an adding machine.

A minute later he said, "Your total is $1,236.23. Now, you boys can come back here when ya want, but iffen things change, I'll have a sign in the winder that says chips are required or something like that. If I have guests, I'll have my broom in the display winder so you'll know not to come in. Now, I live right above this place, so if you'd rather shop at night using a flashlight, you can do that too. I'm alone since Myrtle died, so wakin' me ain't no big deal. Iffen I was yer ages, I'd gather me up a gang of Christian soldiers and go out and kick some serious ass."

James laughed and then replied, "It's a thought, for sure. Thanks, and do you have a name?"

"Nope, and ya two don't neither. When bein' tortured, we can't say what we don't know, now can we? I can get by now, selling this stuff, because I don't have one of them chip readers, but it's coming and when it does, well, I won't be here. Let me get a dolly and I'll help take this stuff to your car."

"Thanks, and you'll get all our business, until things turn rough."

"If things get spooky, let us know and you can come to live with us." Bob offered.

"How can I do that?"

Pulling some paper from his pocket, James wrote down his phone number, with no name. Handing it to the old man, he said, "Just call and we'll come for you."

"By cracky, I'll do that iffen things get rough. I'm too old to help y'all much, but my brain still works fine."

Bob asked, "You ever in the military?"

"I was a career man, twenty years in the army. I retired an E-7, because I wouldn't attend college or kiss some officer's ass. I have to warn ya though, I'm blunt and speak my mind."

"That's the real reason you didn't get promoted higher." Bob said, and then chuckled.

"Ya reckon?" the old man said, and then laughed.

James said, "If you have visitors, play along with them and then call me the first chance you have. I think they'll warn you first, give you a chip scanning machine and leave. What percentage of this town has the chip?"

"Maybe, oh, five percent. We're in the sticks, most won't drive to another larger town to get the chip, it's not needed here right now and most of us don't want the damned thing."

"Once you get it, it takes over your thinking, sends you thoughts, and knows everything about you. Like a GPS, it gives your location to the authorities at all times, as well as sends your vital signs to a computer used to track you. We know, because we have a man with us that had a chip, until we removed it."

"It don't pay no never mind, because I ain't gettin' the damned thing. The Bible warns us of what is to happen during the end of times, and it's surely happenin' as we breathe. I had some ole boy in here last week with what looked like a bar code buried under his skin on his forehead. When I asked him about it, he said, 'worker bees got the bar code, and the elite got the chip.' This crap all started a few years back when the White House started passing all them laws with a stroke of the President's magical pen. All that transgender stuff and gay stuff ain't none of my business, because I'm as straight as they come, but the laws weren't needed. It got so bad my wife and I stopped using public bathrooms."

That's likely part of the NWO, Bob thought, but didn't say anything.

"I think the changes were planned years ago and just now placed into law." James said, and then extended his hand to shake with the store owner.

As they shook, James said again, "Don't hesitate calling me if the brown stuff hits the fence. We'll either meet you some place or come and get you."

"Well, by God, if I leave, my store comes with me. So, we'll damned sure not starve to death. I'll call if I have the need."

"Good; come on Bob, we need to get back."

Two weeks later, James was sitting by the fire, just before dusk, when his phone rang and he didn't recognize the number, but it was a local call.

"H . . . help me. T . . . they . . . beat . . . me."

It sounded like the old man at the store in Newburg, "Are you the grocer?"

"Yes . . . yes. Come . . . for me . . . please."

"We'll be there in a few minutes."

"I'm behind the . . . counter . . . on the . . . floor."

"Hang on, we'll be there as fast as we can."

"Good. B . . . bye." The line went dead.

"Bob, I need you and Nancy to come with me, and now. The old man that owns the grocery store in Newburg was visited by the Feds, and they beat 'em up. Nancy, be sure you bring your medical kit."

"How bad is he?" Bob asked.

"No idea, but he sounded bad and was in a lot of pain."

"Maybe the men who beat him are part of a team and still in the town." Ben said.

"Now, that is an interesting thought. They only have one hotel and it's just outside of town, near the freeway. We might just pay those folks a visit."

"What do you think?" Frank asked.

"Load everyone in the cars and one of you ride the motorcycle. We'll pay them a visit, if we can find them. Jerry, you stay here and mind the store, while we see if we can administer some justice, good ole boy style."

The night was clear, and once at the store they just walked in because the door was unlocked. The old man was found behind the counter, and he'd been busted up pretty good, with cracked ribs, a possible concussion, and cuts to his face and hands. James knew the old man's nose was broken, and both eyes were black and blue. Nancy gave him a shot of morphine and then looked him over closely.

"He'll survive, but it'll take a spell for his ribs to heal." Nancy said.

James' phone rang, so he opened it and said, "Hello?"

"It's me, Jerry; Blake just died. He started shaking and jerking, and by the time I reached him, he was gone."

"Cover him with a blanket and we'll bury him in the morning." Then his phone screen turned black.

Nancy met his eyes and asked, "Is Blake dead?"

"Yep," James said as he moved to the old grocer. He asked, "Any idea where the men are that beat you up?"

His pain gone now, but fighting sleep, the old man said, "Mable . . . Kennedy said . . . they were at the Ozarks . . . Hotel near the highway. Five of . . . them in the . . . bunch."

"Nancy, you take 'em back to camp while we visit the men who did this."

The old man, his pain lessened by the morphine said, "I have a big truck out back; when ya leave town, bring the whole damned store with ya. Keys are in the truck. I need to sleep some, so I cain't help ya —"

"Dick, you and the women stay here and load the truck. I suggest you do the job fast too, because this town will be hot when we're done with our job."

The old man, who Nancy learned was named Homer Poor from the business license in the store window, was loaded in the Jeep and she returned him to camp.

As the store was being loaded in the truck, James and the rest moved for the hotel. Now, for the first time, they were about to turn bloody, but all realized Americans had to move, and now. For too many years they'd said nothing nor took any action, because they'd left it up to the political clowns to keep things under control. They'd not done their job, and now this small group was about to start the bloodiest conflict in this nation's history. It was time to clean America up, starting at the floor level and then slowly moving up.

When they pulled into the parking lot, they saw just a single floor building and all the rooms opened into the parking lot. Two men went around the back, just in case someone tried to get out by using a window.

James and Bob entered the lobby and made their way to the desk.

"May I help you gentlemen?" a young man in his mid-twenties asked. He was an average looking man, with auburn hair, round hippy glasses, and had Liberal written all over him.

"What room are the Federal Agents in?" Bob asked.

"I'm not allowed to tell you that, sir, it's a violation of my customer's privacy. Besides, I don't think you need to know."

Holding his pistol out, with the barrel less than an inch from the man's face, James said, "You either tell me or I'll start kicking doors in, and I'll kill every sonofabitch I see. But, you'll not see that, because you're the very first bastard I'll kill. Don't think this is a bluff, son, or your brains will soon be on the wall behind you."

"Uh, don't shoot me, mister. I have a wife and two kids at home."

"Room numbers?" Bob asked.

"There are five of them. Two in one room and three in the other. Rooms 105 and 106."

"See that wasn't so hard, huh? Let me see your cell phone." James said.

When the clerk handed it to him, it was dropped to the floor and then stomped hard by James. His boots shattered the cell into little chunks of plastic. Bob then moved behind the desk and cut the phone cords to the main hotel phone system to pieces.

"Let's move now!" James said.

Bob said, "No, just a second. Now, program me two keys to get access into the rooms."

Lowering his head, the clerk made the card keys and then handed them to Bob. As the two men stood talking, Ben said, "I'll unlock the doors, and when all of us are ready, I'll swing the doors open."

"Sit in your chair, and now." Bob said to the clerk.

"Why?"

"I'm going to tie you up and blindfold you, that is, if you want to live. Or, I can just shoot you, hell, it doesn't matter to me."

"I'm sitting."

Bob tied the young man to his chair and then blindfolded him with his own necktie.

As they left the office, James said, "We need to hit both rooms at the same time. So, I'll do one room while you do the other."

"How are we going to do this? I was just going to toss a grenade in and wipe 'em out." Bob said.

"We can do that, and it may save us casualties, too."

Once at the vehicles the group was told of the grenades and how they were to enter the rooms as soon as both exploded. There were to be no survivors.

They then moved to the room doors.

Bob was worried. As a combat veteran with a Combat Infantry Badge with a star, he knew things never went as planned in combat. Something would go wrong, but what? This looked simple, open the doors, toss grenades and then mop up after the explosions.

James was at his door, so when their eyes met, Bob nodded. The magnetic strip was placed in both doors, the green light came on, and the doors were swung open. Two grenades were tossed in and from one room they heard a yell of surprise. A few short seconds later there came two explosions, and everyone entered the rooms.

The walls were dripping blood, and all five men were dead.

"Take their weapons, clothes, ammo, money, watches and anything we may need later. If you find any chips or registers for the chip scanner, destroy the scanners but bring the chips." James said, and then grinned. He had an idea.

Twenty minutes later as they were leaving, two cop cars pulled in, blocked the exit, and the officers left the car and knelt down behind the squad car doors, and both had weapons drawn.

Ben raised the sniper rifle, sighted in the man on the left, and then squeezed the trigger. The shot was loud and the officer fell hard, where he jerked and shook, because he'd taken the round in the center of his face. The second policeman sent four or five shots toward Ben and then ducked down behind his door.

Ben, sighted in the man's knee in the crosshairs of his scope, which was below the door and squeezed his trigger. The officer screamed and fell back. Bob ran forward and fired two rounds into the downed officer's head.

Running back to the vehicles, Bob screamed, "Let's go!"

As they were leaving town the chips were tossed into the river because if nothing else, it'd cause confusion for the people manning the NWO computer consoles.

As they moved, Bob said, "It feels so wrong to kill an officer of the law."

"Yes it does," James said, "but they were chipped or they'd not be working. I'm sorry, but from now on, we're at war. If they are part of the establishment, they're our enemies. We need to start thinking like a military unit and not a bunch of civilians."

Ben said, "I'm sure if your roles were reversed, he'd be glad he took you out. I think he'd be bragging how he took out a redneck."

"I hear you, but I was raised to respect the law, and now I'm killing the enforcers."

Ben replied, "The laws they're enforcing are not legal and not in our Constitution, which is a piece of paper we never should have gotten away from as a nation. The first and second amendments are now useless to every American. The President is not to make laws, just enforce the laws passed. This crap where he signs just anything into law is not legal. The sonofabitch has used his last executive pen to sign laws into effect. I'm sure we're not the only group fighting them now."

"Do you think others are resisting as well?"

"Turn on the TV when we get back and see. By them coming into small hick towns like this, they're really stirring up a hornet's nest. These folks are the very backbone of America, always have been, and they'll not put up with this bullshit long."

Less than an hour later they pulled into camp, parked under a large oak and covered the vehicle with a tarp to keep it out of sight from above. They made their way to the fire. As they all took seats, the weapons taken from the Federal Agents were looked over and the women each got a pistol, along with the magazines to go with it. One of the pistols and a shotgun taken from the hotel room was kept for the old store owner. There was a box of ammo for each weapon.

Money taken was handed over to James, and the rings, expensive watches and jewelry went into a pile to use for trading later. The men were suddenly tired and hungry.

The grocer was lying beside the fire and meeting James' eyes he asked, "Are those bastards dead?"

"Yep, everyone of them, along with two state policemen."

"Don't feel bad about killin' those cops. They're all chipped and can't control themselves. They're all like them people in one of them zombie movies."

"What's your name?" Bob asked with a grin.

"Don't laugh, but it's Homer Poor."

"Why would we laugh?" James asked.

"I caught hell in my school years because of my name, and the fact we were poor, to boot. Now, just call me Gator. It's been my nickname since I was about 7 years old, 'cause I learned to eat anything. Ya call out fer Homer and I'll not answer. Hell, ain't been nobody call me that since my momma died."

"Hush!" Ben said, "I hear a helicopter."

CHAPTER 16

In Air Force One the Captain said, "This is your Captain speaking. Lieutenant Colonel James Murdock and I are in contact with the Cheyenne Mountain missile complex. They inform me they have no Presidential suite, but they do have a VIP room for you, Mr. President, and your lovely wife. It's small, but they claim you've used it before as a senator. I was informed they will do all they can to make your stay a pleasant one for both of you. Crew, to your landing positions. We have just been approved for landing and will be on the ground shortly."

The aircraft banked slightly and the whirring sound of the wheels lowering filled the cabin. Minutes later the wheels gave a loud screech as the tires met the runway, leaving a black strip on top of others that had landed before them. The flaps came up, the engines reversed, and the pilot applied the brakes.

As the aircraft moved toward a parking spot the Captain said, "Mr. President and First Lady, it's currently 0400 hours at the Cheyenne Mountain missile complex, with nice weather. The temperature outside is 50 degrees and there is a slight wind from the west at less than five miles an hour. Skies are clear, and I want to remind everyone to remain seated and buckled up until I bring the aircraft to a complete stop. We will be parking shortly. As a reminder to all new passengers, the first people off the aircraft will be the President and First Lady."

Inside the complex, the commander, Colonel, General select, Brian Null, a twenty year United States Air Force veteran and senior command pilot, USAF Academy grad, second in his class, and a fast burner up the rank ladder was on a classified phone line.

"Yes, sir. I fully understand, but his death must appear natural. I can't just shoot the man. I will think of a way to kill him, but to kill a President is a serious matter, and a full investigation will be conducted. I promise you, sir, he'll never leave this complex alive. Yes, yes, goodbye."

Colonel Null shook his head and wondered how he'd get out of the mess he was in now, or even if he could where would he go? The NWO had a long reach and unlimited funds.

"Sir," a Staff Sergeant said as he knocked on the Colonel's door frame, "the President and his group are in the conference room as you requested."

"Oh, yes, thank you, Jim, and say hello to that beautiful woman you're married to when you see her again."

"I will, sir." The young man smiled.

The Colonel stood and made his way to the briefing room.

The briefing was a standard one that explained the complex, the jobs of some of those assigned to the mountain, and the past, present and future of the base. He also read their mission statement and their goals as a unit. Once he'd covered that, the Colonel called his intelligence officer, a Major, forward to give the current intelligence status. ISIS is currently the top dog in the World.

"Sir, the situation in the middle east is unchanged, with cars and people continuing to be used to kill innocents and noncombatants. So far this week, there have been an even half dozen suicide bombers and four cars or trucks exploded. The numbers dead are roughly 68 with over 200 injured. Then, closer to home, we now have claims from ISIS that they were responsible for the dirty bomb that took out the White House. They claim it was in the back of a rental truck and being driven by a suicide bomber at the time of detonation. Of course, the area is so hot with radiation we've not been able to exam the center where the device was exploded. The best we've been able to do is to fly over the area with drones and record the damage done. Of course, there are no witnesses and we have thousands being treated for radiation sickness."

"Your report is excellent, sir, except I'm not interested in world news, Major. I need you to tell me what is happening here, here in my country."

"Uh, initial reports indicate a massive uprising in mainly conservative states, with armed resistance against the UN removing any private weapons from homes. A spokesman for the resistance said they are simply 'doing what the second amendment was written for, protecting our rights.'"

"Not good, and I expected resistance, but not like this. This is pure chaos."

"They claim they'll stop fighting when the order to stop removing arms is given, the UN troops leave American soil, and they are assured no legal action will be taken against anyone who resisted the illegal confiscation of personal weapons.

We have some evidence that the New World Order is involved fanning the flames of war on both sides. The resistance is receiving sophisticated weapons from Europe, but so far our agents have not been able to learn anything, except that some weapons running is taking place. We do know a few Senators and Congressmen and women, we have their names, have taken money from the NWO. Our military, as a whole, have refused to take weapons from private citizens and are trying to avoid taking a side."

"Why is my military not doing the job they should?" the President asked.

"Uh, Major, don't answer that question, I will." the Colonel said.

"Well?"

"Sir, with all due respect, the order to take weapons from private citizens violates the second Amendment to the Constitution of the United States, as you know. All military members, officers and enlisted take an oath, just as you did, to defend the Constitution against all enemies, foreign and domestic. Our military does not see your order as a lawful one under the UCMJ, our manual for Courts Martial, or our legal code books, and they are correct. We are bound by law, as well as our oath, to protect the U. S. Constitution and not laws you've signed into action with your executive pen."

"By God, Colonel, it's law now!" the President screamed, his anger fueled by the double whiskeys he'd had on Air Force One.

"Again, sir, no disrespect intended, but you, as the President of the United States, are the Executive Officer of our Government. You cannot technically draft a law from your personal desires or wishes. Sir, you have no law making authority and are limited to signing a bill into law or vetoing it when it comes to your desk from Congress."

"You are wrong, Colonel! I passed a law to force all Americans to surrender their guns and it will be obeyed. I am the absolute law in this country now!"

"I hope you are correct, sir, but your military will not become involved, and neither will your state law enforcement officials."

Remember the chip implants, the President thought and then smiled as he said, "I'll not argue with you; excuse my outburst, but I've been through much in the last few days. I need a few days of rest and some good food."

"I can understand, sir." Colonel Null said, and then looking at the Major, winked, and added, "Continue with your intelligence briefing."

"At last count, 25% of active duty personnel and 70% of all guard and reserve units have had the implant. Out of thousands of implants, there were only two cases where the person's body would not accept the foreign object. In both cases, the hand became infected, so the chip was removed. We were, however, able to tattoo a barcode on their foreheads.

The last of my briefing is the slide you see, where the armed resistance to the taking of private weapons is taking place the most often."

"Looks mostly to be the Southern states, Rockies, and Midwest."

"It is, sir, and Texas, as well as Florida, are hot spots right now. The Texans refuse to give up their guns and Florida, which has a very high percentage of veteran retirees, has told you to, quote, 'Go to hell,' unquote. In both locations, fierce combat between the UN and private citizens has taken place."

Standing and needing a drink, the President said, "The First Lady and I are tired, and need breakfast and some sleep."

Good, if I can slip some anthrax into a letter or document, I can cause an illness or maybe death. Regardless, he'll need a hospital. Odds are, even if not killed, he'll be removed from office. Hell, I might get lucky and kill 'em both, Colonel Null thought, and unknowingly smiled. The Colonel stood and said, "Chief Hill, see to the needs of our Commander-in-Chief. Mr. President and First Lady, if you'll follow Chief Hill, he will take care of you."

As the President and Colonel moved toward the door, Chief Hill yelled from the very pit of his stomach, "Tennn-hoooit!"

Everyone stood.

Near the door, the Colonel said, "At ease." The Chief then moved forward to lead the President to his quarters.

Later the same day, a young man with two stripes took the President some messages and letters from various sources. A special carrier plane had brought all the correspondence to the complex for the Commander-in-Chief. It was the usual stuff he read everyday, and he thought nothing of it. It was just after supper when he poured four fingers of whiskey in his glass and began opening the mail.

He took a large gulp of whiskey, moved to the bed and laid down. He placed his drink on the night table. His back was propped up so he was actually almost sitting and he was comfortable as he slipped his reading glasses on. The First Lady was reading a novel as he went over his papers.

All went smoothly until he opened a card from his mom in Alabama. A fine white dust moved into the air as the letter opener moved across the top of the envelope. The particles were so small, if not for the light and surrounding darkness, he'd not have seen it at all. He removed his reading glasses and saw a fine mist settling on his wife and wondered what it was. When he glanced at the letter, it was a simple card from his mother, and even the date stamp showed Mobile, Alabama.

Glancing at the folds in the card, he saw tiny particles of the dust.

This is not normal; I need to contact security. This stuff almost looks like baby powder, he thought as he picked up the phone. How can this be? Because I would swear this is mom's handwriting.

"Security? This is the President. I need to have you report to my quarters now. I opened a letter with a powdery substance in it. Both the First Lady and I have inhaled this power."

Men soon arrived wearing special suits with self contained air, and as one man took samples of the powder, another, a doctor, looked his two patients over closely.

"How does he look, sir?" a Senior Master Sergeant asked.

"Take them to the complex hospital and place both of them in the same room, but I want them isolated. I have no idea what they've inhaled, but I suspect its anthrax and, if so, I'll want a specialist flown in. If they develop meningitis like symptoms, a little testing will confirm or disprove my guess."

"Sergeant Wilson, I want photos of everything, and I mean all of it. Get photos of the letter, the powder, the powder in the creases of the paper, just everything in this room."

"Including the whiskey?"

"Yes, and take it to the lab too. I want this whole room tested."

"Yes, sir."

"Who do you think did this doc?" Airman Jones asked.

"Right now, son, almost every man and woman in this nation wants the President dead. So, take your pick."

"Oh, I see, sir."

"Place them in the plastic isolation tents on the stretchers and let's move them to the hospital. If we treat them fast enough, we may be able to save them. Tell the lab I want the results as soon as they have them."

"Yes, sir." an airman said, and then left the room with two samples contained in bags in his hands.

A Staff Sergeant asked, "Why use the isolation tents as we move them to the hospital, sir? I was told anthrax is **not** contagious."

"It's not, but we have no way of knowing right this minute what they were exposed to, if anything. It may be baby powder on that letter, but I doubt it. I'm simply taking a precaution."

They called the control center, had the hallways emptied of normal traffic and made their way to the hospital section of the complex. Their medical center was as capable as any hospital in the world, just lacking some specialists, but they could usually be flown in if needed.

"Nurse, I'm sure these are anthrax patients, so look for a sudden onset of fever, headache, and stiff neck as complaints from them. The powder is currently in the lab being tested. I want them kept in isolation, and I have requested a specialist be brought in to treat them. In the meantime, remember they are the President of the United States and the First Lady, so treat them well."

"Yes of course, sir." a male Lieutenant nurse said.

"Start an IV with antibiotics and antitoxin. I have no idea if we reached them fast enough or not, but if they start having breathing problems put them on a ventilator, and use continuous fluid drainage."

"Uh, yes, sir. I fully understand."

The doctor quickly showered in the decontamination shower, dried off, and then returned to the hospital after he dressed in scrubs.

"Sir, while you were out the lab called, and the powder sample tested positive for anthrax. They double checked the samples and results were positive for *Bacillus Anthracis both times. They said the genetic makeup was slightly different with a silicon element discovered."*

"Terrorists often use silicon with Bacillus Anthracis so it sticks to the lungs better and increases the fatality rate."

The Nurse walked near the desk shaking his head.

"How are the patients?" he asked.

"Complaining of some flu like symptoms. The President has had violent vomiting and diarrhea, along with severe stomach cramps. The First Lady does not have the same symptoms. That has me a bit confused, but I know little of anthrax."

"Be cautious," a Master Sergeant medic said, "because we know the letter was handled by the mail room clerks, the person or persons that delivered

the card to the President, and only God knows who else. I suspect in the next few days, more with the same problems will show here."

"*It sounds like the flu, or food poisoning to me. Run his and her blood to the lab and have it looked at closely. I want a full blown blood test done on him. I suspect we'll find something else involved with him." the doctor ordered.*

"*Who here would poison the President?" the nurse asked.*

"*I have not said he was poisoned, only that it's a thought. Once his blood is tested, we'll know what we have on our hands. If he was poisoned, it'll open up a whole can of security worms."*

The nurse asked, "When does the infection usually start after exposure to anthrax? You know, if I didn't know better, I'd think they both developed meningitis."

"Infection usually develops within a week after exposure, except I have no idea how adding silicon to the spores will impact that infection time. I'd suspect, only I don't really know, it may cut the time down tremendously."

A full Colonel, the Hospital Commander, entered and said, "I've contacted the Center for Disease Control and they have a specialist on the way here as I speak. They said we usually have up to a week before the infection starts, but with the silicon helping the spores stick to the linings of the lungs, well, they don't think we have that long. Since the letter address to the President was from his mother, the Non-Commissioned Officer in Charge (NCOIC) of the mail room thought it was personal and didn't open it."

"I don't think we have a week either, but the lab results will tell us much more." the doctor said.

Picking up a chart, the Colonel looked it over and said, "Looks to me like you've done all you can for both of them. All we can do now is monitor them and wait for our man or woman to arrive."

I'm surprised the President survived the arsenic trioxide I put in his whiskey bottle. Only I was guessing how much to put into a fifth of whiskey. I'm even more surprised his blood hasn't been taken for testing by the Hospital yet, but

that's just a matter of time. In the meantime, I need to gather up things in the event the man doesn't die, Colonel Null thought as he cleaned his 9 mm pistol with an oily rag. His cleaned M4A1 was on his bed and his ammo pouches were beside his rifle, as he took a sip of some seven year old Irish whiskey.

He suddenly picked up the secure line and dialed a number.

"Hello, Colonel, I was just discussing you. You have news for me, ja?"

"My automobile is in the garage with a serious problem and I do not think it will recover."

"Oh, and what is the nature of this illness?"

"Anthrax and arsenic, according to my mechanic. We will need a new one soon, or so I was told."

"Good, Colonel, and what of you?"

"I need out of here and now, if possible."

"I can understand that. You will have military orders and a plane in air to you within the next thirty minutes. You will be ordered to use the aircraft to travel to your next base. There will be another Colonel on the aircraft to take command of the complex and he may or may not be a member of the New World Order, so say little to him. Any questions?"

"No, sir. Thank you."

"Good day, Colonel." The call was over.

Forty-five minutes later, his phone rang.

"Colonel Null speaking."

"Sir, this is Senior Airman Wilkes; I have a C-130 inbound to pick you up, and they have your replacement and new orders for you. I was instructed to have you waiting on the flight line when they arrive. Their ETA is fifteen minutes, sir."

"Thank you, I'll be right up."

He then left his room, walked to the small air terminal and straight to the counter, so the airman could see he was ready to leave.

"Sir, if you'd like something to eat or a drink, the VIP lounge is open for officers and senior NCOs."

"That's where I'll be."

"Uh, let me take your luggage and I'll book it for the aircraft, sir, and see it's loaded for you."

"Thank you. I appreciate the assistance." He then passed his bags to the young man and moved for the lounge.

The man walked into the lounge, up to the bar and ordered a double bourbon. He sat on a stool at the bar making small talk as he drank two more. Finally, he heard a loud speaker announce, "Attention, please, Colonel Null your aircraft is now available for boarding. Colonel Null, to your aircraft, please."

The Colonel downed his drink, walked to the flight line and saw a C-130 running engines as a load master waved him forward.

The ramp was down, so walking to the Master Sergeant, he yelled, "Colonel Null?" He then pointed at himself.

He was motioned to get on the aircraft and once on, he saw two squads of paratroopers in the canvas red seats. One squad was on each side, so he sat next to another Colonel. The ramp was being raised as the aircraft taxied for takeoff. By the time the bird was at the end of the runway, the ramp was closed. They took off, gained attitude and began cruising at 20,000 feet.

As the aircraft moved, he noticed the paratroopers were rigged for a free fall jump, with oxygen masks, oxygen bottles, communications and slightly different parachutes and gear.

Must be a special operations bunch or some Rangers on the prowl, Null thought as he remembered his five jumps at the Air Force Academy.

An hour later, a man who could have only been the Load Master yelled as the ramp was lowered, "Stand Up!" He indicated for the men to stand with his hands, because it was hard to hear in the aircraft.

"Move to the ramp!" Again he saw the man use his hands to show what he wanted done.

Moving to the ramp, the group stood waiting for a green light, which meant for them to leave the aircraft. Null naturally moved close to them and pulled out his phone to get some photos. At this altitude, the ground was a blend of various shades of greens, and browns.

Suddenly the light turned green and the men left the aircraft as a group, but when the Jump Master left the ramp, he had Colonel Null's right arm in his two hands. Holding onto the

Colonel, the man just stepped from the ramp, let his weight shift, and they both fell from the aircraft.

They'd no sooner cleared the ramp than the vise like grip on the Colonel let go of him.

"Base, this is Blackjack One, mission accomplished." the Jump Master said to headquarters, using his communications system.

"Roger, Blackjack, copy, mission complete."

"Roger that, base. Out."

Falling now at terminal velocity, Null's brain was working so quickly nothing stayed focused in his mind for over a microsecond. Due to the altitude, his thinking began to slow as oxygen deprivation struck him fast and hard. Seconds later, he lost consciousness and awoke a few fast seconds before his body slammed into the side of a mountain head first, going just slightly under 120 miles an hour.

CHAPTER 17

"**The chopper is off** in the distance, moving in grids or patterns, like helicopters do when searching for someone. I think that someone is us." James said.

"Want us to put the fire out?" Donna asked.

"I think it would be smart, and pray they don't have infrared capability on the bird." Ben said as he stood.

"What's that infer-red stuff?" Gator asked, as three of them poured water on the fire.

"It's a computerized method of seeing heat in darkness. If the chopper has it, we show as red people on their screens. All they have to do is shoot at the red folks. It's like a computer game really, and no details are shown of us."

"Will the vehicles we drove here show?" James asked.

"I don't know what the motor temperatures are right now, but the hotter they are the better they'll show. If they're cool, no, they'll not show."

"Some things in the woods give off heat." Gator said.

"Of course they do, but they'll see us well enough to see our heads, shoulders and limbs."

"Oh, not good then."

"I don't know if they have it or not, so relax, but load your weapons." Ben said, and then placed a round into the breech of his sniper rifle.

When the chopper was nearer, Ben said, "Spotlight on both doors, and you can be sure they have machine-guns under those lights. Everyone get under something and don't move until the chopper leaves."

The aircraft moved over them, the light flashed and moved in all directions. It then moved forward a little and began searching with the lights again. Three different times the helicopter was over them, but it eventually flew into another grid.

"Okay, everyone come out now. I suspect they're gone, but they may come back at some point. I'm pretty sure they didn't have infrared capability or some of us would have been picked up on the screen."

"How can you tell if it has this or that on a helicopter?" Gator asked.

"Good question, and usually you have no idea, unless it's mounted on external pods. I mean, if that chopper had had a cannon, it would have been mounted on a pod, it had nothing hanging from it at all, but I know there were machine-guns under those lights. When you see a chopper, the best thing to do is stop moving and if you have time, crawl under cover."

Donna said, "That light went all over me and I expected to be shot any second."

James was holding her hand and he squeezed it. She knew he was telling her he loved her, because they'd been squeezing hands over forty years.

"Things look differently from the air. I've had helicopters looking for me and I wanted them to see me, and we still had trouble finding each other. Often colors and shapes blend together. You're wearing jeans and gray shirt, so you'd be hard to see with a fast glance." Frank said.

"What now?" Gator asked.

"Stay up or go to bed, but I suggest no fires." Ben said.

"I think over the next week, night time fires will be a fond memory." James said, and then grinned. It was a full moon, so everyone saw his teeth.

"Do you think they'll bring in dogs?" Nancy asked.

"They would if they knew we were in a general area. They have no idea even what direction we took after we left the hotel. For all they know, we could be in Saint Louis or Kansas City by now." Ben said.

As he met Nancy's eyes, James said, "Yep, the clerk was blindfolded, so he has no idea which direction we left and once the attack started, I never saw any of the other guests at all."

"I suspect they were smart and stayed in their rooms."

"Let it go, because they have no idea where we are, or even who did the killing. They have nothing to go on."

"I hear you, but I just thought of something we forgot. The front desk had a security camera, so if it was working properly, they'll know what two of us look like."

"Well, I saw cameras outside too, where the guests come and go, so they'll have us on tape, if they were working, but many don't."

"How badly did you mess up the hotel?" Gator asked.

"Not bad really; expect we totaled two rooms for sure. The rooms will need to be built from scratch just to get all the blood and bits of flesh from the walls. Chunks of sheet-rock were blown to hell, and I suspect all the furniture was no good." Ben said.

"I know the cops will keep the rooms as is and secured for a year, and they'll pay Mable Kennedy to keep the doors locked and sealed. You did say her name was Mable, right?" James asked.

Gator, grinning, replied, "Yep, and I was sweet on her when I first got here, but her husband didn't like that much, so I let her go. Bill, her old man died last year, so I've taken her out for supper a time or two."

Donna suddenly said, "I don't mean to change the subject, but how will some of us get our medications now, since we don't have the chips installed?"

James smiled and said, "I've given that some thought and taking a legal prescription from Nancy to the pharmacy, like we did before, would just get us arrested now, because the chip is needed. Gator, do you know the town of Licking well?"

"I had an older brother that used to live there, so I know it good enough. Why, ain't much in Licking."

"Does it have a pharmacy?"

"Yep, they do."

"Police station?"

"No, they don't, but they do have a jail with an administration room out front. I think they have two cells and both of them are probably rusty. Last I heard, Bubba Skaggs was the policeman and he don't cause any trouble. Why all the questions?" Gator batted his eyes and looked confused.

"Tonight, we're all going to rob the Licking pharmacy, but we're to take drugs, not money."

"Those of us requiring certain drugs, speak with Nancy so she can write them down and once in the pharmacy, she'll grab shipping containers of the drugs. If we have time, I'll clean the damned place out, and leave them nothing." James said and then added, "I'm concerned that the NWO may take complete control of the distribution of controlled substances, which would allow them to kill millions of people by simply stopping delivery of their meds."

"Some folks on heart meds, high blood pressure, diabetes, or even simple infections will die if medications are withheld." Nancy said, and then batted her eyes a few times as if the whole concept of withholding medication was unthinkable to her.

"That's the main reason we'll hit the pharmacy this evening. While some may die in the coming months, hopefully it won't be anyone in our group. I want no one hurt if we can avoid it, but if a gun is pulled, shoot to kill. Without blood pressure meds, we'll lose Donna, me, Gator and Dick. We also need to be prepared in case someone comes down with something, too. I want to clean the place out."

"Why don't you and I go over there and look the place over? You've never been in the place and I was in there years ago, nigh on five years back. The whole place may be changed around by now."

"Well, get on the bike, Gator, we're going to town." James said as he grinned.

"Why the motorcycle?"

"Two reasons, it'll use less gas and it'll take us places a car can't go. Now, get the helmet on and let's go."

The drive to the Licking pharmacy was uneventful, with James enjoying the cool air on his face as they traveled. The drug store was smaller than most, but the pharmacist was situated behind the counter in an open area. Drugs were seen on countless shelves behind the man, and that was all he needed to see.

Gator neared the clerk and said, "I'm new to the area and take Azor and Labetalol for my high blood pressure; do you carry them?"

The pharmacist glanced up and said, "Sure, and while we're smaller than pharmacies in large towns, you'll find we can fill almost any prescription you bring us. What we don't have in stock we can order from Rolla and have it in a couple of hours."

"Well, by cracky, I'll be back later today with my prescription. What time do ya and the store close?"

"Nine sharp so be here before that or you'll be out of luck."

"I'll be back in plenty of time to get my medications."

The two men mingled around the store, watched a couple of purchases, and then took three cases of various canned soups, three bags of charcoal, and boxes of bandages for minor injuries to the checkout.

"I hope ya don't need no chip thingy in my hand, 'cause I ain't got one of 'em yet." Gator said.

"Ya don't need one here. Mister Jones, the Pharmacist owns the place and he refuses to get one; calls it the mark of the beast. I fully agree with him. The last Federal man to come in here, the Boss pulled a gun out of his holster and stuck it in the man's face. The man left, but he was threatening to put us all in a FEMA camp."

"Good, so he carries a gun? He's a smart man these days."

"Oh, yes, and it's always in his shoulder harness. He showed it to me once and called it a 9 mm which I thought was a wrench size, or something like that."

Once outside, James placed the soups in the hard saddlebags along with the other stuff. The lids wouldn't close, so he secured them with bungie cords.

As they were putting their motorcycle helmets on, Gator said, "The pharmacist has a 9 mm pistol concealed on his left side, in a shoulder holster, since he's right handed."

"I hope we don't have to hurt him. I'm sure he's insured against robberies and stealing narcotics is a felony, but I don't want to add murder to my list of bad deeds. Especially since he's refusing to take the mark."

"We have to do what needs doin' to survive, my friend. Lets' hope later this evening things will go smoothly."

Later that same day, Gator and James entered the pharmacy once more. Nancy was in Gator's old store truck, as Dick and Ben covered the front door. Glancing at her watch, it was 2045, so within minutes the robbery would go down. Blake and Donna were watching the rear doors, just in case someone ran out during the robbery. Minutes after the first two entered, Ben entered and soon had a clerk helping him find something for his 'lower back pain.'

Frank took a prescription from Nancy to the rear of the store and gave it to the same pharmacist that had been working earlier. Gator and James stood behind their man, so it looked as if they were simply in line for service.

The man walked to his computer, entered the information and then said, "Mister Sals, I'd love to fill this for you, but the government has your doctor down as refusing the chip and there is a one thousand dollar reward for her."

"I don't understand. She's a nurse practitioner, but you mean she ain't allowed to write no prescriptions?"

"No, the government considers her a criminal because she doesn't have the microchip in her left hand."

"Oh, wait, I have another prescription from another doctor, so let's see if this one works."

"Sure."

Frank reached in his coat, pulled out a loaded and ready Ruger .45 auto, and said, "Remove the pistol from your shoulder harness very slowly. This is a robbery and if everyone does as they're told, no one will be hurt."

The pharmacist removed his pistol, placed it on the counter, and then said, "Son, we don't have a thousand dollars in the whole place."

"It's not your money I want, so keep it." James said.

Gator moved to the front door and had Nancy slowly back the big truck to the front door. She then entered, ran to the pharmacy and began stacking boxes of drugs on the counter. As most of the crew loaded drugs, James had the cashier tied to the Pharmacist and then left Gator to watch over them.

James placed the man's pistol in the small of his back and then went outside. As he stood watching the loading, Frank looked down the street and said, "Squad car coming, and it looks like the cop Gator told us about."

"Bubba Skaggs?"

"I guess that's his name. What if he stops?"

"Then we try to get rid of him."

"If push comes to shove?"

"We try to take him prisoner, but if it turns to shooting, kill him. We know all cops have the chip, all of them, so he's an enemy from the start. Killing someone with the mark of the beast will not keep me from sleeping any night."

"I'll show him my CIA badge, and let's hope it carries some weight."

"When he stops, I'll be up by the cab, and as you talk to him, I'll try to take him prisoner." James said, and moved to the cab of the big deuce and a half.

Bubba pulled into a parking slot and got out of the car, pistol in hand. Frank neared and showed his CIA badge. He then said, "This man and his staff have refused the chip, so all his meds are being taken by the government. Over the next few days, vendors will remove his other items from the shelves."

"Well, I'll be damned. I don't see the big deal. I got a chip and it didn't hurt or nothin'."

"You don't see it as the mark of the beast?"

"No," Bubba laughed. He then added, "That's foolishness, and in order for the chip to be the mark of the beast, there needs to be an anti-Christ and there ain't one. Let me see your badge for a minute, because I need to report this to the highway patrol."

"Sure." Frank said, and tossed the badge to Bubba.

When Bubba leaned over to change the frequency of his radio, Frank pulled out his .38 snub nose and fired two rounds into the cop. The first bullet punched a hole through his body, from his left arm and out under the raised right arm. It then struck his dash and disappeared. Bubba screamed as the second bullet hit him in the head, right behind his left ear. His scream was short lived as the bullet blew a big chunk of skull and brain from his head. His body began to jerk as it shut down.

Frank opened the car door and pulled the portly man from his vehicle. He then took the man's wallet, badge, gun and other gear from this still shivering body. From the squad car, he took a shotgun and an M4A1 with six magazines. There was little else of use to them in the vehicle.

"Hurry, people, a cop was just killed!" James yelled.

Everyone knew the cop's heart beat and other vitals would soon alert someone with the NWO, and since the chip had a GPS capability, the exact spot of the dead man would soon be known. As far as they were located from a large city, James knew they had time to load all the drugs, but he didn't feel comfortable, and his senses were warning him to move, and move now.

Leaving Frank outside, he entered the store and made his way to Nancy. Once near he asked, "How much longer will you be?"

"Not sure, but maybe ten minutes, why?"

"You must have heard the shots. Frank had to kill the local cop."

"I'll sort through what's here and I'm sure some of this stuff I'll not need."

"No, take it all, and leave his shelves bare. I need to get back out front, but hurry this up if you can."

On the way outside, James took a can of cold pop and a chocolate bar, leaving five dollars in the till.

Twenty minutes later, just as the tailgate to the old truck was raised, Ben yelled, "Chopper!"

Everyone ran to a vehicle and they drove away at a normal speed, so they'd not draw attention. Just as the truck was about to turn a corner, Ben said, "They're landing in the pharmacy parking lot."

Nancy, the driver, asked, "Do I keep driving or what?"

"Keep driving and —"

"It's back in the air."

"They must have dropped some men off and plan to come after us."

"No one knows the vehicles we have, no one. The folks inside never saw what we were driving."

Frank laughed and said, "How much traffic do you expect is on any given road around here at this time of the night? They're lining up right behind us now."

"Shit, we can't lead them back to the camp."

"What now?" Nancy asked.

"I don't have any idea." James replied.

CHAPTER 18

"**Null is dead,**" the voice on the phone said. "But, from what I understand the President will live."

Colonel Alfred "Al" Cash, Colonel Null's replacement, replied, "Sir, I've not been briefed on the President's condition yet, but the First Lady died yesterday, the day I arrived. I will be briefed on the President's health in about fifteen minutes, during what is called 'stand up' or my daily briefing."

"I don't see how he can be alive, when he swallowed strychnine and inhaled Anthrax. Let me know immediately if his condition changes either direction."

"Yes, sir." The phone went dead.

Minutes later, in stand up, the Colonel turned to his commander of the hospital and asked, "Colonel, what is the President's current condition?"

"Initial lab reports show he swallowed strychnine along with inhaling Anthrax, beyond any doubt, and his liver function is failing and his heart is weak. A security check of his room indicated, well, at first all looked well, but strychnine was discovered in the whiskey decanter. The President is well known for enjoying good Kentucky bourbon and whoever attempted to kill him, obviously knew this."

"Will he live?"

"Good question, and my first thoughts are no. However, some of the best doctors in the world have been consulted and we're doing all we can to keep him alive. Now, I will say this much, if he does live, he'll not be able to function as the President."

"I see."

Suddenly, the doctor's cell phone vibrated and when he glanced at the screen, it was a Code Blue VIP.

"Excuse me, sir, this call is about the President. I need to step into the hallway for a few minutes."

"By all means, Colonel." Cash said, and then added, "Weather, brief me as the doctor takes his call."

Ten minutes later, after the weather and security brief, the hospital commander returned to his seat, glanced around the room and said, "Ladies and Gentlemen, the President of the United States died at 0803 this morning. Right now an autopsy is being done, but I think every person in this room knows the cause of his death. Tomorrow, his body, as well as the First Lady's, will be picked up by Air Force One."

Looking at his Chaplain, the Complex Commander said, "Sir, would you lead us in prayer?"

The newly formed Congress and Senate were a mess, with heated arguments that almost led to blows taking place daily. The politicians argued over the chip, the mark of the beast, the anti-Christ, as well as guns and the United Nations. Most suspected the requirement to have the chip installed was a violation of basic human rights. The Southern states more or less told the rest of the world to go to hell, there would be no chip implants below the Mason-Dixon Line.

Finally, the House Speaker said, "The floor recognizes the honorable Bill Black, of Mississippi."

"Thank you," Black said as he stood, "Mister Speaker. I want to inform the Government of the United States of America, that effective at 10:28 am this morning," he looked at his watch, "the great state of Mississippi will secede from the Union. We will not and cannot allow the implant of those unGodly chips into our bodies. This damned Mark of the Beast is not taken casually in the Southern States and Mississippi has decided to lead the way by telling y'all to kiss our collective asses. We may have lost our last war with y'all, but we'll not lose this one. God is on our side."

The whole congress turned loud with talking, yelling, and cat calls.

The Speaker finally reestablished control and then asked, "How many other states agree with leaving the union?"

A majority of hands went up, and the Speaker marked off states as he looked at the hands. He knew his home state of California would not leave the Union, because they were flat ass broke, and if not for Federal Assistance, they'd not be able to pay anyone.

"My count shows over 37 states wish to leave the Union."

"The Union is too Liberal!" someone shouted.

"Congressman Tooms of Missouri, you have the floor."

"I'd like to remind Congress of the last Civil War, where we had hundreds of thousands of dead on both sides. That horrible war happened at the time it was perfectly legal for any state to leave the Union. Now read a high school history book. Y'all make Abe Lincoln read like a God or something, when in fact, he was an open racist. Lincoln didn't give a damn about black folks and only fought the war to preserve the Union. But unlike the last time, Missouri will now leave the Union over implants, not states rights. The people of Missouri, like all the Southern states, refuses to submit to the power and control of the anti-Christ and have the implant. *It is the Mark of the Beast!*

For years the liberals in the nation, have twisted and distorted things to the point of stupidity. Not long ago, we were arguing over bathrooms for transgender folks, while they only constitute 3% or less of our population. We don't even have all bathrooms modified to handle our disabled and they are approximately 20% of our population. Kids are taught the Muslim Religion in schools as American men and women die in the Middle East fighting people of the Islamic faith. Our own children were sent home if they carried a Bible or chewed a piece of cheese into the shape of a pistol. *Shame on us!*

How about medical coverage for our Veterans? I'm sickened each time I hear of a veteran dying because they were unable to see a doctor at a VA hospital. Or, how about medical assistance for our elderly, or even providing our homeless a warm place to sleep? Stop giving funds to our enemies. The United States has such a deficit right now, it will never be paid off. And, do you know who is responsible for this debt? All you damned Liberals!"

"You're a damned liar!" the Representative from Michigan yelled.

The Speaker went back to banging with his gavel again, as he screamed, "Order! Order, please."

Men and women began to walk from the room. Soon, all that remained were the Liberal states. They were all standing and confused. Two thirds of Congress had just walked out the door and left the United States.

"Uh, can they do that?" The freshman Congresswoman from New York asked.

"They just did. Does this mean a civil war?"

"How can we have a war, when we don't even have a President sworn in yet?"

The Speaker thought, *I need about six drinks to even get through today. What a damned mess.* He then said, "We must prepare an announcement for the new President to declare a state of war against all the states that just walked out."

"Some of the Liberal states are surrounded by Conservative states. Hell, we can't let the conservative states leave; they have a lot of money."

"It's illegal to leave the Union." the Speaker reminded everyone.

"Look, you are all forgetting one very important issue here." a Congresswoman from Rhode Island said.

"What's that?" the Speaker asked.

"The armed forces will side with the Conservative States and not us. They have sworn an oath to protect and defend the Constitution. Here we wish to more or less abolish it completely."

"Shit, what a mess. I'd never considered that." the Speaker of the House said.

Three days later, as the President of the United States was sworn in, the Conservative States of America swore their leader in, as well. The news cameras from all states were on the US President as he moved to a podium and prepared to speak.

"My fellow Americans, I am deeply honored to be your next President of the United States, but I have a rough time ahead of me, as do you as citizens. I have asked the Selective Service to draft 100,000 men and women for immediate service to our nation. The draft will continue in effect until an unknown time in the future. I fear the states that illegally left the Union must be brought back into the fold by the use of brutal force.

Tomorrow morning at 9 am, I will speak to Congress and request a declaration of war. This state of war will exist between the United States and the states who have broken our country in two. These states, who have taken to calling themselves the Conservative States of America, will be brought back into the Union, by force if necessary. Once before the CSA tried to create their own nation and it did not happen then. I assure all of you who can hear and see me now, it will not happen this time either.

Additionally, since 95% of our armed forces have gone over to the other side, taking their arms and munitions, I have asked the United Nations for 500,000 combat troops and they will be arriving starting tomorrow. These troops will arrive with their own weapons, ammo and other vehicles they'll need to fight this war."

"Uh, Mr. President," a reporter yelled out, "is war our only option?"

"I'm afraid so, Mark, and if they want to return to the Union by morning, that is fine as long as they meet our demands."

"What are those demands, sir?"

"Each state will have to pay a five billion dollar fine and agree to immediate chip implant, which is done for safety and quality of life issues. No more questions please."

Getting into his limo, the President said, "Oh, what a mess. Intelligence tells me radical Muslims were behind the President's death and I know better. My gut instinct is the New World Order, but how in the hell did they poison the man's drink? The only persons that could have killed him were at the complex."

His aide, Robert Hill, asked, "Where to now, sir?"

"Take me to what passes for the White House these days. I can't believe they found anthrax in the President, as well as strychnine. I want security beefed up and I want it in place today."

"I'll see it's done, sir." Hill said.

Minutes passed and then the aide's phone rang.

"Hello? Yes, yes, let me ask him."

"Sir, it's your chef and he wants to know if you want what is on the menu or something different tonight for supper."

"Steak, baked potato, and salad. Tell him, in the future to ask the First Lady. I'm entering a damned war and he wants to know what I desire for supper?" He removed a decanter from the bar and poured himself a large glass of Kentucky whiskey.

"Sir, has anyone given thought to the Democrats and Republicans trapped where they may not want to be?"

"I haven't, and why should I even care?"

"I think they could prove a valuable asset to you and our cause."

"Oh? Tell me more."

"The Republicans we can round up and use them as hostages in certain situations. Telling the enemy if they do this or don't do that, we will kill x number of them. Then, our folks could be very useful as spies."

"Excellent idea. I want you to order that the voting record of every city under our control forward a listing of all Republicans to the police. I want all of them rounded up and placed in FEMA camps. If any of them give you any troubles, shoot them."

"There will be resistance, sir."

Smiling, the President said, "Yes, of course there will be, and so much the better."

In the Conservative States of America, a tall thin man walked to the podium in Atlanta and said, "Ladies and Gentlemen, here is the first President of the Conservative States of America, William P. Patterson."

Patterson was an average looking man, in his mid-fifties, of average size and weight. His brown hair was worn short, his beard neatly trimmed, and his green eyes alert. A beautiful Southern Belle moved to him and he took her hand in his. Both raised a hand to wave at the people watching and cheering for them. The First Lady was ten years his junior and she was still as pretty as when in college. They had three children, two boys and a girl, all adopted.

Walking to the podium, Patterson said, "We have a hard time ahead of us which will not be easy in the months to come, but I feel God is on our side. Unlike the last civil war, I don't expect the government of the winning side to be as gentle as the Yankees were in 1865. I know I will personally place a rope around the neck of the sonofabitch they currently call the President.

Most of our military forces are with us in this fight, so unlike the last war, we are starting with a well organized fighting force on our side, with plenty of supplies. However, the might of the whole world may be thrown at us, but with God's help we will win.

Effective immediately, we will pray and say a pledge of allegiance to the flag in all government and school buildings in all states at the beginning of each day. Our police will round up all illegal aliens and then send them home, billing their nations the cost of transportation. Refugees who do not want to see our crosses, hear our Christmas music, or join us in prayer will be asked to leave. The one and only law here is American law, so obey it or go to jail. I have asked all Muslims to return to their homelands or to the United States, because we see a real conflict with their religion and ours. There will never be Sharia law here, only our laws, based on the word of God. The Conservative States of America will not honor any previously made relocation agreement between any foreigners and the United States of America. Under our new laws, only those people who wish to become Americans will be allowed to relocate to our country. That means only one language, English, and all military age immigrants, male and female, will serve two years in our military. By serving honorably they will be granted residency.

Also, public assistance will no longer be available to anyone not physically or mentally disabled, as stated by two doctors, and those of you who are lazy, drunks, or addicts, your days of freeloading the system are over. If you are able to work and cannot find a job, the government will put you to work and see you are compensated for your time, at minimum wage. This assistance program will allow us to do more with our money and also allow all able bodied persons to receive help. If you are a baby machine for the benefits, those days are over. From this moment on, the only place food-stamps are to be used is in government stocked food warehouses. No cash will be given, no phone service, no cable TV, and if you come to us for help, don't pull up in an expensive car. If you do, your car will be confiscated and government food-stamps will be given to you as payment in full. We will use the 'blue book' to determine the value of your car and to pay you in food-stamps. From now on in this nation, unless you are disabled, if you don't work, you don't eat.

I have also reinstated the draft. All males and females between the ages of 18 and 45 that have not previously served in the military are eligible to be drafted. First offender criminals of all but rape, murder, or other violent crimes, will be given to either the Army or our Marines. If they fail to complete their four year military obligation, they will be placed in prison and their sentence will start at day one. No credit for military service good time served will be given."

"What of a flag?"

"We are working on that. We, unlike the USA, will use the old American Constitution to govern our people. So, your rights are almost the same, but less Federal control. We will leave the management of state rights up to the individual states. I foresee a small Federal Government, with more powerful and larger state governments. Finally, it is the right of each citizen to own as many guns as they wish, if they attain them legally. However, we will continue to do background checks, mainly to keep guns out of the hands of those folks who are mentally unstable. Open carry and concealed carry are both legal as of this second, and we encourage all our law abiding citizens to carry a firearm, especially with war coming."

"How long will this war last, sir?" a reporter asked.

The President smiled, shook his head and then said, "Until it's over, son. If you have more questions, join my press secretary tomorrow morning here at 9 am. Thank you, and God bless the Conservative States of America."

The President moved to his limo and once seated said, "Get me out of here."

The First Lady looked at him, smiled and then said, "William, you make a simply dashing President, dear."

He laughed, looked at his aide and said, "I thought a couple of the reporters were going to start yelling when I brought up no public assistance for those who can but won't work. I'm tired of a society that is lazy and wants freebies. I'll put their asses to cutting grass along the highways if I have to do the job. We need to instill some self respect into many of our folks. I didn't think it was time to bring it up, but soon all males right out of high school will do two years of mandatory military service before they can enter the work force or college."

"Oh, the rich will not like that at all. They are privileged, don't you know?" the aide said.

"I mean everyone who can pass a physical will serve, with no exceptions. I think my four years in the Marines made me into the man I am today."

"You were so dashing in your uniform, baby." the First Lady said.

"Along with my golden second lieutenant bars and my national defense ribbon." he said, and then laughed.

"I've told the chef to fix us a Southern meal tonight. So, we're having baked quail, beans with cornbread, biscuits, collard greens, and fried potatoes."

"Would you like a before supper drink, my dear?" he asked.

"Yes, of course with a man like you. Pour me some Kentucky bourbon, the best whiskey in the world."

As he poured two fingers of the amber colored liquid into her glass, he said, "The Irish may argue with you about the whiskey."

The President's phone rang, "Hello?"

"Why don't you obey your orders?"

"I don't take orders from anyone except the people of Conservative States of America. I've told you before, I will not be bought."

"You are a dead man then."

"Listen to me, you bastard, I will not be bought and all men are born to die, are we not? Death does not scare me, but some things in life are worse than death, like the loss of self respect and integrity. By the way, my intelligence section wants to know if your wife knows about the stunning redhead you went home with last week. I have pictures, compromising photos I may add, and I have the address in Frankfurt, sir. I want —" The line went dead.

He tossed the phone to his aide and said, "I want a secure phone; get rid of this. See the images we have, you know the ones, are sent to Germany; overnight them."

"Yes, sir."

In Darmstad, Germany, when the mail was delivered on Monday, Frau Thierse, poured a cup of tea and made her way to the sofa. There were the usual bills; water, trash, newspaper delivery, and a manila envelope addressed to her. She was surprised, because the return address was a high school in the state of Texas in America. She spoke English very well, but had no American friends in Texas.

She opened it and read the letter first:

"Dear Frau Thierse,

Enclosed you'll find images of your husband and Ms. Adolpha Hanish on the 18th of this month at her home. They seem to be quite friendly and I'm sure you'll agree, they are much more than just casual associates. I thought you should know of this. By the way, the woman lives at:

Frau Adolpha Hanish
123 Ahorn Straße
Frankfurt am Main, Deutschland
Your friend,
Hans."

She turned the envelope upside down and a good thirty 8X10 color images fell. The image on the very top was her husband, kissing a beautiful nude woman's breasts and the other images were obviously shot as they'd made love. In anger, she tossed the images on the sofa and stood. Since her husband was with the police, he kept a 9 mm handgun in the house. Anger overwhelmed her as she moved to the desk, removed the pistol and inserted a round into the chamber. She'd wait for the sonofabitch to get home, kill him, then kill the bitch he'd slept with, obviously on one of his many "business trips."

CHAPTER 19

James was worried about the chopper looking for them, and seeing an old barn on the side of the road, he had Nancy drive to the locked gate; he got out of the truck and cut the lock off with bolt cutters he carried. They then pulled the truck into the barn and closed the only half of the door still standing. There was a full moon out, so once out of town, Nancy had turned the lights off and driven in the dark. She was still able to see the gravel road in the bright moonlight. Frank and Ben got out, sniper rifles in their hands.

The chopper was nearing and the search lights on both sides were bright.

"You try to take the gunners out as I try for the pilot." Ben said.

"Will do, if I can." Frank replied and grinned.

It was then James clearly saw the truck tracks leading right to the barn.

The helicopter saw them too, because he dropped down to about 6 feet and the search lights were moving in all directions.

When the aircraft moved closer to the barn door, Joda yelled to be heard, "Now!"

Frank fired twice and the lights suddenly swung down to look at the ground under the bird. Ben could just barely see the pilot's head, and that was due to his console lights. He fired twice, once at the pilot and once at the co-pilot. He knew the pilot was dead, because his face and helmet had exploded. The co-pilot, unknown to Ben, had taken a round through the chest, out his back, then the bullet ricocheted in the cabin and struck him hard in the left thigh.

The chopper nose raised about eight feet and then suddenly fell to the ground. The aircraft landed hard, sending broken rotor blades in all directions, and a second after landing, a loud *whoof* was heard as the wreckage burst into flames. Two men were heard screaming and when James neared the co-pilot's door, his legs were trapped in the metal of the console panel. Knowing they'd never be able to free the man, Ben pulled his pistol and shot the man in the head. The second man, a door gunner was half in flames when pulled from the aircraft. As Nancy and James looked the man over, Frank and Ben took the two machine-guns and all the ammo. Frank also took two pairs of Night Vision Goggles (NVGs) in a case with spare batteries.

The guns and ammo were loaded in the truck as Nancy gave the lone survivor a shot of morphine. She then covered the injured man with a blanket she'd thrown in the truck earlier.

They then jumped in the truck. Frank had Nancy don a pair of goggles, and they continued to move toward camp.

Three nights later, using the battery powered TV, they tuned in a local station. They watched the weather and medical news, and then the reporter moved closer to home with the local news.

"The United States FBI was investigating a deadly pharmacy robbery which took place in Licking, a small town south of Rolla and off highway 63. Bubba Skaggs, the town sheriff, was shot twice, execution style, with one shot to the head. The Pharmacy lost every single prescription drug in the store, even those locked in a controlled substance room. The United States indicated it was an open act of terrorism."

The cameraman had footage of the stripped bare pharmacy shelves and then the smoking remains of the helicopter crash.

The reporter continued, "When a state police chopper responded to the pharmacy's calls for help, investigators were dropped off at the drug store, and the aircraft then followed a large truck they believed carried the suspects. At some point in the search, the chopper radioed they were taking fire. Officials have since learned the aircraft was shot down, with three out the four crew members killed. The survivor was given medical aid and morphine for his extensive burns by these criminals. The Missouri state police claim they have no reason to treat the robbery as a crime, because it was committed before the announcement of the official forming of the Conservative States of America. Because it is listed as an act of terrorism against the United States, not against the CSA, no charges will be sought. More news as it becomes available."

In the studio a man said, "The new Conservative States of America announced that they will not go to war, unless the United States invades them or demonstrates through an act of violence that they intend to harm the new nation. 'All we want, as a new nation, is to be left alone,' the first President of the Conservative States of America said. The words cast an eerie veil over the whole statement, because just prior to the first civil war, President Jefferson Davis had spoken similar words."

Joda said, "President Davis' exact words were, 'All we ask is to be left alone.'"

The news anchor said, "We now join Jim Braylock, as he covers a speech about to be given by the President any moment now."

The TV screen then switched to the new President of the United States who was walking to a podium with two advisers. He moved behind the microphone, took a sip of water and then cleared his throat.

"My fellow Americans, as of one day ago, a state of declared war exists between the United States of America and the Conservative States of America. I have asked the United Nations to assist us in our struggle and they have agreed. May God guide us as we take arms against our brothers, sisters, mothers and fathers. I have announced a state of martial law, which will remain in effect in our nation until such time as the Conservative States of America are brought back into the Union. With me enacting martial law, due process will be on hold until I announce otherwise. I will not take any questions at this time, and have work to do."

The camera zoomed in on the anchor man, who said, "The President of the Conservative States of America announced today that those individuals within our nation, including all officers of the law, must have the NWO chips removed immediately. In 60 days, those with the chips still installed will be listed as spies. Our government's primary concern is infiltration of spies from the USA. At this point, martial law has not been declared, which may change over time."

The newsman flipped a sheet of paper over, "And, finally, tonight in other news UN troops have gathered at both the Missouri and Kentucky borders for a possible invasion. Satellite images indicate over 250,000 men and women, most with arms, positioned ready to attack the two states. The Governors of both states say they are ready to fight, with the old US military in defensive positions and aircraft prepared to launch at a moment's notice."

When the station went to a commercial, James turned the TV off, surprised at what he'd just heard.

"Well," Nancy said, "they'll not be looking for us, and the chips won't happen here."

Gator said, "I'd not rush anything right now, and for damned sure ain't going home yet."

Ben moved from where he'd been standing and sat on the log. After a few seconds he said, "The possible invasion worries me. While the military sided with us, I'm not sure they'll have all they need to fight."

Joda said, "I'm sure some Conservative states, or those that left the union, may be surrounded by Union states."

"We don't even know, other than the old Southern states, who is in the CSA." James said.

"Well, from the news, we know Illinois is still in the USA and Kentucky ain't. On the Northeast coast, maybe New Hampshire is one, but the rest lean Liberal."

"I hope y'all realize we're not but a little over a hundred miles from the city of Saint Louis and the Mississippi River." James said, and then added, "But, first they have to cross the river."

"They're UN troops, so they have lots of gear and equipment." Joda said, then added a small log to their fire.

"They can have all they need, but they have two things against them. First, they are foreigners and second, they don't know the area like the natives do."

Nancy asked, "Should we leave then and return home?"

James thought for a minute, listening to the damp wood pop and crack in the flames before he said, "I can't just up and leave. I loved the United States and spent half my life serving her in uniform, but she's changed—and not for the good, either. She's immoral, corrupt, and controlling, and that that's not the country I served. Her politicians all act as if they've been bought and I think the CSA is worth fighting for, and dying for, if need be."

"I agree." Ben said, and few seconds later Frank and the rest of the men agreed.

"I don't think I was born a fighter," Nancy said, "but I'm sure my medical skills will be needed. So, I'm staying."

Donna hesitated, but finally said, "I'm sorry, James and all of you, but I'm no warrior."

"Neither am I." Carol Hall said.

"I'll leave." April said.

"Me too." Joan said and then added, "This is as rough as I've ever lived, and I don't like it."

Donna began to cry and said, "I . . . I'm just . . . not used to . . . this stuff."

James moved to her, kissed her, and said, "This, baby, has been easy. Usually in a war there are few of the comforts we have here. Every man here has served in the service, so we know what to expect, and right now this is a good life. I suggest, come morning, you take the mobile-home and go back to Texas. I don't suspect you'll be bothered now, not in Texas, and those damned Texicans will never surrender." He used *Texicans* instead of Texans to tease his Lubbock born wife.

She squeezed his hand and said, "I love you, James. I don't know what I did that made God send you into my life, but I'd do it again if I could."

"When you leave, Carol," Ben said, "make sure the kids never forget who their daddy is, okay?"

Soon the women were crying and the men were heard trying to reassure them, while Gator sat by the fire, watching. He had no one, not really, not since his wife had passed on. All the emotion going on around him watered his eyes and for a minute or two, he felt his heart breaking for these couples. Each and every one of them was a damned fine person.

Frank, wanting to end the emotional roller-coaster asked, "Hey old timer, ya going back with the women?"

"Who in the hell ya callin' an old timer? Me?"

"You're the oldest one here, ain't ya?"

"By God, I've half a mind to get up and lay a whoppin' on yer ass. Ya can tell 'em at the hospital an old timer done beat yer butt, but good."

"I'm teasing you, Gator. But, you've not said anything important yet."

"I'm thinkin', which ya young studs rarely do. Now that we're under the CSA, the abortions will end, except for special cases. I get sad every single time I think of the millions of babies that died under the flag of the United States of America. We committed genocide, no other way around it, and I pray God will forgive us for not stopping it."

"Abortions were legal." Nancy said.

"Does legal make it right? At one time ownin' slaves was legal too, but we all know that was wrong. In the 1800's it was legal for a white man to kill black folks, Injuns, and Mexicans all day long, and he was breaking no laws. We all know murder, of anyone, is wrong. The sad part is, the Democrats were the power behind all of these social illnesses. Now, a little girl has to get permission to take an aspirin given by her school nurse, with a note from a doctor, but that same little girl can go see a doctor after school and have an abortion without telling anyone. It's so wrong."

"I didn't say it was right, I said it was legal."

"I hear'd ya. My wife told me, oh, maybe a year before we married that she'd had an abortion when she was only 16. I never held that against her, because it was her daddy's idea, and she was just a kid when it happened. I discovered after we were married I didn't need to hold it against her, because she was hard enough on herself. She'd cry at times over the loss of that baby and there wasn't a damned thing I could do for her."

"Some women suffer and others don't at all." Nancy said, while growing uncomfortable discussing this with Gator, only she didn't know why.

The old man's eyes clearly showed pain when he said, "Just before my wife's last breath, she prayed and asked God to forgive her for killing her first child. Now, ain't that one hell of a note? Think of the millions of doctors, lawyers and other intelligent folks those abortions killed. Lots of women used to say, 'Don't tell me what to do with my body.' Seems they forgot the fetus is not their body, but a separate body and of a unique individual. The only difference between an abortion and murder is the age of the victim, and one is legal. Killing is killing, in my eyes."

Silence.

James, not liking the conversation but against abortions, finally said, "Once home, each of you will need to call us so we don't worry about you. Do not pick up any strangers and use some common sense. Openly carry your guns; we're the CSA now, and I know carrying guns is legal. I have no idea how food prices are, cost of power and utilities, or anything in Texas right now. Donna, I suggest later tonight you call your momma and get an idea of what you'll be facing."

"I think by taking turns driving, you can make it home without stopping, except for gas, and expect a good twenty to thirty dollars a gallon."

"I expect that."

"Then once in Houston, fill the tanks up again, because the flow of gas may stop or the prices may go even higher."

"Now," said Ben, "I suspect tonight after supper, we can all have a few beers. It may be months, or years, before we all see each other again."

And some of us may be dead was thought by all, but said by none.

The next morning, the mobile home was idling as the women loaded their bags and took a seat. Most of the gear and equipment stayed behind for those left to do the fighting. Tears were flowing on both sides as Donna kissed James and then made her way to the driver's seat. She then closed the door and drove away.

The men slowly made their way back to camp.

"I think," Joda said, "we need to let the authorities know we're here."

"No, I disagree, because if we do that, they might put us on a list, or in some damned computer, and who knows who'll get a copy."

"The world is falling apart all around us, and you suggest we do what?"

"Park our asses and wait. The damned Yankee Liberals will get at least this far with their invasion. Remember, we're just a few miles, 103 miles exactly, from Saint Louis. It's a fairly Liberal city too, so they'll be here soon. They'll want to take Fort Leonard Wood, if nothing else. I feel, the fewer folks that know about us, the better."

"If you think it's safer."

Nancy said, "Even our enemies aren't thinking like themselves. When we found Ben, he was a mental mess, with the chip monitoring his body and mind. The New World Order doesn't care about anyone but their leader. All the rest of us are expendable."

James said, "I'll bet if you told the average person about the NWO, they'd think you're crazy, because they trust our government to protect them. What they don't realize is our politicians have sold out to the highest bidder. Hell, the last one that refused to sell out was Kennedy and you know what happened to him, only it wasn't Lee Harvey Oswald that killed him, he was the scapegoat. He was killed by an NWO sniper."

"That's pretty heavy thinking." Gator said.

"The NWO is patient and they've been around since the early 1700's influencing history in many ways. At first, everyone thought the NWO was actually the Masons, except that isn't true. If they can wait this long, they'll do what it takes when they finally do grab for keeps." Ben said, and then meeting the eyes of Frank, he added, "Keep your sniper rifle close, brother, because I suspect when the UN comes, it'll leave a lot of pretty little blue helmets with bloody holes in them."

That evening over a supper fire with darkness falling over the land, Gator said, "Oh, shit. Look to the east."

All heads turned to look in that direction and at times small dim flashes of light were seen. Some of the lights were brighter than others.

"The shit has hit the stump! Turn on the TV and let's get an update."

The TV was switched on and a serious looking anchor man was in the local station. He read a bit and then his eyes met the camera.

"If you've just joined us, the war between the United States and the Conservative States of America has started. Approximately two hours ago, the US launched a UN amphibious assault across the Mississippi River, landing on the shores of Saint Louis, and met little resistance. Our Marines and Army have been rushed to the river, just as word of an airborne invasion west of the city has been reported. Initial reports have the paratroopers landing as far west as the Gasconade River, in central Missouri. I take you now to Lynn Combs, who is on the scene in Saint Louis. Lynn?"

A black woman wearing a helmet and flack vest popped on the TV screen, "Howard, I'm standing less than a half a block from current fighting and it is gruesome. Initial reports by our military stated that we have experienced a little over 1,500 deaths and the enemy at least double that. However, the military released a statement saying, and I quote, 'Tanks and troops led by CSA commander General Thomas A. Jackson, have pierced the Union lines in a bold move. His thrust was from Iowa into Illinois, and his last report stated he's just south of Chicago. He reports resistance is stiff, but the enemy is withdrawing to the big windy city.' End of quote. The General was ordered across the river from where he'd been staging, minutes after the report of a Union invasion being attempted. As usual, when performing an amphibious landing, our Marines led the way. They are also spearheading the attack on Chicago. I repeat, both the

Conservative States of America and the UN led United States military have attempted amphibious landings, with the UN on our soil, but still within a block of the Mississippi River. CSA forces are in the middle of Illinois, grouping for an attack on the Windy City. This is Lynn Combs for Channel 9, 'for all your latest news.'"

"Medical centers are reporting hospitals are overflowing with wounded in our city and the Saint Louis Mayor has his hands full, using school gyms and other city facilities as makeshift hospitals. There has been a call for all types of blood, and you can give blood at any one of the medical centers around town."

The camera switched to a man standing at the main gate at Fort Leonard Wood.

"This is breaking news, with Howard Miles. Authorities at Fort Leonard Wood just announced they are under heavy attack by UN paratroopers. While you can obviously see the attack was not made on the main gate, officials tell us they are being attacked on the east and south sides of this huge training center. If you listen, you can clearly hear the pop of small arms fire and the boom of cannons."

The camera panned to the east, and since it was dark, flashes from explosions were clearly seen. After a few seconds the camera returned to the reporter.

"Authorities at the base claim that UN paratroopers are scattered all over the Ozark Mountains, in Missouri and Arkansas. If you see them, you are urged to call your local law enforcement agency. We have reports of attacks at the university in Rolla, a report of an attack on the police station in Cuba, the takeover of a hospital in Bourbon, and witnesses have seen large groups of men wearing blue helmets throughout the Southern part of the state. Again, paratroopers are reportedly scattered throughout the Missouri and Arkansas Ozark Mountains. Call the police, if you see any troops with blue helmets. This is Howard Miles, reporting. Back to you in the studio, John."

"The Governor of Missouri just moments ago declared an emergency and has initiated martial law in the state until this invasion is beaten back. Off and on all day, this martial law decree will be reported by the Emergency Broadcasting Center on your televisions and radios. This is not a test. The Conservative States of America have been invaded by the United States. Please stay tuned to WXXB, Channel 9, 'for all your latest news.'"

When a commercial came on, the TV was turned off.

"Damn," said James, "what a mess."

"Hush, I hear something!" Joda said just above a whisper as he raised the coffee pot and poured the contents on their fire.

CHAPTER 20

Frau Thierse remained on the sofa when she heard the front door open. She'd placed the images from the United States in an envelope and left it on the table beside his recliner. She was on her third bottle of wine and feeling no pain. Beside her, under a newspaper, her husband's 9mm lay with a shell in the chamber ready to fire. The safety was off.

"Good evening, my dear." he said as he tossed his briefcase on an overstuffed leather chair and then moved to his recliner. He pulled a thin blanket up and around his waist.

"Good evening, and how was your day?" she asked as she met his eyes.

She is mad, he thought, but said, "It was work, just another day at work." He picked up the mail and began going through it. Seeing the envelope, he picked it up and the images fell out. He saw it was photos of him and Adolpha, and his heart skipped a few beats. *No wonder she's pissed, oh damn!*

"Explain the images."

"T . . . they must have used a graphics program to, uh, change the head on the man."

She raised the pistol and said, "No, you are lying. See, they can change the head on the man, but that is your penis in the photograph. Do you think after all these years, I'd not recognize that small issue? I have her address, too."

"Put the gun down. This is not worth going to prison over."

"I'll keep the gun and as for going to prison, that will never happen. See, I have a reservation with the devil and he's going to provide me a place to stay. Goodbye, you —"

The Boss fired his pistol through the thin blanket on his lap, saw the bullet strike his wife in the center of the chest, and the wall behind her was instantly splattered with blood, as the bullet continued on to strike his bookcase.

She gave a loud moan when the bullet struck her, jerked the trigger on her pistol, and smiled as the bullet struck him in the chest, as well.

He felt the bullet punch a hole through his chest and his pain was severe. He was surprised his wife was still standing. He knew he had to put her down or she'd kill him, if she hadn't already. Pulling his pistol out from under the blanket, he fired twice, both bullets hitting her hard. The first bullet hit her low, about an inch below her belly button, while the last bullet struck her in the face, blowing shards of bone out the back of her skull and splattering the wall with gore, blood, and brain tissue. She fell like she'd run into a clothesline.

As his wife jerked and trembled, her body shutting down, he bandaged himself as well as he could and then moved to his car. As soon as he started the engine, he drove to Adolpha's home, knowing she'd help him.

She lived close, less than 10 kilometers away, but by the time he got there, he was weak from blood loss. He parked his car, walked to her front door and rang the doorbell. As he waited for a response his world turned from light to gray, and then slowly changed from gray to black. He knew no more.

Hearing a slight noise, the Boss opened his eyes to find himself on a stretcher, mounted to the wall of a private jet, because he heard the engines. Raising his head, he looked around and said, "Wasser?"

"Oh, good, you've come around. Here, is some water, but just a little for right now." she gave him a few sips from a paper cup. "You've been shot, and you're currently on your way to a hospital in England, where I have an important meeting with the NWO."

"Why am I not in Frankfurt? They have hospitals there, too." he asked, his mind dazed by his injury.

"The police were looking for you and the charge was murder, but it was never publicized on the television or in the newspapers. They found your wife dead, shot three times. They easily checked the ballistics and the bullets that took her life were fired from your service pistol. I found the pistol on you when I answered my door. A badly burned man with a dental chart identical to yours was found with a single gunshot to his head. He also set a timer on a bomb in his car and it went off, blowing him to pieces. You are officially listed as dead."

"She had photos of you and I having sex, but how is that possible?"

Adolpha laughed and said, "It's good she didn't see the movie, I think."

"Movie? Have you lost your mind?"

"I'm a woman who likes watching myself pleasing men. When I make love to a man in my bed, I have cameras installed that take photographs from different locations, and angles. Later when I'm alone, I watch them to enjoy the faces of my lovers, as well as all the hot action. You, my lover, were one of the best and as soon as you heal, I will bring a big smile to your face again. I suspect someone on my staff, maybe the butler or my driver sold the images. Since the US sent the images to your wife, perhaps the images were sold to the CIA. I will have both men removed and eliminated."

"What am I to do now?"

"Your name has changed and you are now Paul Runkle, with a complete history behind your name. Your other information remains the same, except you are a retired German General, of the Air Force. In the UK, you will be hospitalized and when discharged, you will be well provided for. The NWO considers you too important to eliminate, so you'll be provided a solid cover. Your job with us will continue as usual, once you are strong again."

"What of my reputation and my children?"

"You and your wife were buried two days ago, side by side in your family cemetery. Your children, all of them, have lawyers and are busy fighting over your estate. I find them colder than a hired killer. The television news released that criminals broke into your home, killed you and your wife, but not before you killed both of them. The penitentiary provided us with two men, who we simply shot and then dumped in your home. The police know the difference, but a little money helped them to forget. Everything in life comes with a cost."

"Why all that trouble and expense for me?"

"You, General Runkle, are to be the new leader of the North American Union, NAU, once finalized. I will run the European Union so we'll be working close together at times, very, very close, if I get my way." She then gave a sexy laugh. Meeting his eyes, she added, "I am glad the NWO has need of you, because I have need of you as well. I think once you are out of the hospital, you need a sexy woman to spend some time with you. I think a visit from me will help you heal faster."

"Perhaps it might just do that. Tell someone I have pain, please."

Adolpha called for a doctor and minutes later, the Boss was asleep.

The President of the United States was speaking to the press outdoors, when a sudden gust of wind blew his notes from the podium. He bent over to pick them up when he heard a scream behind him and two men fell, the same bullet striking both of them. Two Secret Service agents were suddenly on the President, as helicopters in the air and police officers on the ground moved toward the building holding the sniper.

"Roger that, we have two down." an agent said as he stood beside the President.

The screaming continued, because both men had taken painful injuries.

An EMT ran up on stage and minutes later the yelling stopped.

Shots were heard off in the distance and then a police radio said, "The suspect is hit and down. I repeat, the suspect is down and he has been hit."

The agents moved off of the President, stood and then helped their boss to his feet.

The President gave both men a pat on the back and said, "Thank you both. I'll see you're taken good care of in the future."

His aide appeared and said, "We have two bystanders down. One was your press secretary, down with a bullet through his hips, and the other was an Army General, who took what was left of the bullet in the left thigh, shattering the bone. Initial estimates, from the medics, is the same .50 caliber round struck both men."

"Where was the sniper at?"

"See that tall building almost a mile off? Just to the left of it is a smaller building. The chopper spotted him on the roof at first, but he was caught on the ground minutes later and I was told he was killed."

"From now on, no more press meetings outside." the President said, and then walking to the microphone said, "Due to the attempt on my life here today, this press meeting is canceled. I ask all of you, and your viewers or readers, to pray for my press secretary, Tobis Jones, and, uh, General David James Carson. I understand both men were struck, but I have no other information at this time."

The President walked to his limo, climbed inside and immediately poured a glass of strong amber colored bourbon. He knocked it back and refilled his glass, intending to sip on this one.

His aide and wife entered and the vehicle started.

The driver asked, "Where to, Mr. President?"

"Uh, back to the White House."

"While you were speaking, ISIS has taken more of Iraq and they executed another five hundred Christians."

"Look, I have my damned hands full here as it is, so what do you expect me to do?"

"Uh, well, I have no idea, sir. I'm just letting you know what happened while you were busy. I do this all the time."

"I'm sorry, John. I've got a war on my hands, one we're not doing so well in, I might add. Muslims killing Christians, rebels in

Africa kidnapping young girls to use as sex slaves, Muslims rioting in the United Kingdom, riots by everyone in California, and I'm just tired of all this crap."

"I can understand, sir. Do you still want to speak with Lieutenant General Dalston at noon?"

"Oh, yes, because I'm pushing his promotion through Congress, and he will be my overall allied leader and Commander for this war. He's got the military skills, the guts and the intelligence to make things happen. I'm pushing for him to be promoted to the highest level as General, five stars."

"I think General Dalston is well qualified for the position, sir."

"Also, I want my daily military briefing moved up an hour, along with the weather and security meetings."

They pulled into a long avenue that went by the White House, when suddenly anti-aircraft guns began to spit lead in the sky, missiles were launched from the front lawn, and cannon shells struck the road in front of them, throwing concrete over ten feet into the air.

Picking up his phone the President pushed #1 and a voice answered, "Yes, sir?"

The sound of a jet passing low and fast drowned out all communications for a minute and then a loud explosion made the world shake, so the President had to yell to be heard, "What in the hell is happening at the White House?"

"We're under attack by the CSA, sir!"

There came a sonic boom and then UN aircraft entered the fight.

"Quickly, as they're busy, drive us to the back door, hurry." the President ordered.

Just as they entered the gate, another loud explosion was heard and, looking around, they saw nothing. Raising the phone, he asked, "What was that noise?"

"One of the UN jets crashed on the avenue you were just on and blew up, sir."

"I see smoke out of my window." the First Lady said.

"Okay, into the house *now!*" an agent said as he opened the limo door.

As they moved for the house, the aide noticed where bullets had struck the specially armored limo and knocked the paint off. He gave an involuntary shudder.

Once in the building, the agents moved them by battery powered elevator ten stories below, to a bunker. Once in the bunker the President moved to his war room and listened to the communications between the UN aircraft.

"Bogey at your twelve O'clock high, Falcon two."

"Roger, Eagle One, returning to base."

"Eagle One, your engines are smoking badly and I don't think you'll make it."

"Break right, break, break! Damn you, break right!"

Turning the volume down, the President realized he'd become like Adolf Hitler in his final days in his bunker. That angered him, because he wanted to be on the offensive. In the room with him were General officers and an admiral from each branch of the services; ignoring them, the President picked up the microphone and said, "Attention, Attention all United Nations aircraft. This is the President of the United States. I humbly ask you to make the Conservatives pay highly for this attack on my home and the home of all Americans. I am safe, so do your duties. Remember, the NWO is depending on all of us."

Once he released the mic button, bullets were heard striking aircraft, with the sounds of guns and cannons loud. The yelling of warnings and directions to fly continued to be screamed over the radio.

"Mayday, mayday, mayday, this is Bear Three One. I'm going down, I repeat, I'm going down now!"

"Eject, Bear!"

"He's out! To the left at about 5,000 feet."

"He's got a good chute."

"Cut the chatter on the radio. Keep it professional."

"Pull up, Gator two six, up!"

"Got the bastard! Hoooaaahhh!"

"Gator two six just impacted on the White House lawn. I saw his canopy fly off, but the ejection seat never fired."

"Negative, I have two parachutes at about three angles, near the nine O'clock position."

"All of us, protect them on the way down. Protect Bear too, second flight!" The loud whine of engines was heard.

"Hawk Three-four, break left, bogey on your six."

"Jesus, Bear's parachute is in flames!"

"Flames? Must be the heat from the burning buildings and the gas stations."

"Roger that, because I see no CSA aircraft in our area. Falcon two just shot the last one down."

"This is the tower, all bogeys are currently leaving California. The air space over the entire state will soon be clear."

"My God, he's going to fall any second now!"

"Just a bit more, Bear Three One!"

"He's on the ground and on his feet! Bear Three One is safely on the ground!"

The sound of an emergency beeper on guard was heard and then 15 seconds later, Bear said, "This is Bear Three One and I'm safely on the ground, but I'd not like to experience that again."

"Bear this is Falcon One, and I have notified Search and Rescue. They are sending a chopper, but ask you to move away from the flames, to the avenue in front of the White House."

"Roger, will do, but tell the rescue bird I need some clean underwear, out."

"Falcon One, this is the President, can you give me an estimate of losses on both sides?"

"Uh, roger, sir. I can report that our losses were seven aircraft and they lost two birds, sir."

"We suffered seven losses to their two? Once you land, Colonel, I will have a car waiting for you. I want you to brief me on how we can prevent losses like this in the future. President out."

"Uh, yes, sir." Falcon One replied and all knew the Boss was in for an ass chewing.

"The air space over the entire state is clear. I repeat, all enemy traffic is clear over the state. All UN aircraft return to base."

"Roger, copy tower let's go home, boys."

The President cocked his head to the left and turning to the Air Force General he asked, "From what you heard, General, how can we improve our attacks?"

"Sir, I think it's crucial you understand our forces were outnumbered over three to one. It appears a few CSA planes were kept flying high over their ground attack and when our aircraft appeared to defend the White House, they had the advantage of not only altitude, but speed as well. Imagine them as Hawks diving on birds or fish. Using that tactic, from the German Air Force and learned during the second World War, it gave them a great advantage, not to mention their overall superior numbers."

"Mister President?" his aide said.

"Yes?'

"Radar has detected flights of B-1s, B-52s, and even C-130s on a direct course for the state. Our intelligence thinks it's a bombing raid, and they plan to carpet bomb the White House."

"Are all aircraft heading here?"

"No, sir, not yet. The aircraft are approaching from all directions except west, sir."

"General, get everything that can fly and fight into the air and do it now, by God!"

The Air Force General walked to the President and said, "Sir, you and the First Lady need to leave this bunker now. There is a tunnel in here that leads to a spot by a river. The exit is well camouflaged, and in a parking lot near you'll find four black armored SUVs. Your aide will have the keys. I suggest you, the First Lady, your driver, aide, and at least six Secret Service agents leave, and now."

"Why the rush? I mean you make this sound like they'll drop nukes on me and I don't see that happening."

The C-130s may carry "daisy cutters," which were used in Vietnam and Afghanistan. The bomb has the ability to flatten a forest into a helicopter landing zone. It's a 15,000 pound (6,800 kg) conventional bomb, delivered from a C-130 and if they drop a few here, you will want to be someplace else. Then, again, they might use a MOAB bomb, which is 22,600 pounds and the blast area is 500 feet. Used or planned to be used against soft to medium targets, it will flatten the White House and all surrounding support buildings, including the air conditioners, power, communications, and water to this bunker."

"What of all the people in the bunker, then?"

"We have emergency backup systems for 24 hours. Once the backup systems come on, I'll have the troops use the same tunnel you used to leave, sir. Of course, all electronics, classified and other high security items will either be destroyed or brought with us. We have thermite grenades to ruin the gear left behind. Now, go, sir, and stay safe. I have no idea of the kind of damage a MOAB can do here."

"John?"

"Here, Mr. President."

"Get the First Lady and a half dozen Secret Service Agents; we need to leave. Be sure to bring the keys to the black SUVs parked near the tunnel. Hurry; I understand there is some danger coming and quickly, too."

Minutes later the hatch covering the tunnel had the padlock unlocked and a code was punched into the keypad. The numbers all turned green and the door opened. The small party left the bunker and moved into the tunnel. Electric lights lit the way and about half way to the exit, the ground shook violently, the lights went out and then came back on, but noticeably dimmer.

One of the agents said, "The main power source has been wiped out, and we're on auxiliary power."

Seconds later, there came another shaking and dust and cracked concrete fell from the roof of the tunnel. The First lady screamed, her eyes large in fear.

"Ma'am, you're safe. The bunker and this tunnel were developed to survive a nuke attack. We're all safe." The same agent spoke again.

They began to trot to the exit, having heard the agent's words, but not even he believed them.

CHAPTER 21

"I hear armor, but it must be ours, right?" Frank whispered.

"Tanks and such could have been dropped using Low Altitude Parachute Extraction System (LAPES). It's easily done, and all they need is an open field." Joda said.

Frank strained his eyes to see better, then remembered the NVGs he'd taken from the crashed helicopter. He ran to the supply cabin, pulled the NVGs and handed one pair to Ben.

He donned the goggles and then whispered, "Three tanks, and they're bad guys. It looks to me like they're looking for a place to spend the night."

"Let them stay here and we'll surprise them later this evening."

Ben said, "I see troops too, maybe a platoon or more of infantry."

The tanks were heard to stop moving and then the engines went into idle. Orders were heard, but it was too far away to clearly hear what was said. Minutes later, the engines stopped. When James took a peek, he saw a big 'UN' on each tank.

"Captain!"

"Yes, sir?"

"Have the men dig in close to the tanks. Have their holes deep enough so if we get into a fight, our tanks can drive right over them. Tell them if they are not deep enough, they'll be buried in a pizza box back home."

"I will tell them, Colonel."

Frank whispered to Ben, "Let them go to work, and near midnight we'll visit our friends. I suspect after the adrenaline of a combat jump, walking for most of the day, and then digging holes, our friends will be tired tonight. Once they are asleep, we'll try to take the tanks out. I want the keys in the vehicles, including the deuce and a half, ready to go. Even if we knock out the tanks, the ground troops will hit us hard at daylight. Everything of any value should be packed now, but absolutely no noise."

Once all of importance was packed away, mostly in the big truck, they moved into the trees near the edge of the clearing, where they could keep an eye on the enemy. Near midnight the last man finished his foxhole and then dropped into it for some much needed sleep. They'd heard the order given for fifty percent of the troops to stay alert.

As prior military men, all those in the trees watching knew staying awake after jumping from an aircraft, combat, and moving all day, the fifty percent alert would actually drop to about 15 or 20 percent, as fatigue visited each man. Near 0300 hours, they'd strike the tanks.

Little movement was seen but snores were heard, as well as someone mumbling in their sleep. The time passed slowly, but James was excited, because all three M1A1 Abrams Tanks had their hatches open. If they could get close enough to drop some grenades Ben had brought with him, then they'd take all of the heavy beasts out. Tom would man the M-60 machine-gun taken recently from the chopper they'd downed at the barn, while Nancy would be his ammo person.

Each of them carried a couple of Molotov cocktails, so they'd not use all the grenades they had. No one had any idea when they'd get more military supplies and explosives, if ever. The plan was for James, Joda, and Dick to drop a Molotov cocktail down an open hatch, followed by a grenade. It was hoped that the resulting explosion and fire would cause the ammo and fuel to explode, thus destroying the tank. The key was for all of them to release the grenades at almost the same time.

Later, glancing at his watch, James said, "Time to move. Frank and Ben, if you see anyone moving after the fighting starts, take them out. Especially if they are an officer or senior NCO."

"We'll keep them off your back and our rifles have silencers, so even as you move forward, I'll have your back covered. I'll use Ben as a spotter, well, at least until you mount the tanks."

Looking at Joda and Dick, James then said, "The key here is for all of us to drop our grenades at the same time. Even if we come under fire, we all drop at the same time. Understood?"

Both men nodded and then they followed James as he crawled toward the tanks. The leader felt his heart pounding in his ears and his senses were finely tuned, looking for any danger. He heard or felt nothing from the men sleeping in the fox holes. He hoped the snipers and M-60 would keep them safe, but things always went wrong in combat, always.

All three made it to their tank because they'd moved slowly, and had camouflage makeup on their faces, necks and hands, provided by Ben. When James was on his tank, he squatted by the turret to wait for the others. After all three were on their tanks, James threw his Molotov cocktail as hard as he could down the hatch, but the rag had not been lit.

He pulled the pin from his grenade, looked at the other two men and they were ready, too. He tossed the grenade at the same time a tank crew member asked, "What was that noise? I smell gas."

James jumped from the big heavy tank and took off running behind the other two men. Rifles began to pop, but they were coming from the trees. The first tank suddenly exploded, sending flames out of the open hatches and making the area as light as day. A bullet *zinged* by James' ear just as he reached the trees. When he glanced at the tanks, thick black smoke and fire were rolling into each other above the burning vehicles.

The second tank gave a huge *ka-boom* as it exploded and sent the turret high into the air, twisting and turning as it ascended toward some low clouds. The third tank shot off with a loud explosion, the turret lifting about six feet, as the flames shot out of the hatches and the round spot on its body where the turret usually rested. Two men, their foxholes too close to the tanks, stood and stumbled around, aflame as they screeched in pain. A silent shot from Ben killed one, but he couldn't see the other, and apparently Frank wasn't going to waste a shot on his burning man.

Less than three minutes later the man, still in flames from splashed fuel, fell to his knees, and fell forward onto his face in the grass, his pain finally gone.

Then the three tanks began to have secondary explosions as the fuel, ammo, and other combustibles went up in flames. The dug in soldiers were firing into the woods now, their bullets clipping small limbs and leaves from the trees. At times a bullet would strike a rock, causing a loud *p-zing* as it ricocheted off into space.

Jerry was good on the M-60, firing in short spurts and careful not to burn the barrel out. James made his way around the burning tanks, which were sending thick black oily smoke into the air. The earlier light had diminished, but thanks to the burning tanks, enough light remained for him to man the other machine-gun. As he moved behind the powerful gun, he could clearly see the silhouettes of the troops against the burning tanks.

Dick was his ammo man, and his job was to make sure the bullets fed into the gun without twisting or jamming.

James pulled the trigger, smiled at the familiar recoil, and then began looking for targets. They were killing now on both sides of the tanks, and it was bloody work. One man, a grenade in hand, stood and ran for Jerry.

"I got 'em." Ben said, and then sent a bullet to pierce the man's head, hitting him almost between the eyes. His skull flew apart, gore splattering behind him. He struck the ground hard, and seconds later the grenade exploded.

A man with a radio in his hand sat up as he placed a call requesting air support, then took three rounds in the middle of his chest, all striking him within split seconds of each other. He crumbled to the bottom of his hole, where he felt the cool soil against his face. Then his vision went from light, to gray and finally faded into black. He gave a long sigh and then died.

Over time, the gunfire from the foxholes slowed and then stopped.

"Stay in position until daylight, then we'll check them. There still may still be some of them alive, so stay smart and safe." James yelled as he took his forefinger off the machine-gun trigger. A white tinge of smoke lifted from the barrel of his weapon to the skies. The smell of burnt flesh was so strong, Nancy turned her head to the left and puked until she began to dry-heave. The sound of the others retching was heard in the woods.

Glancing at the only dead man James could see clearly, it was the man who'd burned to death and his body was in a fetal position, with his hands pulled close to his chest and his fingers curled. Smoke still rose from his blackened form.

Right at dawn, James called out, "Move forward slowly and if you have movement, shoot."

On his side of the tank, a young trooper suddenly stood and made a run for the trees. He almost made it, but Ben's sniper rifle fired, and his scream was loud as the bullet punched a hole through his back and out his chest. A long finger of blood followed the bullet out the front of his chest. The man fell to his side and began kicking at the grasses as his fingers clawed the soil. Less than a minute later, he gave a loud sigh and died.

Two more shots were heard and then James saw a trooper aiming a pistol at him, probably an officer, and then Frank's rifle popped. The man fell unnaturally to land half in and half out his hole.

"Gather all the gear; boots, rifles, knives, ammo, helmets, all of it. Toss it all in the truck and let's get the hell out of here. Let's move, people, the army will send someone to look for these men when they don't call in this morning."

Dick was removing the boots off the feet of a young man, when he suddenly felt a hard blow, and he was knocked on his ass. He heard someone yell for a medic, but he knew Nancy was all they had. Seconds later he heard two shots and then the face of Nancy appeared.

"H . . . he shot . . . me." Dick managed to get out, because the pain was getting stronger now.

"I'm going to give you some morphine to stop your pain, okay?"

An hour later, as the small convoy moved down the dirt and gravel back roads of the Ozarks, James and Nancy, in the truck, were talking.

Between them on the seat, was the captured radio, which would, hopefully, help them avoid roadblocks or check points the US may have established. They were driving parallel to the big Piney River, maybe 100 feet from the riverbanks, close to Fort Leonard Wood, and Devil's Elbow. The countryside was surrounded by high bluffs and just a mile or so further, on their right, was a huge cave James was moving toward, to use as a temporary base camp. They would drive to the end of the bluff, take the next dirt road to the right and then cut across country. They'd eventually come to the top of the cave, leave the vehicles camouflaged there, and then live in the cave. Since they'd leave most of the supplies in the truck and cars, they'd need a guard on top to keep an eye on things.

Thanks to the dead men around the tanks, they now had M4'ss and plenty of ammo. They'd also taken mines, a flamethrower, and other gear from the foxholes. Each man was carrying 10 of the Meals Ready to Eat, MREs, and Nancy had picked up a field surgical first aid kit.

"How far can we see from the top of this cave?"

"On clear days, for miles and miles, but it all depends on the weather. Today looks like rain, so I'm sure later this afternoon when the rains come, we'll not see as far. We'll be able to watch the river and the road below us. You can reach the cave by walking on the loose shale and sandstone rocks, but they'll slide down and make a hell of a racket. No one can gain access to the cave without us knowing they're coming."

"Is there a way out of the place?"

"You can come in the front door or out the back, but the back way takes some crawling and time. You'll come out near where we'll park."

"How much further?"

"Half a mile maybe."

Suddenly the radio came alive, "Base this is Gray Wolf, over."

"Uh, go Gray Wolf."

"Be advised that all three tanks are destroyed, and infantry as well. I count 39 bodies, with one man missing. I repeat 3 . . . 9 . . . KIA. No Charlie Sierra Able bodies found. Add the tank crews as well, because they've been blown to bits. That will change our KIA count to 48, over."

"Roger, our KIA is 48."

"Wait one."

The base, or headquarters radioman, gave the general the KIA count and the man went insane with anger.

"Uh, base, Gray Wolf, and we have found the missing man. The platoon Sergeant claims a group of about a dozen partisans struck the tanks first, then caught the men guarding in a cross-fire, killing them. I'd let you speak with him, but he has a sucking chest wound and is being treated."

"Gray Wolf, this is Base Actual. Can you tell what in the hell happened out there?" the General asked.

"It appears the tank crews were all asleep and most likely the infantry too, sir. I don't think they expected to be hit. From what I've seen, the partisans had one man injured."

"So you're telling me 48 of my people were killed by about a dozen of the enemy, and it *might* have cost them one life?"

"That's about the size of it, from what I see here, sir."

Long minutes passed.

"Gray Wolf, Base. The old man was as mad as a wet hen when he left for his office. I'd hate to be an officer at the afternoon staff meeting."

"Roger that. Tell our ride home we need a pick up, but it will take some time with 48 body bags, over."

"I copy, and they're on their way. I'll have the chopper flight leader contact you when they near. Out."

Nancy and James both grinned, but he said, "There will be some serious ass chewing at the staff meeting, and our odds of ever catching a whole tank crew asleep again will be low after today."

"Dick was alive a bit ago, but he was hit hard. I don't think he'll make it, not really."

"We need to park here in these trees and then check the cave out closely. We're home."

"Sir, the newspapers in Germany report the death of the man and woman who lived at the address where you sent the photographs, except intelligence states one coffin was empty —the man's. The papers say a criminal shot the man we called the Boss, who in turn shot the robber, and they both died. It seems two criminals and both of the others were killed. One reporter claims the discovery of a stack of photographs, which were compromising for the gentleman, sir. There is a big legal battle over the estate by the children, because a great deal of wealth is involved. The woman was definitely killed and the man is suspected by our intelligence of being flown to the United Kingdom for treatment. They discovered a man who looks like him in a British hospital and he's being kept under watch by an agent that works as a nurse."

"Excellent; so perhaps I forced the Boss to retire, then."

"I have no idea, but I will have our intelligence report the condition of his health. If he is healthy, do you want him eliminated?"

The President thought for a moment and then said, "Yes, but it must look like either an accident or not be traceable to us."

"I'll see to this immediately, sir."

Ten minutes later, in the UK a cellphone rang, "Hello."

"Eliminate the German Air Force General."

"It shall be done by morning." She heard the line go dead.

Silvia Ball was a nurse working the same floor as General Paul Runkle. She was to go on shift in about fifteen minutes. She removed a plastic container from her locker, as well as a syringe. She placed them both in her lab coat pocket.

She signed in, got her briefing from the nurse she was replacing and went over the patient charts, seeing the General was improving, but sleeping a lot. She moved down the hallway checking each patient as she always did when coming on every morning shift.

When she entered the General's room he was sleeping, so she moved to his IV and inserted the syringe, dispensing venom from the brown recluse spider. She had a 35 ml Monoject Syringe filled with the poison, so slightly over an ounce entered the bag. She then placed a dead brown recluse spider from the plastic container she carried, in bed with him. She'd killed the spider in the locker room and brought it here for just this reason. She walked from the room.

Near an hour later, as she was adjusting the drip on an IV of another patient she heard the speaker system announce, "We have a code blue in room 103. I repeat a code blue in room 103."

As a member of the code blue team, she moved to the General's room to assist in trying to save his life. The doctor ran in, jerked the blanket off, and the spider seemed to jump in the air.

"Spider!" the doctor exclaimed, and took a leap back.

The nurse ran to the brown recluse stepped on it, and then moved to the General. Glancing at a wall of machines monitoring him she yelled, "Heart attack! Get the paddles now!"

The doctor, over his initial fear of the spider now, moved forward and took control.

The venom injected was more than enough, because the paddles did no good and his heartbeat remained a steady unmoving line on the monitor.

After 45 minutes, the doctor brought it all to an end when he said, "Since the spider was in his bed, I want an autopsy performed on this man. George, I want you to gather the spider's remains in a urine specimen bottle and have them looked over closely. I hope there is no correlation between the spider and this man's death, but there may be. For the sake of the hospital let's hope they are unrelated, because the last thing we need is for the word to get out we have spiders in our healthcare facility."

"Yes, sir."

The nurse went about her normal shift work, knowing in some way she'd just assisted the CSA in removing a dangerous man.

Once her shift was finished, as she returned home walking in the rain, she didn't see the man walking half a block behind her. She entered her apartment, changed and then dialed a number. The man behind her had simply followed her to her door by the dripped water on the brown carpet in the hallway. He listened by the door.

"Mother Hen here, and the problem is gone."

"Great, do you think anyone suspects you? If so, I can bring you here."

"No reason to suspect me, but of course I'll eventually be questioned by the police."

The man outside the door slowly turned her doorknob and discovered the door was locked. Taking his lock picking tools from his coat pocket, he turned the deadbolt. He turned the door handle once more and it opened. Pulling a 9 mm with a silencer, he carefully stepped inside. He heard her still talking.

He walked toward the bedroom, heard her voice growing louder and suspected she was changing or something. At the door, he stopped to listen.

"I promise you, any danger to me and I'll call you for a ride home."

"You'll call no one!" the man with the pistol said as he stepped into her room.

"W . . . who are you and why —"

There were two muffled gunshots, followed by a short scream. His bullets pierced her chest with one blowing a hole in her heart, while the other struck her lungs. She lay on the floor quivering when the killer heard a voice on the phone yelling.

"Hello." the killer answered, a big smile on his lips.

"Who are you, and what have you done to her?"

"She's dead. See, I'm an enforcer for the New World Order and I've just killed my first CSA agent. Tell your Mister President his killing of our man in the hospital was a very serious mistake. I've been instructed to inform you that as of this moment, a state of war exists between the NWO and the CSA. I hope to meet you professionally one day, John, after all, I have your address. Say hello to your wife and three kids for me." The killer then threw the phone on the bed and shot the phone. The killer was unaware his bullet went through the phone, bed, and the floor, to strike a newborn child's head in the apartment below.

He pulled his phone from his pocket, dialed a number, and said, "Silent Night."

"Sehr gut. Kommen Sie jetzt nach Hause."

CHAPTER 22

The President of the Conservative States of America was in his war room listening to the battle currently going on between his aircraft and the UN's. His aide entered, leaned to his ear, and then whispered of the telephone call with Mother Hen, and her killer. He stood waiting.

Standing, the President said, "Go get your family and bring them here. They can live here and keep my wife company." He placed his left hand on his aide and guided him into an empty room.

"Sir, I can't do that."

"Is there someplace you can send them that's safe?"

"I don't know."

"Are you sure he said we were at war with the New World Order?"

"I'm positive, sir, and when he said it I got the chills. Those people are rich and ruthless."

"You're correct. John, fetch your family and bring them here. I think this is the last safe place for them in the world."

"You very well may be right, but I can't make a decision like this without speaking with my wife, sir."

"I understand. Go and then let me know your decision, because you're like family."

"Thank you, sir." John said as he walked from the room.

James and his small group were now attacking UN forces where they found them. Over the last few weeks they'd ambushed small groups, and their arsenal of collected weapons had grown. They were still working out of the cave, and while Dick had little strength, he was alive and getting better with each new day. At the moment, they were seated in the cave listening to Ben explain how to take out a chopper using a LAW. As he spoke, everyone listened to his words closely.

Frank, who was sitting in the front of the cave guarding, said, "Company comin' to visit and they're not our side."

"How many?"

"Platoon size, is my guess."

Ben smiled and said, "Looks like we need to move to a new home. At least this one had a grand view."

"Gather up your individual gear and leave some grenades with the pins pulled under some stuff, because we might get lucky and kill a couple. Ben, I want you and Frank to cover us with your sniper rifles as we shag ass out of our area of operations (AO)."

"We can do that."

Five minutes later, the group was leaving the cave and Frank fired his first round. Since he had a silencer, he started killing from the back of the group and worked his way forward. He killed five men before the platoon Sergeant realized he had dead men.

As the platoon started withdrawing, the two snipers ran up the trail and then Ben fired, having removed his silencer, and a soldier screamed and grabbed his face. He wanted the enemy in the cave now, so he let them see him leaving. Maybe they'd kill a few more with the two mines and grenades they'd left.

At the top of the bluff, as they were loading, two loud explosions were heard, followed by screams. As they drove away, James spotted some of the men climbing over the edge of the bluff. In seconds they were lost to sight.

James led as he moved to another cave he knew of further north.

The President of the CSA had his security team find a place for John and his family. The house used for the White House was huge and there were rooms in the place the President hadn't even visited yet. But he was usually busy and while his war was currently going well, he knew it could all change in a matter of a few short days. The troops at Fort Leonard Wood had pushed the UN troops back across the Big Piney River and they were dug in at that spot. There, reports of pretty blue helmets with bullet holes in them were coming in from all over the state of Missouri.

He poured himself a double bourbon, telling his bartender to sit and watch television with him, as the First Lady helped John and his family get settled. Sitting in an overstuffed recliner, he turned the TV on.

The news was on and a cameraman was panning the trees, near Rolla, Missouri, where UN paratroopers had been caught by locals hanging in trees by their parachutes. Some good ole boys from the small town were shooting them to pieces using everything from BB guns to 30.06's.

The reporter then said, "the footage you just saw is the killing of some of the UN troops that invaded our country approximately three weeks back. While the footage is a bit old, it shows the determination of our citizens. Currently we have thousands of refugees flooding into the state to avoid having the micro-chip implanted. Since they are Americans, they are screened by our security teams and those with arrest warrants or a history of criminal behavior are sent back. If they pass that stage, then they must take an oath of allegiance to the CSA. Able bodied men and women then have a two year military service obligation before they are legally real citizens. If parents, one parent will stay with their children as the other does his or her compulsory service. This is Daniel Williams reporting for WXXC, Jefferson City."

The camera switched to the studio.

"The Conservative States of America accepted the unconditional surrender of the state of Illinois early this morning, and I take you live now to Bill Bodeker in Chicago, Bill."

"I'm standing in the courtyard of the state capitol, and scattered all around me are the bloody bodies of dead and wounded UN troops. CSA medics are working as quickly as they can, but there are just too many. The local hospitals are full, as are the school gymnasiums, and it's gotten to the point that tents are being set up on the capitol grounds. The taking of this one city alone cost the UN over 200,000 troops, while the CSA lost approximate 20,000 dead and wounded.

One of the first things done here by the CSA military Commander was to order the arrest of the mayor and all council members. They are currently locked up, pending trials over their apparent misuse of funds. As a liberal city, there was absolutely no resistance by civilian residents. Guns found hidden in some homes brought an instant execution by the army, unless they showed as the legal owner of the weapons in our computers. The legal guns were then taken from their owners and will be returned at some point in the future.

I want you to hear what Colonel John H. Applegate said as he addressed the fallen town on television."

The next image was of a Full Colonel dressed in battle dress uniform standing in front of a podium. His face was camouflaged with face paint and his cheeks dirty from mud.

"Ladies and Gentlemen of Chicago, I come here today to explain some rules you'll have to obey for an unknown period of time. From this moment on, unless you are certified by two doctors to be either physically or mentally disabled, if you don't work, you don't eat. Those of you with full-time jobs, this doesn't apply to you. If you want to eat and work, register at any of our soon to be posted work detail groups. These groups will look your family up in the computer, and if both adults are working you can then, after work, claim your funny money to go to our warehouses and select your foods. The only place in the world this money has any value is at our storage facilities.

If you are caught cheating about the number of kids you have, claiming you're married when you're not, or using counterfeit funny money, the first time is 30 days in jail, the second time is 6 months in jail. If we catch you a third time, you'll be executed for attempted fraud of the Government of the Conservative States of America. And speaking of executions, the whole state is now under martial law, and that means if you're seen out after dark, you will be shot."

"What about my rights!" a chunky black woman yelled.

"Lady, you are essentially living in an occupied state right now, which means you have no rights." the Colonel replied.

"Ya gonna see some riots then." a man yelled from the back of the crowd.

"I will warn all of you once and *only* once, so please listen to me. If you are out after dark, you will be shot, if you riot, you will be shot, every last one of you. If you need medical assistance for any reason, dial 911 and wait. If you drive and we catch you, you and the ill person will be shot to death. I am warning you, this is serious business."

"What about my first amendment rights! I know my rights." the chunky black woman screamed once more.

"We only honor the first amendment for citizens of the Conservative States of America. You, lady, are basically a prisoner of war in an occupied state, as I said before. You will do what you are told, or face the consequences."

"Some will try them and you know it, sir." the bartender said.

"Yep, and they'll die, too. We're going to clean Chicago of its bedbugs and lice." the President said and then turned the TV off.

"What a mess. Chicago is as crooked as a snake, sir."

"We will investigate the politicians, judges, police, and all of them. I suspect some public hangings will take place soon. From now on, hanging is the method of execution for our nation. Additionally, three violent crimes and you're soon dancing on the end of a rope. You'll hang for raping a child as well as shooting a police officer, even if you fail to kill him or her. Goodnight, Bill, I'm off to bed."

Bill stood and said, "Goodnight, Mister President."

At the morning briefing, intelligence said they had proof the NWO was behind a huge riot the night before in Chicago.

The agent briefing intelligence said, "The following video is graphic and was taken during last night's riots. The only people allowed out after dark are a select few media folks. This cameraman was not one of them and was discovered dead last night after the riots. A total of 1,102 protesters were killed in the riots. We had one loss, one of our Army Privates accidentally shot himself in the left foot."

The movie showed folks moving, mostly men of black or Hispanic descent. It must have been the cameraman's voice that said, "People are carrying signs and it is well after dark." The cameraman focused on two different groups of CSA military men, and they appeared to be assembling a machine-gun on a tripod. "There are no police, but here come CSA troops marching out in an orderly fashion and as you can see, they are waiting, still in ranks. I hope this does not turn violent, but I feel it will."

A Major yelled, "Disperse immediately or we will shoot. You were warned before."

"We know our rights, so death to the Conservative States of America! You sumbitches can't tell us what to do! We know our rights!" a young white woman in front of the line yelled back.

A split-second later, the Major said, "Fire!"

The two machine-guns, placed at different angles, began to spit bullets at a high rate of speed. People in the crowed began to fall, with some screaming, some not making a sound, but all surprised they were being shot at. Protesters began to scream and flee but then the army troops began to shoot into the masses and many more people died. As the protesters broke and ran, the army went after them, using dogs, tanks and armor to track them down.

"Mister President, by dawn, the protesters were all dead, as well as the cameraman. His camera was found and as a result, it was taken by intelligence. As you can see, the rioters clearly broke the law. They were testing us to see if we meant what we said. An additional 128 people were executed overnight in the whole state of Illinois. If we do not enforce martial law as we are, resistance groups will move against us."

"Yes, yes, I agree. I just hate killing for such a small offense, but they know the rules. As for the resistance, no prisoners; kill every one we take prisoner."

"Over the day yesterday, and all last night, we used B-52s, B-1s, and B-2s to bomb California. Our targets were industrial areas, shipping ports, and military complexes. Additionally, the White House was leveled."

"Our losses?"

"Fifteen aircraft, with all but four being fighters. Three were C-130s and one was a helicopter, which we lost during a rescue attempt."

"Their losses?"

"The UN did not have a good day, sir. We downed thirty-eight fighters, three helicopters, four transport aircraft, and six drones. An advantage they have is when their pilots bail out of a bad aircraft, they land on friendly soil. Ours, according to drone images we have taken, are hanged or hacked to death by frustrated civilians. As you know as an Air Force veteran, sir, our pilots are only issued a .38 for protection."

"Start issuing them 9mm with at least 6 magazines for the weapon. Do we currently have search and rescue operations going on?"

"Yes, sir, we do. A Captain Alex Baldwin had his F-16B, a two seat model, shot down early yesterday as he led the first wave of fighters. His aircraft sustained severe engine damage and was losing fuel. At some point, he and his weapons system operator, WSO, had to get out and walk. We've had only one conversation with Baldwin and that was near noon yesterday. To get him out safely is currently a big SAR operation, sir."

Captain Alex Baldwin had teamed up with his WSO on the ground a little after noon the day before, but Dave Hill had injured his left arm during ejection from the aircraft. The arm appeared to be broken right above the wrist. The bad guys were looking for them, but they'd come down at the western base of the Sierra Nevada Mountains. Baldwin kept them constantly moving east to get deeper in the mountain range.

Baldwin had entered the Air Force through the AFROTC program, and had applied for pilot training, hoping he would be smart enough to complete the training. He was a man of average weight and height, with gray eyes that spoke of his high intellect. Generally a quiet man, he knew you could learn more by listening than talking. While not bad looking, only two women in his life ever called him handsome, his wife and his mother. He doubted either one was being completely honest, but he appreciated their kind comments. He removed his flight cap, ran his hand threw his wet auburn hair, and hoped his wife was not worried about him. It was growing hot already.

They both had a survival kit along with a survival vest, and had enough gear to survive, if only food and water could be found. The night before, they'd heard men searching for them and they seemed to be civilians. Neither man wanted to be recovered by the general public, because they were known for their brutality with prisoners. Also, they often hanged their captives or killed them on the spot.

Lieutenant Dave Hill was a graduate of the US Air Force Academy and had graduated as the #2 cadet just a year ago. Smart, good looking, and single, he was popular with the ladies. His blond hair attracted some, while his rugged facial features and square chin, or blue eyes pulled in others. At only 22, his flying mates called him Baby Face, due to his age.

"Alex, I hurt, man."

"I have some morphine with self-injecting syringes, but I don't want to use them until help is near or we find a damned good hiding place. If I give the drug to you now, you'll fall asleep and I would be forced to leave you behind if I had to move quickly."

"Let's move . . . then, because I need something . . . for the pain."

Pulling a map of the area from his pocket, he moved close to Dave, and pointing on the map, with his index finger, said, "We're right here, and I make out a lake to be about three miles from us. If we can reach the lake, it's possible we can follow a running stream uphill for a distance and establish a rescue site."

"Let's go . . . because this . . . pain is killing me. Hell, I . . . may pass out . . . from the pain alone."

"Hang tough, Baby Face, and we'll be safe in a couple of hours.

"Don't start . . . that shit again." Dave said, and then forced a smile.

"Let's move, then."

Both men were wearing camouflage makeup on their hands, necks and faces which allowed them, with their sage green flight suits, to blend in well with the brush. Alex had turned the radio off, to prevent it from making noise that would compromise their position. Silver and gold watches had been removed, as well as all rings, so they'd not flash in the sunlight. Both men were serious about escaping and evading, but Dave's injury was about to get the best of him. They moved slowly, but at a steady rate, and stopped often to listen.

They moved parallel to an old logging road and when about halfway to the lake, a lone man was seen sitting on a log. They froze in position and when the man turned his head, they dropped to their knees. Alex looked the man over closely, not liking what he saw.

The man was carrying an M4, and had what looked like an old 1911 .45 pistol stuck in his waistband. He also wore a pistol belt with grenades and another pistol in a holster. However, he was not dressed in a uniform, but wearing jeans and a brown cotton long sleeved shirt.

After a few minutes, the man stood, made his way toward the two fliers, and at the very edge of the road he unzipped his jeans to pee. When the stream of urine started, Baldwin lunged forward with his large survival knife, the blade going into the man's soft stomach to the hilt. The man's hands came up to block the blade the second time but missed, and once again the blade went in deeply, but this time Alex jerked the blade hard, from left to right.

The fatally injured man attempted to scream to warn others, but his body wouldn't obey his mind. His thoughts were confused and he was unable to pull a pistol to defend himself. He fell to the mud in the road, almost in a puddle, unable to move at all. He felt his killers taking his gear and weapons, and he wanted to stop them, but slowly his world faded until all was black.

"Let me drag him into the woods and then we'll move on. I'll keep the rifle and grenades, because I don't think you're in any condition to use them. I took some other things from his pockets and even have his backpack, but have no idea what's in it. Now, let's move."

Four hours later, the two men were situated on the side of a mountain and going through the stolen backpack. They found four MREs, matches, four filled magazines for the M4 and three for the .45. At the bottom of the pack was a full quart of whiskey, so Alex handed the drink to his WSO.

"Drink just enough to take the edge off your pain."

As Dave guzzled the booze, Alex tried the radio. He switched to beeper for fifteen seconds, then turning the beeper beacon off, he said, "This is Talon One to any aircraft, mayday, mayday, mayday."

"Uh, Talon One, this is Low Rider Six. I read you five by five."

"Low Rider, I need a ride home."

"Understand. Let me call base."

"Roger, go."

Long minutes passed, then finally a voice said, "Search and rescue are headed your way, Talon, so relax. ETA is twenty minutes."

It was then Alex saw about a company size group walking toward him and all were armed.

"Low Rider Six, I have company coming."

"I'm in an A-10 and I can lend you a hand. Uh, but first I need to locate you better. Turn your beeper on for 30 seconds. I'll fly toward you and when I'm overhead, say now."

"Roger, I remember how this game is played."

He switched his radio to beeper and waited as he counted off the seconds. Low Rider came screaming out of the sky, which caused the men moving toward them to seek cover.

As the A-10 flew overhead, Alex switched from beeper to voice, and said, "Overhead . . . 3 . . . 2 . . .1, uh, now. I'm ten meters to the left of when I said now."

"I have you visual. Get your heads down, and keep them down."

The A-10 banked slowly to the right, lined up on the men on the ground and began its approach. Alex saw two puffs of smoke from the aircraft and two missiles moved toward the hillside.

There came two loud explosions, followed by screams. Then the Gatling gun on the nose opened up.

Pieces of bodies flew into the air as the bullets tore apart anyone they struck. Dirt was thrown ten feet or more into the air by the shells, often after passing through a man or two. Shrieks of pain were heard when the gunfire stopped. When the aircraft lined up for another pass, the men on the ground were seen running to the trees, opposite of where the downed fliers were located.

"Uh, Talon One, this is Sandy. I'm a minute or so ahead of Rescue One. I have some napalm, if you need it."

"Sandy, Low Rider here."

As Low Rider explained where the two downed men were, Alex felt like a small animal was chewing on his guts. He was so nervous his hands were shaking violently.

"Talon, get your head down. I'm going to use some shake and bake on the tree line opposite your position. Starting my run now."

An F-18 moved over the trees at a high rate of speed and two containers fell from the bird, and were seen flipping end over end before they struck the trees. When the container exploded, a solid wall of fire shot high into the air and assisted by the momentum of the jet, spread out like a burning wave of flames. The heat was felt by Alex and Dave. Screams were heard as some of men burned to death.

"Uh, Talon One, this is Save One and I have you visual. Do you have any injuries at this time?"

"Negative, I'm fine, but my WSO has a broken arm, over."

"I'll lower a forest penetrator and I want both of you to come up at the same time. Once at my door, do nothing and my crew will pull you into the aircraft."

"Roger, copy."

"Okay, coming in now."

I have to wait for the penetrator to strike the ground or the static electricity will knock my ass for a loop, Alex thought, as he remembered his survival training.

A few minutes later the chopper was right above them as the penetrator lowered.

"Uh, Sandy, I'm taking ground fire from east of the burning trees. Taking fire, taking fire from the trees." Save One said over the radio.

Alex and Dave quickly moved toward the penetrator, and the second it struck the ground, he lowered two seats and pulled two tabs, one of which went under their arms. He slung the M4 over his shoulder, tightened the strap around Dave and then gave a thumbs up. As they ascended by an electric wench, ground fire grew heavy from almost all directions.

"Uh, Falcon, I have to move now, so hang on."

The aircraft moved forward toward the top of the mountains, and Alex knew he was squeezing Dave so hard it was probable his thumb print would remain on his skin for life. He refused to look down, and he was looking at the chopper when a line of bullet holes ran across the side of the bird. It was then the winch began to move again. Soon they were at the door, the winch stopped, and a man wearing a helmet pulled them into the chopper and unstrapped them. He then pointed to red nylon seats and motioned for them to put their seat belts on. One man near a machine-gun was sprawled out on the floor, looking at Alex with unseeing eyes, his neck and chest ripped open by something. A medic moved to Dave, gave him a shot of morphine, and began working on his injury.

CHAPTER 23

The President of the Conservative States of America was seated at a big oval table constructed of solid oak, listening to his Navy Commander explaining why an invasion of California wouldn't work. He listened carefully and then asked, "Sir, is your second in command here today?"

"Yes, sir, he is Admiral James C. Howell."

"Good, because you, sir, are fired. Your replacement is Admiral Howell, who will now tell me how *he* will invade California. Gentlemen, I know in my mind that when California falls, the United States falls. Oh, Admiral Thomas, you may leave, sir; since you're no longer in charge of my Navy, you have no need to know what we discuss. My aide will bring you new orders at some point today."

Standing, the Admiral said, "Yes, sir."

"Now, Admiral Howell, tell me where you think we can land troops from the ocean on California's coastline."

The Admiral stood, walked to the huge map of California and said, "First we strike them at the eastern border of the state, and then we strike them two days later on the coast. It may be possible to land amphibious troops, Marines actually, many places along the shore line. If you'll allow me 24 hours, sir, I can determine the best places. By hitting the east first, I would expect military commanders to rush their manpower and resources to that area. Let's give me 48 hours after they move east, and then I'll strike north and south on their coast. I think we will cause deep confusion and panic."

"How will you know when they have moved enough gear and men to the east?"

"Satellite photographs, sir." the Admiral replied.

"I will give you three days from now to plan an invasion, Admiral, but if you can't do the job, I will replace you. I will replace any man or woman on my staff who cannot or will not make things happen. I grow damned tired of negative answers."

"Yes, sir, I'll have a plan ready, sir."

The Commandant of the Marine Corps said, "If we hit a low populated area, we can estimate 5 to 10 % casualties, while an area like San Francisco or Los Angeles could cost us up to 70%. On behalf of my men and women, who were born to fight, they'll damned sure go where I send them, but to keep my losses low, try to land us in an underpopulated area, Admiral."

"I'll see what I can do, Steve."

"Okay, now, have we had any problems with riots or civil unrest in Illinois?"

"No, sir, but some thieves were captured and executed on the spot. Their bodies were left where they fell."

The President looked around and asked, "Anyone else have anything?"

Silence.

"Okay then, let's return to work."

"According to intelligence," a tall thin man dressed in black said, "the Conservative States of America are planning to invade the US on the California coast."

He was standing in the New World Order headquarters in Switzerland and briefing ten individuals.

"What is their purpose in invading that state instead of another one?" Adolpha ask, her full glossy lips turning heads as she spoke.

"California, ma'am, is the heart of the US. Many large and small cities on the coast are ports for shipping from around the world. Many large manufacturing companies are located in the state, and it's of psychological importance as well. By taking

California, the CSA will show the world they are a government and military to be reckoned with, and they will be."

"And what is the NWO to do as this takes place?"

Giving a grin, the man said, "Nothing, nothing major at all. We'll deal with the winner. Now, my staff tells me there is a good chance the CSA will win this battle, which may rush the end of the war. The state we're talking about is the backbone of the new US."

"This war could last how many years?"

"Our analysts say this one will be over in two years maximum."

"Do they also predict a winner?"

"Yes, ma'am, and it will be the CSA. One reason is folks are tired of the politics in the old US and they're rushing to the Conservative states by the millions. Black folks who have a history of voting democrat have now realized all the party was giving them was lip service and free phones. We have reports of illegal aliens fleeing back to Mexico in huge numbers because large groups of black and white folks are openly looking for them, blaming the war on them. Additionally, politicians in the CSA are sending illegals home as fast as they can round them up, and even Muslim refugees are being deported in record numbers. Soon, very soon, all that will remain are those born there and those with a green card."

Adolpha smiled and then asked, "What exactly do you mean when you say, 'tired of the politics?"

"Before the war, as every member of the NWO knows, we bought most politicians, but we weren't the only ones paying them. Often a politician would be elected and his social status would be upper middle class. Then, at the end of his four years of service in Politics, he'd leave office as a millionaire. How is that possible making what most governments pay politicians?"

"I see. So, as these people fight we do nothing? What of our war with them?"

"Patience my dear. We do nothing. We will send agents into the country, but the days of chip implanting may be over for a while. The Conservative States of America are beyond any doubt a Christian nation. Now, I'm sorry to say it may take a hundred years or more before we can bring implanting back. Hopefully, given time, political parties will change, and the Liberals will return."

"Damn," she said, "I'd hoped for a winter home in Florida this year."

The man laughed and said, "That concludes my lecture; any questions?"

Silence filled the briefing room.

"Have a good day." he said as he moved toward his training aids and began collecting his papers and notes.

Adolpha approached him after the rest left and asked, "Would you be interested in supper at my place?"

"You live in Frankfurt, do you not?"

"Yes, that is my primary residence, but I have a small cottage here." She met his eyes and then winked at him.

"Uh, how do I find this cottage of yours?"

"Here is my card," she said, and extended her hand. When he took the card, his index finger touched her hand and she moaned.

"And what time is supper, and the attire?"

"1800 sharp and wear as little as is legal." She gave a low, deep laugh and then added, "I'll have the champagne chilled and on ice."

"And," he asked grinning, "what is on the menu?"

She ran her tongue seductively over her red glossy lips and then replied, "Me, just me."

Out now in paperback/ebook

"*New World Order: The California Invasion, Volume 2,*"

from W.R. Benton.

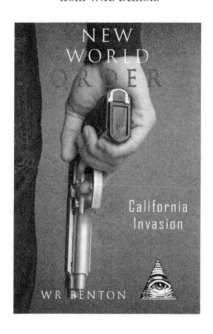

THE FALL OF AMERICA:
Books 1-3

Now available as audiobooks at iTunes, or at Audible.com.

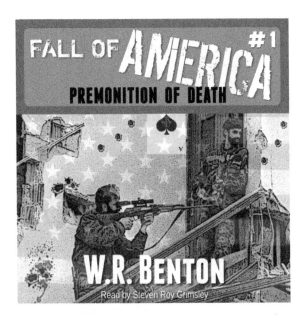

ABOUT THE AUTHOR

W.R. Benton Benton, pen name for Gary L. Benton, was born in the Missouri Ozarks. He is a graduate of Wayland Baptist University, Plainview, Texas, with a BS in Occupational Safety and Health. Benton's writing has been endorsed by writers Don Bendell, Matt Braun, and Stephen Lodge, as well as actor James Drury, "The Virginian," actor Robert Woods, Mississippi Senator Terry Burton, and many others. He's been interviewed by many local Mississippi television and radio stations.

A true cowboy at heart, Benton spent over 26 years on active military duty with the United States Air Force and retired in 1997, with the rank of Senior Master Sergeant (E-8). He lives on an imaginary ranch with hundreds of horses and thousands of make-believe cows. He has four dogs and two cats, all real. You can discover more about W. R. Benton by visiting his websites, www.simplesurvival.net or www.wrbenton.net.

Be sure to visit him on Facebook at
www.facebook.com/wrbenton01
His books can be seen on Amazon at the following link:
http://www.amazon.com/author/wrbenton/
and at
http://modusoperandipress.com

"Simple Survival - A Family Outdoors Guide" is more than a book—it is an outdoor resource bible that every family should have a copy of. This is one of those books that you should have in your camping bag along with the tent and other equipment.

Gary L. Benton

However, reading it at home before you go off on some outdoor adventure would be a great help when potential situations happen.

Available at Amazon and other online bookstores

Impending Disasters - This helpful and comprehensive book covers most major disasters and how to stay safe if you decide to evacuate or stay. It has a section on prolonged survival, which will assist keeping you alive after the natural disaster has done its

damage. Many people die following natural disasters, from one mishap or another, but you can learn to survive.

Learn to deal with Tornadoes, ice storms, hurricane, flooding, blackouts, riots, and much more. Contains easy to understand information, and critical gear/equipment lists you will need.

Available at Amazon and other online bookstores

On a trip to the Lake Clark area of the Alaskan bush, a sudden arctic weather system forces down the small plane of Dr. Jim Wade, and his son David. Both have survived the crash, but not unscathed. Food, fire and shelter are all a priority. Following the death of his father, now it is up to David to figure out what to do next, and how to survive, on a remote Alaskan mountain—in winter!

This is a fictional story of survival, resilience and of the spirit to live. It is both authentic and accurate, having been written by a former Air Force life support survival instructor. For ages 10 and up

Both are available at Amazon and other online bookstores

Set adrift, a family of three are cast out to sea in a rubber raft, where they must find a way to conquer one terrifying tragedy after another or die in the process.

In this gripping story of survival everyone will be tested to their limits. Christian faith and hope are hallmarks of this tale that will touch your heart..

Made in the USA
Middletown, DE
25 July 2020

13644423R00136